A Pack of Lies

A Pack of Lies

Jo Thomas

www.foxspirit.co.uk

conversion by handebooks.co.uk

ISBN: 978-1-909348-80-6

Published by:
Fox Spirit Books
www.foxspirit.co.uk

I continue to dedicate the life of Elkie Bernstein to four amazing women: to the memory of Alice Beck and Jennifer Thomas, as well as to Samantha and Jennifer Jackson, who support me through everything.

I'd also like to thank the awesome Fox Spirit Books team (Adele Wearing and Darren Pulsford) and the Skulk (who I'm too lazy to name individually), as well as offer particular thanks and recognition for my alpha and beta readers: Dylan Fox, Ole Andreas Imsen and Nick Marsh.

Tusen takk to Berit Ellingsen, Johan Ludvig Brattås, Margrét Helgadóttir, Martha Hubbard, and Martin McGrath for extra help with Norwegian names, words and phrases. Any language problems arise because of my poor skills, not their advice.

I finally understood the English paranoia about language in Norway. No. That's uncharitable. Maybe I should say 'Anglophone' or 'monolingual', not English. Anyway, suddenly I got it, that fear that people saying words that you don't understand are saying them about you.

I guess I've been there before—Bernstein's not exactly a common name in North Wales—but I don't remember not knowing at least a handful of Welsh, enough to talk politely to neighbours who never spoke English. It was a shock to be in a place where I only heard words I recognised if my hosts chose to do so.

I told myself it was nothing, that it would pass, that I was a temporary guest at the Institute—as long as Olsen could bring himself to release me back into the wild.

Lie 1: Everything's Fine

In a glorified kennel run in Norway, my life changed.

The run was actually a cell of sorts. I just had difficulty thinking of it as anything less than an animal's run. It was designed in much the same way, although it had the illusion of privacy because there was nothing but a blank wall opposite the glass wall and door I'd come in through. But we were confined and I could hear Ben's neighbour inmates—sniffing, sobbing, panting.

'Elkie? Elkie, what's wrong?' Ben asked in Welsh.

He had that little-boy-lost look, wide-eyed and full of potential that would probably never be fulfilled. I looked away and swallowed down the sickness I could feel in my throat. Now wasn't the time to share anything other than the cheap chess set I'd brought him.

'Nothing,' I said, also in Welsh because why share it with everyone.

I laid the board out with care, concentrating on the black and white squares, the fold down the middle, the smooth texture. We'd played with something similar at primary school but then it had been draughts, not chess.

'Do you know anything about chess?' I asked, back in English because we might as well seem harmless to the security team.

In my head, the real little boy version laughed and said, 'King me!' as we played draughts indoors on a rainy day during playtime. In real life, he said, 'is this where you explain about the horsie and the prawns and—'

'Ben, a "yes" or "no" is fine.'

'No. It looked boring.'

Yeah, I used to think that, too. Right up to the day I'd been looking at ways of weaning Ben off the all-action games and I realised strategy might be a necessary skill in this cell. That day, holding the board and getting ready to show Ben what little I'd picked up from the Internet, I realised it might be an important skill for me, too.

'Not enough blood and guts, eh?' I asked.

A rhetorical question. He'd always liked games that

involved hitting computer generated characters until they exploded in blood better than puzzles and planning. He had to be pretty ill with slow reaction times to drift over into anything less than a trigger happy world. We both knew it. I had the scars to prove it.

'The kings,' I said and put them in their starting positions. 'They can move one space in any direction.'

'Sounds pathetic.'

I hid the two pieces in my hands, put my hands behind my back, swapped them around a few times.

'But important. The game ends when the opponent's king is captured—checkmate—or can't move—stalemate. Which hand?'

'Just because it's the king?' Ben asked and picked my left hand.

I held out the black king and he took it from my palm, careful not to brush against my skin. He held the piece up to look at it closely.

'There aren't any hidden weapons,' I said drily as I put my white king in its starting place on the board.

I didn't make a crack about how monarchy doesn't make sense at the best of times. There are people who are held as important, through skill or inheritance. Like Ben's ability to find other werewolves, not the commonest creature in the world, and set them on a mission despite his own restricted movement. Whoever held Ben and kept him was winning.

I didn't even point out that he was in the most effective stalemate ever, caught in Olsen's Institute without Internet connection. What I'd just realised was that Olsen was a rival king, and not the right person to be siding with. It's only a small leap from proving a group of people a valid section of society to proving them a superior set. That's the kind of fear that puts nationalist parties like the BNP and UKIP in government, and it was eating away at my innards. There was also the possibility that, as the chess analogy began to fail, Olsen could use Ben and his powers for this false superiority.

I got on with explaining all the other chess pieces instead, setting them out as the diagrams I'd found online had shown me. For the sake of completion, I won the first game. But I didn't stand a chance against Ben after that. Even without proper instruction, the former golden boy put me into stalemate once and checkmate twice before he would let me press the buzzer to be allowed out.

I say 'let me'. I could probably have pressed it regardless of his wishes. I'd gotten used to being able to cope, physically. I just didn't want to do that to someone I used to have a crush on, who I felt responsible for.

'You're just tired of being beaten,' Ben said.

'Yes.'

In more ways than one. Just because I was in the habit of surviving, of coming out of the other side alive, didn't mean I really won or came away without bruising. There wasn't enough chocolate hazelnut spread in the world to make it feel better.

'Just one more game?'

I smiled. 'I thought you didn't like chess?'

'It'll do,' he said.

But he stood up and backed away from the desk, into the barred bedroom. The door didn't close on him but the separation, the gap between guest and inmate, was obvious.

'Conn, let her stay,' he whispered.

Tall, lanky, greying, and not my idea of a knight in shining armour but he'd come to my rescue. He was probably about old enough to be my father and I'd gotten used to not having one of those.

'I'm tired,' I told Ben. There was no way I was letting anyone else answer for me. 'I'll come back tomorrow, if I'm allowed.'

Ben turned wide-eyes on me again. Was he doing it intentionally? Was the little-boy-lost a ploy? I'd never assumed that Ben would be the kind to manipulate like that. His games were different. Well, I thought they were. After a few attempts at strategy, I was starting to doubt everything.

'Elkie's already said she'll be back tomorrow,' said Conn and his word, his presence, was enough for Ben to accept 'no' for an answer.

Head low, Ben shuffled back to the desk we'd been playing chess at—where I was still sat—and picked up the black queen.

'Here,' he said and thrust it at me.

'Keep it for me until tomorrow,' I said, keeping my hand closed and not understanding what he was trying to tell me, if anything. I stood. 'Anyway, I have my own set back at the farm.'

He looked at me.

'So we can play when I've gone home. We just need to send each other the moves and keep track with our own sets,' I explained.

He nodded but he didn't put the black queen down. Instead, he held it tighter, until his knuckles went white.

'Elkie?' Conn sort of asked. A gentle reminder of his presence and my request to leave Ben's run. Cell. Whatever.

'Coming.'

It was almost a relief to walk out into the corridor, in sight of the obvious CCTV cameras once more but at least not trapped like an animal.

'Olsen would like to talk to you again,' Conn said.

He didn't stand around waiting for my response. His shoulders were tense, stiff with discomfort. For me or for the inmates we walked past?

'What about?' I asked.

It wasn't like I had anything to say that Olsen would be interested in hearing. It's not like he wanted to hear excuses for the werewolf deaths I'd been part of. There was no excuse. I'd been stupid. I should have gone to the police with the first death. Maybe.

Conn shrugged. 'Just... be careful. He cares a lot about his... charges.'

That BNP-esque paranoia raised its head. Unlike Conn's, which just seemed to sink lower.

'Oh?' I asked, and then, 'Where am I staying tonight?'

'We have a visitors' wing.'

I nodded. Kind of obvious that a large hospital in the middle of nowhere would have facilities. I'd banked on it when I'd booked the flight over. I still wasn't convinced I wouldn't end up in my own run, though.

'They didn't all come through here,' I said.

Conn said nothing. He just kept on walking, shoulders heavy as he led me back through the hallways of an old country house now being used as a mental health institute. One that housed people who thought they were werewolves and the odd man who actually was. Like the one in front of me.

'The werewolves I killed, I mean. They didn't all come through here. They can't all have come through here if he didn't know how many Ben found.'

Conn still said nothing. His shoulders came up a bit, though, making him look firmer and more resolute. This was something he cared about, that I had seen and killed his kind.

I stopped. 'And it's not murder if they attacked me first.'

Conn stopped and looked back at me. There was an odd expression on his face that I couldn't quite place. Maybe he agreed with me. Maybe I reminded him of something. Maybe it had nothing to do with me, just what was in his head at that moment in time.

'Is it?' I asked.

'I really don't know,' he said. 'Legally, no. Morally, knowin' they're comin' after you and not alertin' authorities or tryin' to stop them? That I don't know.'

It was only what my conscience had just been telling me but that didn't mean I was happy to hear it from somebody else.

'Alert the authorities? What was I supposed to do? Go to the police and say, "Sorry but this naked dead guy in the wood was actually all furred up and trying to bite my head off"? Or how about "Sorry about the dead lawyer but he was making sure I didn't stop Ben's dad pimping his son's bite out"?'

'Really?'

'Yes,' I answered. 'Old Man Lloyd made money out of Ben and his being turned into werewolves.'

Conn snorted. 'No. I meant were you really tryin' to stop the Lloyds' business?'

'Biting people so they turn into werewolves is not a business.'

'It doesn't do any harm if they're making sure the clients are looked after when they first turn, when they're at their most dangerous.'

'Unless the clients are bastard lawyers who take it on themselves to intimidate the local teenagers,' I said.

'True. But why men want to become werewolves is arguably nothing to do with us.'

'You mean it doesn't matter that they're all men wanting to prove how high they can piss up a wall by killing other people.'

'An unfortunate reality of life,' said Conn.

He turned again and started walking. I followed, not really wanting to be left in the middle of an unfamiliar building.

'So your Old Man Lloyd could have done with a better vettin' process. In your opinion.'

'I'd prefer no vetting process at all,' I said grimly. 'Any man who wants to be a wolf isn't all right in the head.'

Conn cleared his throat.

'Present company not excluded,' I said.

'Oh?'

He wasn't upset. I think he might even have been amused. That didn't make me feel any better. If he was relaxed enough to be amused, he felt like he had some control over the situation. I had none.

'I don't know you from Adam. All I know is you haven't tried to kill me and don't seem to want other werewolves to kill me, either.'

Conn laughed. 'True.'

It wasn't. He had that air of boy-scout capability—prepared, well-meaning and earnest—that said he really was a knight in shining armour. But that didn't necessarily mean much if we found ourselves on different sides.

'Life isn't that simple,' he said, as if he could read my thoughts. 'There's more options than "yes" or "no", "either" and "or". There are shades of grey. There are multiple sides.'

It was my turn to say nothing.

'You deserve a chance, Elkie. I'll do my best to make sure you get it.'

Olsen didn't look up from his computer as I entered, or stop talking in Norwegian on the phone. Conn closed the door behind him, leaving me standing like a defenceless idiot in the middle of the floor. The thing that never seems to change is that my potential enemy has almost all the advantages and I have to fight just to even things out.

Before coming to Norway, things were black and white, life or death. Life was looking after the farm and surviving day-to-day. Death was waiting for Ben to send the next werewolf—or what happened if I didn't manage to beat them. Between Ben's game and life on a farm in the middle of Welsh nowhere, I was not prepared for being in an office with a werewolf who may or may not want me dead. Especially one on the first floor with two large windows and one strong wooden door between me and freedom.

I helped myself to the chair facing the middle-aged professor, half-listening to the lilting conversation that some part of my brain insisted I'd understand if I just listened hard enough. Not that it did any good. The sounds slipped and slid through my ears—close to English but not enough to be understandable. I forced my eyes down to watch my carefully folded hands. Don't hide the thumbs, don't wring, don't hug or hide the body. Don't show weakness.

I waited for the phone call to finish, then counted ten slightly too fast heartbeats. 'You wanted to see me?'

Good. Not too pitchy or tight. I probably stank of nerves to a werewolf nose but it didn't show. Not in the human ways.

'Yes,' he said.

That was it. He still didn't look at me and his attention only wavered long enough to check something on his side of the desk before returning to the computer screen. He started tapping on the computer keyboard and I waited, as if it were no big deal and I were here by choice.

Technically, I was. I wrote to Olsen, I invited myself to the Institute. I just didn't want to still be here, even though I'd only got there that day. I had a ticket for a plane back to the UK in five days but I really wanted to be on it now.

'What about?' I asked. 'I was only in here a few hours ago. I don't know any more or less than I did then.'

He looked up as he clicked the mouse. Whatever he was working on was complete. I rose in importance to the matter in hand. I suspect I was still just a distraction, a minor plot point, a small move in his long-term strategy.

'The things we didn't talk about,' he said.

He shouldn't have been scary. He had all the classic signs

of an ageing office worker with slightly stooped shoulders, greying hair and low prescription glasses. But he had control of whether I got on a plane in five days time or not. He also had a few rooms with werewolves in, including this one.

'Oh?' I asked.

He raised his hands, steepled the fingers as he leant forward. 'You killed werewolves.'

My fingers twitched without my consent, wanting to curl into balls and hide under my arms. I held them in my lap.

'How?'

'You want a list of methods?' I asked, incredulous.

'Like knowing your friend, Dave, used an icicle? No. I mean how are you capable of it? What's so special about Elkie Bernstein that she can beat not one but several.'

I did a rough count, as I always did when I started to wonder how many werewolves I'd been on the wrong side of. 'Including the one with the icicle—Conn said he was called Giovanni—I've seen twenty-two werewolves die.'

I said it quietly but firmly. Part of me wanted to reinforce the 'fear me' message to this... person. Part of me wanted to keep quiet in case that made me so dangerous I had to be locked up or so intriguing that this werewolf had to try his luck.

'Seen?'

'I didn't kill them all,' I said. 'I just happened to be there.'

'Repeatedly.'

I looked down at my hands. Their twitching was small and slow but it was obvious that I was pushing against an instinct to hide them. My discomfort was already obvious to both of us. I took a deep breath and tucked my hands into my sides, hugging myself.

'Dave Williams killed Ben Lloyd's father with parvovirus,' I said. 'Did you know werewolves can catch canine diseases?'

Olsen leant back in his chair. 'No. I didn't.' He paused and looked at me as if I were lying. 'One instance isn't a scientific study.'

I resisted the urge to ask whether he'd run any trials. His werewolf population would be too precious to him for him to take the joke, grim as it was.

'I've just been lucky,' I said. 'Ben was never interested in hiding the fact that they were coming after me, so I could at least make some preparations.'

And then there were those like Old Man Lloyd who probably weren't a risk in themselves but got caught in the crossfire between me, Ben and Dave.

'And those preparations were good enough,' said Olsen. 'And Williams? How many has he killed?'

I counted off on my fingers. 'We're both responsible for the three that attacked us after they were turned by Ben and his dad. Not the fourth—Ben got that one. Old Man Lloyd himself. We both buried the one that fought the dog under a cairn. Diarmuid. Giovanni.'

'Seven.'

'That I know of.'

Dave would have said if he'd met more werewolves. He was too proud of killing them not to.

'So you're responsible for eighteen deaths and you claim your friend is the dangerous one?'

Well, I wanted to be seen as dangerous enough to be left alone. The way Olsen shifted in his seat made me wonder if keeping my mouth shut would have been a better plan. If nothing else, he had werewolf strength and speed on me. And the door was shut.

'He planned on specialising in clinical lycanthropy and killing any patients that turned out to be real werewolves,' I said.

There is a difference between self-defence and murder. Really there is. There must be.

Olsen's lips twisted into a half smile. 'And that happens so often.'

'He basically poisoned Old Man Lloyd and Diarmuid.'

They had never attacked him. Nor me. Not then.

'And you let them die instead of getting them help.'

I swallowed. It was exactly what the small voice in the back of my head told me on a regular basis. The one that currently said that maybe it wouldn't be such a bad thing if I weren't allowed on that plane. Not the same little voice that pointed out I probably wouldn't be on that plane because I was dead, of course.

'Neither of them wanted help,' I said, remembering

Diarmuid insisting I didn't take him to the hospital. 'It's not like I could have carried them in to hospital against their will,' I added, trying to make the memory go away.

'You could have called an ambulance.'

I stared at my lap. It wasn't exactly the first time that had occurred to me. 'Ambulances take time to get out to the middle of nowhere.'

'I didn't realise parvovirus was so fast acting.'

I forced myself to shrug but I couldn't look up. Or say that only accounted for Old Man Lloyd, not Diarmuid.

'Your friend Mr Williams has been seen killing. By Conn as well as you. Giovanni's death has been reported to the police. It has to be investigated and I have little doubt there's enough evidence to find him guilty of murder.'

Olsen paused as he picked up some papers on his desk, looked at them and put them down again. It was a fidgety move that dragged my attention back up from my knees.

'I agree that he's dangerous and I can't afford to have him leave this facility. I will be suggesting he's not of sound mind if he believes a former patient of mine was a werewolf.'

'So don't mention werewolves when I'm questioned?' I asked. 'You really think I need to be told that?'

But at the same time I was wondering what I'd tell Dave's parents. His father was my business partner, and Dave was... Well there was a lot of history there. So it wasn't like I could shrug it off and say he was staying in Norway. I had to tell them he'd been arrested for murder. Without spilling how we'd effectively been partners in what could be considered further crime in our younger days.

'No,' said Olsen. 'But I think you need telling that I find you dangerous.'

Possibly too dangerous. More dangerous than crazed men who wanted to be wolves and went around hunting women. If it hadn't occurred to me before, this was the point that would have made my position obvious. I was not on Olsen's team because I was the opposition. He was even trying to hold back a snarl that revealed the tips of white teeth.

'Are werewolves so common that I'm going to start falling over them in the street?' I asked.

He frowned at me.

'I didn't kill anyone who didn't attack me first,' I said.

I preferred not to think in terms of 'anyone' and stuck to 'anything', usually. It was just that I doubted Olsen, being one of those anythings, would appreciate the phrasing.

'If they don't come after me, they won't come to any harm,' I added.

As if they definitely would come to harm if they attacked me, as if I could always win, as if I wouldn't get old or injured and slow. I am Elkie, hear me roar.

'Life is rare and precious,' said Olsen.

'Really.'

'Particularly werewolf life. I can't risk losing even one when they could be rehabilitated. There are werewolves with potential to be something... special.'

Their life was more important than mine. I didn't like the way that sounded. Olsen had the power to hold me here. He had the power to ensure that I apparently committed suicide, or starved, or attacked another patient and lost, or became addicted to prescription drugs, and on and on. He was a physical threat because he was a werewolf but, as a director of the Institute, he didn't have to resort to the obvious.

'So rehabilitate them before they find me,' I said.

'I don't know who's a werewolf before they reveal themselves,' said Olsen.

By killing someone.

I snorted. 'That's probably your first mistake. Maybe you should try controlling the supply instead of mopping up someone else's handiwork.'

He picked up the paperwork again and this time his hands shook as he fussed with it. Somehow I doubt it was fear.

'That way you can vet them,' I suggested, thinking about the conversation I'd had with Conn as he'd led me back to Olsen's office. 'You can choose men who don't have to be the pack leader.'

He could prove werewolves were valuable members of society by choosing men who wanted to be a part of it. Instead of trying to convince men who thought they were better than society that they didn't have to throw their weight around.

Or kill me. That was the important bit to me.

Olsen put down his papers again. 'You're saying that it's

their fault?'

'That they attacked me? They chose to do it. You can't go around physically attacking people without expecting them to fight back.'

'Blaming the victim for your own failure to control your temper?' Olsen said, his tone flat. 'How... enlightened.'

I said nothing. I wasn't sure what he was getting at.

'Be careful where you wander in the Institute grounds. We have very thorough programmes for both human and special cases that can do without your interruptions. Some individuals show great promise.'

I shivered, wondering what a promising werewolf was for Olsen.

'We're done?' I asked.

'The police will be calling tomorrow to question you, along with Conn and your friend.'

'So don't mention werewolves. I know.'

Olsen smiled. He had the sort of face that should have been good looking, if pale and lined with late middle age.

'Oh, no,' he said. 'Please do. I shall be giving the police my professional opinion of your state of mind and you talking about men who can change into wolves would fit my assessment perfectly.'

I forced a laugh. 'Wolves. Yeah. I doubt they'd like you using their name in vain. I've never met a canine that deformed. You're not wolves.'

Olsen's eyelid twitched.

'Or that bloody stupid.'

His eyelid twitched again.

'Are we done?'

'Yes,' he said, in a not quite even voice.

Lie 2: Werewolves Don't Scare Me

The only thing that stopped me from collapsing back against the door of Olsen's office was knowing the bastard could hear me through the heavy wooden door. I managed to walk down the corridor and around a corner before I gave in. It wasn't until I'd taken a few deep breaths that I realised the place was empty. Where were all the people a building like this could hold?

I crouched, supporting my butt against the corridor wall, with my head low over my hands and knees. I took deep breaths until I could hold myself together, a sigh got me back to standing, another couple of breaths to clear my head and then a final, unintended 'ugh!' pushed me away from the wall. If there was no-one to stop me, it was time to look around.

'Should I be grateful that Conn hasn't been appointed my babysitter or not?' I asked the walls.

And the walls, as expected, didn't answer my question. They stayed bland and white, empty aside from the occasional off-white blank canvas. I was pretty sure that the walls by Olsen's office had painted canvasses. I couldn't remember what. There had been one with blocks, one with broad modernistic brush strokes, and... others. I couldn't even remember the colours.

Then I felt something, or didn't quite hear something. I'm not sure what. I turned on the spot, looking back the way I came. Or to the corner, at least. There was nothing to see.

'It's nothing.'

I'd taken a left outside of Olsen's office instead of a right and ended up somewhere unknown. So if Conn had brought me from the other direction and ...

There it was again. Footsteps. Slow, measured because the person taking them is concentrating on something, on prey, on *me*.

It felt like I was a long way from the main entrance and reception I'd walked through earlier today, maybe the other side of the building. I had no idea how to get back there, back to other people.

'Easiest way to work out where to go is to see what they use the rooms for,' I said.

The nearest door had a sleek modern handle that looked out of place on the old-fashioned solid wood, no obvious lock and a little blank plaque next to it, the kind that a plastic or card notice can be slid into. That at least said it wasn't intended as another relatively high security containment like Ben's.

I tried the handle on that nearest door. It turned as the footsteps—paw pads?—came a little closer. My mind filled in details like sharp canines and heavy breathing.

'What's behind door number one?' I said, then leant on it.

I know old wooden doors—they stick—and this one was no exception. The weight was considerable but it barely caught against the jamb. A nudge opened it easily enough.

'An empty office. Disappointing.'

The light from the corridor showed a room laid out almost exactly the same as his. There were no signs of life, no plants or paperwork, just thick dust on everything. Nothing to use as a defence against whatever was padding along behind me. Had it got to the corner, yet? But if this office were anything to go by, Olsen didn't have half the staff he hoped to rule and he definitely needed more cleaners.

I left the door open and stepped backwards into the middle of the hall. A slight head tilt brought the corner of the corridor back into view. Something was just there but I couldn't see it. Years of being hunted just told me so.

'At least the plaques make sense.'

Each door had one and each was supposed to be a name tag. Why hadn't I noticed one outside Olsen's? I guess I hadn't really been looking. But if every door with a name tag was an office... I shivered, thinking about more men like Olsen. If I listened carefully, I could hear breathing. Arrhythmic and layered. Two of them. Two werewolves stalking me. Again.

'Door number two,' I said and walked diagonally across the corridor.

A larger room. Probably a meeting or interview room. No mirrored window to suggest observation. More dust. I sneezed then closed the door.

'Offices and public facing rooms,' I said. 'It would make more sense if I were near or over the reception again. But only the rooms have natural light, not the corridor. Side corridor?'

Looking out of a window would make things easier. Maybe. Could I afford to take that time with two werewolves behind me?

I opened the meeting room door again and looked straight through. Across the darkness, there was a building on the other side an impressive distance away. I'd forgotten how big it had all looked outside. I'd also forgotten how late it was. Even with it being mid-December and getting dark obscenely early.

I shut the door again.

'So. If I want to find people, what do I need to do? Go back towards Olsen's office or find some stairs?'

Back towards Olsen's office meant confronting my stalkers. I'd never dealt with two at once before. Even in a relatively narrow space like a corridor, I didn't fancy my chances. Maybe I could just keep wandering around until I wasted away and only the memory was left behind to worry about catching a plane out of Norway.

I wanted to run but held myself to a slow walking pace. I probably ought to have opened more doors in case the stair wells were hidden but it didn't seem worth it. As they all had those empty name plaques alongside, they probably just hid office space. Each one of those missing name tags represented a werewolf that Olsen hoped to bring into his pack to do... something.

At least the two following me stayed back behind the corner. Maybe they watched me from around the wall. I didn't look back. I was too scared. I'd been hunted before and knew that this was only holding off the inevitable. They were probably enjoying the fear sweat that was starting to dampen my clothes.

I knew what would happen to me, that day or the day after or the day after that, because I was personally responsible for eighteen of those rooms not having an occupant. And I knew someone else who was bound to be on Olsen's list for removal based on being jointly responsible for three of those empty offices and a further three on his own. Dave Williams, former best friend, former lover, son of my business partner and potential thrusting young buck, was screwed.

'Shit.'

The sound of my own voice made me stop. It came out louder than I intended. It echoed along the corridor more than I would have expected.

'What am I going to tell his parents?'

I'm sorry but your son murdered someone in Norway. There were extenuating circumstances because he was previously attacked by a werewolf so he decided to go on an insane quest to kill them all before they killed him.

I'm sorry but your son is being held in a mental institute in Norway. There are extenuating circumstances because both he and the man in charge of the institute know that he's not crazy. At least not about the werewolves existing part.

I'm sorry but I left your son behind to die in Norway. There are extenuating circumstances because he's a lying, cheating, murdering bastard. No offence.

'I almost hope Olsen does kill you, you idiot,' I said.

A pause.

'Except I can't do it. I can't tell your parents you're gone. Not when I have something to do with it.'

Assuming I had the opportunity. Assuming the two who watched me didn't get me before I was the bearer of bad news.

I started walking again, my pace a little faster than before. With each step I reminded myself that the potential wasn't real and that the rooms would remain empty. There are not that many werewolves and, of those that exist, there are not that many that are sound enough to be in an office. As evidenced by the two pairs of footsteps that hurried to stay in eye and ear shot of me.

I turned my head slightly and they stopped, somewhere behind me. I knew if I turned my head a little more, I'd probably see them stepping into a doorway and out of sight.

The corridor kinked. Not a true end or turn but there was the first bit of natural light since the meeting room from a window over the stairs. Not as grand as those in the main reception, this must once have been the servants' access between floors.

There should have been a narrower, darker corridor running from the kink but it had been closed off with plywood nailed on to a wooden frame. The door cut into the plywood had the fittings to be padlocked shut but the padlock lay on the floor, open and ready to clasp something. Forward, down or up.

'It's like a choose your own adventure,' I muttered. 'And not a good one, either.'

I heard voices echoing up the stair well. Two women speaking in that language that almost but not quite sounded familiar. If I crept closer and listened, would I understand anything?

It was possibly the stupidest thing I could have done. I forgot to account for the unlocked door. The door, weak and makeshift, exploded over me. I managed to stumble to the side so that the attack bounced against my shoulder and I tucked into the wall. Surely those voices must hear it?

They didn't. The Norwegians kept talking, their words a backing track to the growls and pants of my attacker.

'Back off,' I growled back, hands searching my pockets, the wall, the floor, anywhere for anything I could use to fight back.

The misshapen muzzle widened into a grin that was neither human or wolf. A tongue licked pointed canines.

'You're not the big, bad wolf,' I said.

There were no weapons, the nearest people either couldn't hear or didn't care to. There were two more of these monsters behind me. I was about to die. The only reason I wasn't already dead was because this idiot enjoyed rubbing it in.

I looked around, desperate for escape or weapon to make my stand with. Those two more monsters weren't behind me. They were behind my attacker. The three of them were going to jump me. The three of them—

My attacker folded when the first of my stalkers hit him about the waist. The second stalker grabbed for his head and neck. There was a sickening crunch. There was a growl that may have meant 'Go!'

I went, as fast as I could run down the steps, stomping as loudly as I could. I didn't bother with stealth or security. I needed to be near other people. Either other targets or people who would protect me.

The two Norwegian women were still talking and I ran out onto their corridor, noisy as I could. They didn't acknowledge my presence but I heard the first word that made sense to me. The one that faced towards me was in a suit, a manager or a psychologist maybe, and said 'engelsk' among a mouthful of words. The sound was enough for me to understand it.

'I'm not English,' I wanted to shout but didn't. It's the sort of thing that would seem rude.

The other one, in a uniform so I guessed a nurse or an orderly, nodded and carried on talking. I almost didn't catch the movement of her fingers reaching towards something in a pocket.

'Excuse me?' I asked in low and careful English when there was a pause in their conversation.

Still, neither of them really looked at me. The suit held up a finger as if to say 'just a minute'. They continued talking in Norwegian.

I chose to ignore the exclusion and leant against the corridor wall. It felt exactly the same as the corridor above had. Except the canvasses weren't off-white blanks but finished works of varying qualities and styles. And there weren't two werewolves killing a third down here, either. I closed my eyes and thought of Welsh hills.

There were footsteps, first walking away and then walking back.

'Elkie?'

I opened my eyes and there was Conn. The women had left me.

'The nurse called you, right?'

He was the engelsk, not me.

He nodded. 'Beeper.'

'Head of security,' I said, pointing at his chest. 'Unwelcome guest,' I said, pointing at mine.

Conn smiled and shook his head. His thumb bounced of his chest—'dog warden'—and then he pointed back at me—'farmer'. He shrugged and put his hands in his pockets. 'We're both dealin' with feral mutts. I'd just rather find them a place where their sheep worryin' tendencies aren't tested than get rid of them altogether.'

I closed my eyes to consider. I was still leaning back against the corridor wall, still looking relaxed and calm. I must have stank of panic from meeting Olsen and the other three werewolves, though. He could probably smell the blood from upstairs and it didn't appear to be upsetting him.

'So normal humans are sheep in this scenario, are they?' I asked. 'A prey species.'

'Only in their ignorance,' Conn replied.

I didn't answer. I needed to turn the analogy around in my head a few more times. It wasn't the first time I'd thought of Conn as a dog warden, and I was a farmer in real life, but I wasn't sure it really applied to the werewolves. Well, the werewolves other than Conn.

'We're on the same side,' Conn said.

'More or less.'

As long as I seemed reasonable and didn't start hunting, I had a gut instinct that told me Conn wouldn't be happy with any attack against me. He was the kind of person that believed in second chances. So, did he know about three werewolves being loose upstairs? How could he not? Had he been one of them?

'We're all the same species,' he added.

'True,' I said. 'But humanity's the most dangerous thing on the planet.'

I opened my eyes again and he was nodding that slow nod that speaks of understanding with gentle disagreement.

'Now is not the time to correct me. I've had about as much as I can take today,' I said.

'You could probably do with a lie down. And something to eat.'

My stomach rumbled.

'Canteen first, then,' Conn said.

I pushed myself away from the wall. 'Good idea.'

He gestured up the corridor, towards the front of the building. I started walking and he fell in beside me after a couple of heartbeats staring back at the stairs.

'I prefer to think of it as humanity having the most potential on the planet. At least for the moment.'

More twisting around corridors and up and down stairs before he seated me in a huge refectory. It was empty aside from us and a handful of staff just starting to clean up and close things down. A swift count of doors and windows meant an escape shouldn't be too difficult. Shame about the Norwegian winter outside.

'Sit,' Conn said, gesturing towards a table with four chairs. 'I'll be right back with two of whatever is being served.'

'Only one set meal?' I asked, but he was gone.

The charitable assumption would be that, as things were closing, there was unlikely to be much choice available. Given the empty rooms I'd seen, I was more inclined to take it as a sign of how few people really worked or lived here. The Institute wasn't as grand as Dave had made it sound when he'd wanted to come here. But Olsen's plans must be as grand as Dave had thought if he was going to need a place this big.

The one choice, by the way, looked like some attempt at pasta with meatballs. I would complain more but I was hungry. The contents of the plate were gone almost as soon as Conn put it down in front of me.

'So everyone deserves a second chance,' I said as I put my knife and fork neatly side by side on my empty plate.

'Aye. Even Englishmen like me.'

He was still pushing food around, fork in right hand and knife untouched beside his plate. I'd thought only TV Americans ate like that because I'd never seen anyone do it for real.

'Olsen won't be giving me a second chance,' I said.

The odds were stacked against me going home with his permission. Whatever he'd said in our interview, it made no sense to me—with the benefit of thinking time—that someone who'd shown themselves to be a successful werewolf-killer would be released back into the wild. Given that three werewolves had just fought over me, my second chance had vanished.

'I'll make sure you get one,' said Conn.

'Because you're such a nice guy.'

He put his fork down, meal half eaten, and leant forward on his elbows. This was serious.

'Mainly because I always believed everyone deserved a second chance and I have to make sure I stand by that now—'

'Or what?'

He rubbed his face with both hands. Opened his mouth a

few times and then finally said, 'Or I'm not me anymore.'

He had to force himself to help people so that he didn't give in to whatever it was that was really his driving need, his obsession. More or less.

'Is it that difficult?' I asked.

He just looked at me and there was no need to say it. Yes, it's that difficult being honest about yourself. Yes, it's that difficult holding on to your humanity when you know you're standing on a cliff looking out at the sea of insanity.

'So why else?' I asked. 'You said "mainly", so there's more than one reason, right?'

'Giovanni was an ecologist.'

A mental right turn that I didn't understand.

'What?' I asked.

What did this have to do with what was going on?

'Amongst other things, he studied wolves,' Conn added.

I gave up trying to work out where Conn was taking me. 'He wanted to become a werewolf?'

Conn started pushing his food around again.

'No,' I corrected myself. 'He wanted to be a wolf.'

Conn didn't answer my question. It wasn't the direction he wanted to take us in. 'More precisely, he was looking at preservin' a natural environment that's good for wolves without conflictin' too much with human settlements.'

'You mean without them eating livestock.'

He shrugged. 'Or worse in a bad year.'

'The big, bad wolf,' I said.

'Has been a genuine threat for a large part of humanity's time on earth.'

I thought about it. I wouldn't want my cattle eaten by wolves but I don't think I'm dumb enough to leave them unattended in a place with hungry wolves. That's why farmers had employed lots of cattle-herders and shepherds in the dim and distant past. Modern British farming wouldn't spend that kind of money on babysitters, they'd shoot the wolves or keep the livestock closer instead.

'As much as I love wolves,' said Conn, and I had to wonder which kind of creature he was really talking about, 'it doesn't do to forget that they have the potential to do harm. They don't *mean* it. But they don't care enough about us to bother about it.'

He smiled and shovelled a forkful of food into his mouth.

'Giovanni taught you this?'

Conn shook his head and swallowed his food. 'I was learnin' this kind of thing before. Giovanni just gave me the chance to talk it over.'

The fork pushed some more food around. There were maybe three more mouthfuls left on the plate. It was almost like waiting for the school bell to ring at the end of the lesson.

'But he taught me some interesting stuff I hadn't realised about how wolf packs work,' added Conn.

The fork moved. Two mouthfuls were left on the plate. I tried not to stare at it. I wasn't hungry, I'd eaten my fill, but it claimed my attention.

'Tick tock,' I muttered.

'Am I takin' too long?' Conn asked.

There was no sincerity there at all. Not even a hint of pretence.

'I thought I said that quietly,' I said.

'Next time, use your in-head voice, not your mouth.'

I pushed my plate away from in front of me. 'Internal dialogue. Got it.'

'Not that he was an expert, mind,' Conn said.

I blinked. 'Back on Giovanni?'

'Aye. Keep up.'

'Get to the point.'

Conn laughed at me. 'There is no point. Not today. I'm just makin' conversation about a shared experience.'

'Right,' I said. 'So Giovanni wasn't employed as an expert on wolves but he had an interest and worked around them. What else do you want to tell me about him?'

Conn gave me a level look and forked up another mouthful of food. One to go.

'He was part of a programme lookin' at maintainin' the wild wolf population in Italy,' he said eventually.

Eventually I managed a 'There are wolves in Italy?'

'Both wild and in captivity. Not something I knew until Giovanni told me.'

Conn hadn't touched the last bite. This conversation was going to go on for longer. I tried not to swear.

'How did he become... you know?'

Conn shrugged. 'He was that way when he came and wouldn't tell me or Olsen about it.'

A man who wanted to be a wolf, who became a werewolf, would he hand himself over to an Institute?

'So how did he get here?' I asked. 'Did he do something that got him locked up for his own good or did he come willingly?'

Conn said nothing but he ate the last mouthful.

'Giovanni wasn't an inmate,' I said.

Conn chewed and swallowed. 'He was a visitor. Like you.'

'I bet he was a lot more welcome than I am.'

Conn just looked at me.

'He had questions, didn't he?' I asked.

It had to be that. However he'd become a werewolf, he'd wanted to know about — What? Controlling his obsession? Furthering it? Wolves?

Conn shrugged. 'Even if I know the answers you're lookin' for, I'm not in a position to give them to you. There are confidentiality agreements.'

He put his fork and unused knife on his plate and picked the lot up. Conversation time was over.

'Wait,' I said. 'How about if I guess it?'

Conn stood up and walked away. I picked up my things and hurriedly followed.

'What? Not even "hot" or "cold"?'

We put our plates on the counter where the one remaining member of staff nodded to Conn and whisked them away. He didn't even look at me. My feelings of danger and paranoia came back with a vengeance. I hadn't even got to ask if he knew about my stalkers and attacker.

'You've been playing with Ben too long,' said Conn.

He walked off again and I followed. I hoped he was taking me to wherever it was I was spending the night. It might not be the smartest move but it was better than standing in the refectory.

'So we both need to up our game,' I said. 'But aren't you going to give me any clues?'

Thinking of Ben and games reminded me of the chess set, and that Conn was more on Olsen's side than mine, whatever he said. He was making odd moves, like a knight piece jumping about, but I couldn't be sure if the result was as innocent as it seemed until I knew what the overall plan was. But he'd said he'd make sure I got my second chance, and I believed him.

'What do I have to do with Giovanni?' I asked. 'Why were you telling me about him?'

'We'll get there eventually,' Conn said.

There were some stairs and another corridor, but he'd taken this trip slow enough that I could mark the way back.

'Your room,' he said, stopping by a door. 'The canteen should be open for breakfast from half five.'

'Farm hours,' I joked, 'Just like home.'

He grinned. 'They're an hour ahead, here. You'll be a late starter.'

I nodded and reached out for the elegant, modern door handle. No sign of a lock.

'Wait a minute,' said Conn, and he handed me a plastic card.

I looked at it blankly.

'Electromagnetic lock.'

That didn't help.

'Hold it up to the empty name plate.'

I did as I was told and there was a clunk from the door. The name plate now had my name on it. There was another word, 'Besøksrom', that I hoped meant 'guest'.

'Now it'll open,' said Conn.

I tried the handle and it turned.

'You're not down to visit Ben until tomorrow afternoon. The police should be arriving to interview us tomorrow morning. I'll find you when they arrive.'

'*Iawn*,' I said. Fine.

An Honest Bit, or: Intermission

My back-pack waited for me in my room. I only registered it enough to huff out a 'so that's where you went' as if the bag had grown legs and walked from Ben's run on its own. After that, I collapsed face down on the suitably minimalist single bed and slept.

There may have been some snoring and some drooling. There was definitely a night-terror because I woke when I rolled into the wall, trying to get into a defensible crouch. My sleeping brain had forgotten I was in Olsen's Institute, not my house back in North Wales.

I shed my sweat soaked clothes, had a quick shower in the Spartan en-suite and tried to sleep through the last couple of hours before the canteen opened. Not that I had anything to do after breakfast, so I would have quite happily slept in if my body would have let me. It didn't.

I ended up unpacking my back-pack into the small chest of drawers that doubled as a bedside cabinet and then staring at my mobile phone while I sat on the bed. I'd turned it off at Gatwick and hadn't bothered to turn it on. I had it so I could respond to the mountain rescue alarms and everyone knew I was too far away to help for at least four or five days. But part of me wanted to turn it on and send out my own emergency message. If this was what the rest of my life was destined to be like, Olsen could keep it. Captivity was bloody boring—no matter how short he planned my captivity to be.

I was back in the canteen for half-five prompt. Thankfully, I didn't have to do anything other than pick up a tray and hold it out as I said 'Hello', 'Good morning', 'May I have some food?' and 'Thank you'. The staff stared at me but didn't answer. They handed me a cup and pointed me in the general direction of a coffee machine and a buffet of open sandwiches. I drank, wondered if I could have asked for tea, and ate one of everything on offer. The jam sandwich straight after a salmon one may have been a mistake.

I returned to my visitor's cell after rather than explore and end up hunted again.

'Come on, Taff,' Conn called to me when he knocked on the door.

I made a rude noise back and opened the door. 'The Taffs are *hwntws*. In fact, Taffs are from one valley in the south. I'm a *gog*.'

'A *gog*? So that's what the word means. I'd wondered.'

'What?' I asked.

'Not important. Old conversation. Time to go meet the friendly local police.'

I froze in the doorway. My local police were anything but friendly. I'd been near one too many deaths that had to go through official channels. If they knew about the ones I'd hidden, they'd have locked me up years ago.

'They really are,' said Conn. 'Friendly.'

When I didn't move, he turned and started to walk away. He knew I'd follow him. It put my nose out of joint that he was right.

When I caught up, he said, 'There's nothing to worry about. It's a clear cut situation. It's up to you how much you tell them about the things that have no immediate relation to the matter in hand.'

Which meant it was up to me how much I told them about werewolves and my possibly poor state of mind. Probably not a good idea to mention two stalking werewolves killing a third werewolf attacker the day before, then.

'Just go in there and be honest,' he said.

Which is pretty much when he thrust me into a room with two uniformed officers—one male, one female—and a nicely groomed woman in a suit.

'Hello,' I said.

'Miss Bernstein?' asked the suit.

I nodded and looked behind me. Conn was still there and he smiled at me. 'It's okay. They won't bite.'

'Thank you, Mister —'

'Just "Conn" is fine,' he said and was gone, door closing softly behind him.

The male uniform muttered something and the female uniform smirked.

The suit ignored them and smiled at me. 'I'm Ida Marie

Bakken. You can call me Marie.'

'You're another shrink?' I asked.

'Given the nature of the incident, the local police thought it would be best if you were interviewed by a mental health professional.' She smiled. 'Obviously, it seems a little strange as we're here but stress and trauma aren't exactly Professor Olsen's speciality.'

'No,' I said.

'Why don't you sit down? As... Conn said, we won't bite.'

No, I thought, you're not an inmate. The only thing that reassured me that these three hadn't been stalking me last night was two of them being women.

I looked around the room. Aside from the lack of dust and an increase in plant population from zero to three, it could have been the empty meeting room I'd walked into yesterday while exploring.

'Could I—' I swallowed and tried again, 'May I sit in the corner?'

I pointed to a chair that faced out of the room so that I would be able to see the door and all three officials without putting my back to a window. If it was okay to be honest, I might as well admit I had problems exposing my back.

'That's okay,' the suit said, although she scribbled a note as I walked across the room. 'So you came to Norway to visit a friend who's...'

The suit's introduction to questioning tailed off. The uniforms eyed me with something between amusement and sympathy.

'What?' I asked, letting my unease show in my uneven voice.

I looked at each one of them, only briefly making eye contact. The male uniform covered his mouth. The suit pursed her lips.

'Nothing important,' she said and scribbled another note.

This one, I knew, would be about me putting my feet up on my chair and hugging my knees when I sat down. Part of me wanted to laugh about how easy this was. Part of me was just relieved that I was in a roomful of people I could do this with and not find myself leapt on as easy prey. The case they were asking about, as Conn had reminded me, was clear cut and had very little to do with me. As long as I didn't drag in too much history, I was safe from these people and could afford to indulge my fears.

'Dave and I are visiting an old friend,' I prompted when the silence had gone on a lot too long for my comfort.

The suit nodded. 'Benjamin Lloyd.'

'Yes.'

The suit and the uniforms seemed to be waiting for more.

'Sorry,' I said, 'But if you're interviewing me, Marie, what are the two officers for?'

The uniforms looked at me as if I'd grown a second head. This was possibly not the question they expected of someone who was distressed and upset. I have a lot of practice at being both, though, and have learnt to think at the same time.

The suit simply smiled. 'Løvlien and Nygård are here to make sure procedures are followed and that the interview counts towards the investigation.'

I frowned. That didn't sound like the official version.

'Or words to that effect,' the suit added.

She made another note.

I said, 'Oh.'

'You've been interviewed by police before?' the suit asked.

The uniforms didn't obviously tense but I could feel their attention, their focus sharpen. People that guard are not so different from people that hunt.

'I volunteer in mountain search and rescue,' I said, not really answering the question. 'The police have been known to get involved in incidents, too.'

The uniforms didn't ease off.

The suit nodded. 'So, you and... Dave were coming to visit... Benjamin.'

'Ben,' I corrected. 'Yes.'

'And you met the victim. Tell me about it.'

I took a deep breath. Then another. Then a third.

'Not exactly. Dave and I came over by plane. We got here yesterday,' I said. 'Conn met us at the airport.'

The male uniform shifted in his seat a little as the suit made a note.

'You knew... Conn before this?'

'I've met him before,' I said. It couldn't do any harm to

admit it, right? 'Ben's been here a while and he had Conn bring me some legal documents, oh, maybe six months ago.'

'Legal documents?' the suit prodded.

'Ben gave me his family's farm.'

No, I don't really know why, either. It's not like we were ever a couple or anything.

'When Conn brought me the documents, he left contact details so I could come and see Ben,' I said, summarising inaccurately. 'I organised the trip over.'

The suit made a few more notes. I rubbed at my neck and wondered if jumping out of a first floor window was a viable exit strategy.

'Conn picked us up at the airport and drove us here. We had a flat tyre on the way. While Conn changed the wheel, I walked his dogs.'

Short sentences are easier to get out in stressful situations. It also sounds slightly better than the childish 'and then we' I would have otherwise been reduced to.

'Conn said the— the victim's name was Giovanni?'

The suit nodded.

'Well, he came across us—Dave, me and the dogs—while we were walking. We didn't expect to see him. He was upset but Conn turned up and it was all being sorted and then—'

'And then?' the suit prodded.

'Dave disappeared and reappeared with an icicle.'

'You know,' the female uniform drawled in excellent American English, 'that's only the perfect weapon if you don't have witnesses.'

Dave had assumed I would back him up, that I would agree with the cold-blooded killing of a werewolf. Not that I could say that to the police.

'There was blood,' I whispered, 'And the dogs were barking, and Dave was screaming.'

'What was he screaming?' asked the suit.

I shrugged. 'I don't know. It was probably just a scream.'

'How long have you known... Dave?'

'We grew up together,' I replied.

We've lived, played, worked and slept together, with everything that implies. The last part of that was not my greatest moment, in retrospect.

'Has he ever—'

'Done anything like attacking a total stranger with an icicle before?' I interrupted, not wanting to know what the actual question was. I had a horrible feeling both Dave and I could have said 'yes' to whatever the suit was going to suggest. There are many small steps on the way to becoming a killer. 'No.'

The suit frowned. 'I was intending to ask if he ever showed signs of violent temper.'

'No.'

The uniforms both shifted. Movement in stereo.

'No,' I said again. 'He's never been one to lash out physically.'

He could say mean things in the heat of the moment but he didn't attack in a temper. Opponents were better handled when they didn't expect to be attacked. He hadn't attacked Giovanni in a temper. While the actual event hadn't been planned, it was exactly what he intended to do to every werewolf he identified. More things not to mention in interview.

'Do you know of any reason why he would attack... Giovanni?' the suit prodded some more.

'Not really,' I said. 'We didn't know him from Adam.'

'And this werewolf thing?'

I shrugged. 'It's the area of psychology he wants to focus on. That's all I know.'

Or how the real world deals with it, anyway.

'Does he think werewolves are real?' the suit asked.

'How would I know?' I replied.

Both Dave and I had seen the evidence for ourselves but the fur-skins seem to melt away or disappear as soon as the werewolf dies. There was nothing we could point to and say, 'This is proof,' without a werewolf being willing to admit it. There were none of those here or, if there were, Olsen wouldn't let them.

'How would I know what he thinks?' I tried again, softer and less defensive. 'We... we've grown apart since he went away to university and I don't know what's in his head anymore.'

The suit looked at me. I looked at her. I wasn't exactly faking when the tears blurred my vision. I blinked them away and then wiped away their tracks from my cheeks.

'He left me behind.'

It would have been so much simpler if he hadn't. If we'd stayed growing together instead of apart.

Lie 3: I Don't Miss Having A Father

I didn't need to lean against anything and pull myself together when the police and their mental health person had finished with me. They were far too focussed on making sure the obvious facts were really the obvious facts. Which they were.

Dave had killed Giovanni. The Norwegian authorities didn't need to know small details like Giovanni being a werewolf, or Dave having a history of both attacking and being attacked by werewolves. The only other thing they needed to question was Dave's sanity, and talking to me wouldn't exactly prove that. If anything, the police were the safest, gentlest threat I'd dealt with in a long time.

'Everything okay?' Conn asked.

I don't know how but I'd found my way to the main reception. I'd just turned away from the interview room and walked. Without being followed by werewolves, even if I had been listening so hard I thought my head would burst all the way there.

'Yeah,' I said. 'Have they talked to Dave, yet?'

Conn shook his head. 'He's up next.'

I nodded and looked out through one of the windows.

'Can we take the dogs for a walk?' I asked.

There was silence. I felt the receptionist and the woman he'd been talking to boring holes in the back of my head.

'It's snowin',' said Conn.

'Welcome to winter in Norway,' I replied. Then I looked down at my jeans and trainers, 'Although I should probably get my coat if we go.'

I needed outdoors and open space. I hadn't been outdoors since walking in from Conn's car, if that counts as being out in the world. If it doesn't, I hadn't been out since I saw Dave stab Giovanni with an icicle, over twenty-four hours before.

Conn muttered something that may have been 'kids', then, 'Fine, go get your coat.'

'We're going for a walk?'

He shrugged. I grinned. For about five seconds.

'Erm. Which way is my room?'

He laughed. 'That way.'

And I was running, feeling all of about seven or eight, excited about a chance to break free, no matter how temporary. The buzz lasted as long as it took to return with wellies, gloves, scarf and winter coat.

'At least it's not horizontal rain,' I said and walked out the front door, forcing Conn to catch up with me for a change.

He caught up quickly, parka hood pulled up close around his head and scarf covering everything up to his eyes.

'Aye. That gravity defyin' rain is a pain in the arse. And we need to go this way.'

He edged into my personal space and I turned to accommodate, changing my path away from the big mansion-like building to angle along the drive towards a group of trees barely visible in the falling snow. I wouldn't be able to see an attacker. But they wouldn't be able to see me.

I laughed. 'Typical Brits. Ancestral enemies united in our distaste for weather.'

And it wasn't great weather, snow flurrying all around us and laying what I would have called thick before I came here. Perfect for covering attackers' prints. But it also covered mine.

Conn hmmed.

'It's the name, isn't it?' I asked.

He didn't even bother to pretend. 'Elkie Bernstein doesn't exactly sound like native Welsh. But what would I know? I wouldn't have expected Ben to have sent you that silver cross you carry.'

I laughed. 'And I thought "Conn" was an Irish name, not English.'

'I'm from Cumbria.'

'Hen Ogledd!' I said. 'You're Welsher than I am.'

'What?'

'Didn't they teach you anything in school? Cumbria used to be Rheged, a British kingdom.'

Conn shrugged. 'I just remember something about Irish-Norwegian Vikings and the Harrowin' of The North.'

My turn to hmm.

'Before our time, I guess,' I said eventually.

He paused. Yeah, maybe using the phrase 'before our time'

was a mistake. Most of what I was dealing with dated back to before my time with werewolves.

'Before our current concerns might be better,' he said, as if he'd read my mind.

'Oh, my concerns have some history,' I said drily. 'How old is Olsen, anyway?'

No answer.

'Old enough to know better, at least?' I prodded.

Conn laughed.

'How long has he been a werewolf?'

'Longer than me.'

'How long has he been trying to catch others?'

'Longer than me.'

Conn leant in again, changing my route so that I walked along the drive, past the stand of trees.

'He's my concern,' I said. 'He's the one who decides if I stay or go. He's the one who could decide if Dave lives or dies. He's the one who decides to make Ben work for him or keep him locked away.'

He's the one who has killer werewolves loose in his house.

Another turn, on to an asphalt lane that ran off the main drive. I hadn't noticed it yesterday. But, then, I hadn't been looking.

'There's no reason for you to be kept here unless he can make a big deal out of your mental state. If you gave Marie the right answers, he hasn't got that hold. There's no legal reason to hold you.'

It was as if Conn didn't know about the werewolves that had stalked me and what that meant for my getting out of here alive. Or maybe he was better at hiding things than me.

'And he always follows the rules?' I asked.

'There's a framework he has to move within if he expects to stay in charge where he is. If nothing else, his paperwork has to be solid.'

I said nothing.

'I'll do my best to get you your second chance,' Conn said.

I didn't point out that yesterday he'd assured me he would get me that second chance, not just try.

'We're almost there,' he said and I looked up to see a small cottage through the snow.

'Groundskeeper's cottage?' I asked.

Conn shrugged. 'Maybe.'

The wooden door was gloss painted green. There was a Christmas wreath nestling over an old fashioned knocker. It was like something off a chocolate box.

'Fancy more walkin'?' asked Conn, 'Or would you be happy to just throw the hounds out into the garden and have a cup of tea?'

'Is there a biscuit with that cup of tea?'

In the shelter of the porch, Conn pushed back his hood and I could see the smile wrinkle his face. 'Chocolate digestive or rich tea?'

'One of each?'

He leant on the door and it opened with a minor protest, which he ignored. 'Sure.'

As he almost fell in, the pack of five dogs I'd met the day before swirled around his legs. Then they saw me and swirled around me, instead, barking and sniffing and rising up on hind legs to look at me. I wouldn't have to worry about a third person joining us without warning, the pack would make too much fuss and noise.

'In, the lot of you,' Conn said and the dogs obeyed. 'That includes you, Elkie.'

I did as I was told, just another mixed breed following the leader to the kitchen.

'If I take a dog off you,' I said, 'Can it not be the little one?'

'Jack? Too much terrier for you?'

Jack looked like a broom without a handle. It was hard to tell if Conn was right about a terrier being under there.

'Terrier? In that case, definitely not that one. I'll never get him out from the rabbit holes.'

There was a chuckle and I realised I'd missed this. This was the sort of conversation people had with friends and I hadn't had this since Dave and I were at school, if then. The odd flirtation didn't count.

Another door was opened and the pack was sent out with nothing more than a pointed finger.

I unwrapped myself from my winter coat and hung it over the back of a kitchen chair. 'Sorry. I forgot to take my boots off at the door.'

'No matter,' Conn said from the sink, filling the kettle. 'If you want to take them off, stand them by the back door.'

I felt homesick for a home I'd never really had. Conn made an excellent imaginary parent. I had a momentary fantasy of introducing him to my mother, then brushed it away. I was being weird.

'Biscuits are in the fridge,' he said.

I didn't say it was an odd place to keep them. I just went and got them, obedient and daughterly. The well-stocked fridge had an odd mix of childish treats and well-balanced diet. A lot of choice for someone on their own. When I tried to put that much fruit and veg on my weekly shop, it started going off in my fridge before I could get around to eating it all. Maybe that's just me.

There was more weirdness as I turned around to see Conn setting out two cups and two bowls. I watched him drop a tea bag in each and said nothing.

As he poured out milk, he called out 'Moll! Sadie!'

There was the thunder of footsteps on the stairs. I wasn't sure whether it was people, more dogs, or a herd of small elephants. The thunder became two young but large dogs. They had a foxy, pointed look to them, thick whisky coloured fur and high curling tails. The size difference meant one was either the runt of their litter, or there had been a massive coincidence of two breeders having litters at about the same time.

'Erm....'

Conn turned to look at me.

'Don't they need to go out with the other dogs for a pee break?' I asked.

The two pups exchanged a very human look. The kind that says 'this girl's a fool'. That shouldn't be possible. How did they understand what I said? They couldn't. Not really. I was imagining it.

'No,' was all Conn said.

He was fishing tea bags out of drinking vessels, squeezing them out in a way that would have made me wince if I wasn't busy questioning my sanity.

The two bowls went before the two pups, each head-butting against Conn's leg and getting tousled ears for their efforts. He turned to me and pointed at the larger one.

'This is Moll,' he said.

The pup looked at me and cocked her head.

'And this is Sadie.'

The smaller pup gave me a mirror image of Moll's look. Everyone appeared to be waiting for something.

'Erm. Hello,' I said.

Conn nodded and turned back to our cups.

'This is a little weird,' I added.

The pups stared at me. The larger one, Moll, stretched out into that yoga position and licked canine teeth.

I narrowed my eyes and stared back. I've seen off werewolves. I don't take threats from puppies.

Moll huffed but looked away. Sadie, the smaller pup, snorted and stuck her muzzle in her bowl of milky tea. Moll growled a little at her sister and then stuck her muzzle in her own bowl and lapped away noisily.

'True,' said Conn.

'What?'

'It's weird,' he said.

'Not just me, then. Good.'

He laughed at me as he put my cup in front of me. There was another moment of peace—even with two dogs noisily lapping up tea—as he got his own tea and then the weirdness continued.

'Giovanni was goin' to run an errand for me.'

Moll growled as if displeased. It couldn't have been the words. That would have been me projecting too much werewolf experience on a couple of pups.

'What kind of errand?' I asked.

'Takin' Moll and Sadie somewhere safer.'

How would being with Conn be unsafe for them? This was the man who rescued strays and gave second chances. Unless the local werewolves had taken a dislike to fluffy dogs, in which case Jack should be looking for a new home, too.

'Why?' I asked but got no answer.

'Where?' I tried next.

Conn sipped. 'The UK.' Another sip. 'England.'

I considered, cocking my head like the pups had done.

'Just how English are we talking?'

He grinned. 'Home Counties.'

I groaned.

'A bit theatrical for a slight detour on the way home from the airport,' he said.

'I didn't drive all the way to Gatwick,' I said.

'So rent a car.'

I sat up. 'An exchange. I'll do it as an exchange. A favour for a favour.'

'What's the favour?'

'Help me get Ben and Dave home,' I said, 'And I'll take those pups anywhere you want.'

'That's two favours,' Conn said.

'That's two pups.'

'Some would say makin' sure you get out of here counts as a favour,' he countered.

'Then you should have opened bargaining earlier.'

He smiled around his cup.

'And you've already said that it's the police doing the work on that one,' I added.

He called the other dogs in and fussed over brewing another cup of tea but he eventually got to asking the important questions.

'Why?' Conn asked.

'Why what?' I replied, playing dumb.

'Why do you want Ben and Dave on the outside? They're less of a problem if they're confined to one place.'

I watched the pack of five mongrels and how they didn't really approach the two pups. They sort of milled around and licked and rolled but the youngsters were obviously not to be bothered.

'It's easier,' I replied. 'But that doesn't make it right.'

Conn's only response was 'Another cuppa?' even though he already had them in hand.

'Not yet,' I said, but still sipped from the mug he put in front of me as if he hadn't heard.

'Lunch, then?'

I thought about trudging through the snow to the canteen, once more under Olsen's power with werewolves that were obviously hunting me. I thought about staying in the kitchen so homey it was a cliché.

'Yes, please.'

He fussed in cupboards and the fridge. I didn't watch, I was too busy staring at the pups.

'I may not like Dave,' I said slowly, carefully, 'But I can't leave him somewhere I assume will be dangerous to him. If anything happens, I will be responsible. At least in part.'

'Olsen has to obey the law,' Conn said.

I thought of my stalkers and attacker. Some or all of them were those werewolves that showed 'promise'. They weren't following any law I knew of.

'Bollocks,' I said. 'He just has to make sure he doesn't get caught. Or send one of his werewolves to do the job.'

'He doesn't have any werewolves that would do that kind of job,' said Conn with a flat, final tone.

Maybe he didn't know about the others, then. He'd known something was going on, had looked back, had probably smelt it but maybe he didn't know everything Olsen was up to.

'It can be made to look like suicide,' I added.

Conn sighed. Had he been the one to make it look like suicide before on Olsen's orders? How long had he been with the Professor? Did he stand beside the mad scientist because he believed in the mission or because he tried to mitigate the worst?

'Or he only needs to bend it,' I added. 'The law, that is.'

The puppies were playing between themselves, play growling as the smaller, Sadie, pulled on Moll's ear. The dogs were squirming and wriggling, trying to get in on the action but not quite daring to step in.

'I can't go home and talk to Dave's parents knowing that the words I really ought to say are "sorry but I left your son behind to die". I'm not even sure I can manage "your son is under arrest in a strange country for murder".'

'Bad news is always difficult. But Williams did kill someone and he has to answer for it,' Conn said.

I nodded. But hoped that justice didn't include dredging up so much of the past that Dave and I ended up facing charges for perverting the course of justice, and maybe more murder. It's hard to prove self-defence when the bodies have conveniently disappeared. It also makes it hard to prove murder, and that was the main reason I carried the silver cross Ben had sent me.

'And I don't think a man with Olsen's ambitions for werewolf-kind should be left in charge of a werewolf like Ben,' I added.

I collapsed over the table and gently banged my head against the smooth, worn wood.

'I can't believe I suggested using Ben for search and rescue. Olsen'll have an army of killers within a bloody month.'

He probably already had a squad, based on yesterday's performance.

'He won't go that far,' Conn said. There was a quiet confidence in his voice but his body was so tense he could have been turning the just eaten digestive biscuits into a diamond. 'Olsen only wants to show that werewolves are worth something.'

'No,' I said. 'He wants to prove they're worth more.'

Conn unfroze. 'That's not necessarily true.'

'He values each and every werewolf that attacked me more than he values my survival.'

'All life is precious,' Conn said.

I sat up. 'I don't know how they became werewolves, whether they chose it or whether they were accidents. I don't know how rare werewolves really are and whether I've just wiped out half of them. I don't really care. What I know is all of the ones that Ben sent came intending to kill me. It was self-defence on my part.'

'So you've said. And that's what Ben's told me since—'

'You talked to him about it?'

'While you were with Olsen yesterday.'

I took a deep breath and tried again. 'They came to kill me because they wanted to kill me. Whatever their reasoning or rational. The other werewolves I've seen here are obviously referrals or transferred from other institutions. Olsen's trying to produce a master race out of killers and people who are known to have mental problems.'

The werewolves who had followed me down the corridor where not men who just happened to take a misshapen form. They were hunters, killers, werewolves.

'I wouldn't call it a master race,' was all Conn said.

'That's because you're one of them.'

Conn turned around slowly, a blunt, spread-covered knife in hand. 'Are you telling me to check my privilege?'

'What?' I asked. 'Am I supposed to know what that means?'

He gave me a look that suggested I'd missed something important and turned back to whatever he was preparing. I got back on topic.

'I wouldn't mind so much if he were, I dunno, finding the best and brightest and... is there a word? Raising them up? To werewolf-dom. I've got to admit you're stronger and faster with better noses.'

'Upliftin'. And we lose some of our colour vision.'

'Really?' I considered. 'So what can't you see properly?'

'Colours are just harder to see, really. Everything's a little greyer but red and green are more so. But I can see in lower light as well, like a canine can.'

'Oh.'

Conn put a plate with a sandwich and salad in front of me, then sat down behind another.

I lifted up the bread to look inside. 'I'd rather have some chocolate hazelnut spread.'

'This is healthier. You were telling me your opinion on Olsen's attempts to better werewolves,' he said.

'Don't the hazelnuts count as part of my five a day?' I asked.

He took a bite of his sandwich.

'Yeah, well,' I said, returning to more important matters, 'If Olsen were actually choosing people based on their abilities, I'd kind of understand the superiority thing. But he isn't.'

'Are you sure that's better?' asked Conn.

'More logical,' I said. 'Not right.'

Conn nodded.

'You're not any better than me,' I said.

Conn raised his eyebrows.

I cleared my throat. 'No offence.'

'None taken.'

'And you're the best one I've met.'

'Again, none taken,' Conn said around a mouthful of

sandwich. There was an extended pause as he chewed and swallowed, which I used to stare at the two puppies still pulling each other's ears, then he said, 'So you'd rather he created werewolves than tried to rehabilitate those that already exist?'

'This isn't rehabilitation,' I said. 'Have you really listened to him?'

'It's rehabilitation.'

'He cares too much about holding on to the werewolves that come to him,' I said.

'He let Giovanni go. And Diarmuid.'

'He said Giovanni was a patient here.'

Although, to be fair, Conn had also given me that impression right up until I'd asked him yesterday.

'Oh.'

'He doesn't want to let them go. He'd not let any of them go, if he could,' I said.

There were rooms waiting for them, offices for them to further the great work in, meeting rooms for them to compare insane strategies. All with little name plaques and blank canvasses. Just waiting for them to fill an old country mansion.

'He's trying to make some sort of weird pack.'

I tried not to look at Conn's attempt at an equally strange pack when I said that. It was difficult with seven dogs lounging around the cottage kitchen but I just about managed it by staring at a couple of pictures behind Conn. A colour one of him with an adult dog like the pups. A black and white of him sat next to a woman who was older than Olsen and reminded me of someone I'd seen over the last couple of days, I just couldn't think who.

'Wolves don't pack like dogs and humans,' Conn said, as if it had any bearing on the conversation. 'They typically pack in family units. Two parents and their offspring that haven't gone off to start their own families yet.'

For a moment, I was thrown back to chess—which I would no doubt be playing in a couple of hours with Ben when it was my approved visiting time. I could see the king and queen as parents, their older children lined up beside them as full adults, the rooks and bishops and knights, and this year's cubs as pawns that might just grow up to be something more useful if they made it to the other side of the board.

'Was that a vote for "Olsen's plans are unnatural"?' I asked to break away from the image.

'Would you rather he took money from men to turn them into werewolves like Ben's father did?'

'Old Man Lloyd wasn't very selective, either.' I replied. It was his clients that got me involved in this mess in the first place.

'Choosin' those with enough money to pay for the change and the care while doing so is selective.'

I avoided giving a response by picking up my sandwich and eating. There wasn't much I could say.

But Conn obviously wanted a response of some kind. 'Please tell me you didn't suggest more selectivity to Olsen when you talked to him.'

I thought through the conversation as well as I could while I chewed. I swallowed and then, 'May have done.'

Conn swore.

'He's supposed to be an intelligent man. How could he not come up with that idea himself?' I asked.

I shivered. The idea of a werewolf with Dave's brains was a scary thought.

'Because his obsession had him focused on findin' other men like him, not creatin' them.'

'But he's had care of Ben for ages,' I said. 'Surely Old Man Lloyd's business plan has come up at least once... ?'

'I have no idea. I'd just rather you didn't spell it out to Olsen as a possibility. Again.'

He'd seen this before, I realised. Conn knew of other people who'd sold their bite or whatever other methods that might work. He'd known this was possible and had hidden it from Olsen, the self-made alpha of his artificial pack. Maybe not actively hiding it... just not mentioned it. Did that mean he didn't know about the loose werewolves or was just hiding them?

'I'll never say a word about it again,' I promised.

With luck, Olsen would keep on being focused on capturing existing werewolves rather than making new minions of his own.

'Please don't,' said Conn.

I stuffed some more food in my mouth and left the topic lying. There wasn't really any more I could say, now I'd just realised I'd dropped two helpful suggestions in Olsen's ear. I really needed to up my game.

'Look, Elkie, all you need to do is go home.'

I looked at the two pups and then back at Conn.

'Aye, and take those two somewhere safe for me on your way.'

I nodded.

'Everything else...' Conn waved his hand. 'Everything else is outside of your control.'

I nodded again and swallowed. 'But Ben and Dave—'

'I'll do my best to find a way to get Ben and Dave somewhere other than the Institute if you're so convinced that they're not safe here with Olsen.'

I didn't interrupt and correct. I was fairly certain Ben was too important for Olsen to kill him. Particularly if Olsen couched everything in terms of a game that would interest Ben. Dave, on the other hand, was probably intended for a coffin.

'That's the best I can do,' said Conn.

'What more can anyone ask?' I asked.

He was all that was available to me. If his best wasn't good enough, there was no-one else to turn to.

Lie 4: I've Got Nothing To Hide

Conn took me to see Ben through the full-on security team, who could be said to sniff around as much as Conn's weird canine pack, and along the corridor with a plastic wall.

'They're not,' Conn said as we stepped from security gate to corridor.

'Not what?' I asked innocently.

He breathed out heavily through his nose. I knew what he meant, that the guards were normal humans, and he knew it.

'Do they know?'

'About how special our "special cases" really are? Not that I'm aware of.'

I shrugged and stopped to look at the first 'special case'. I'd seen them the last time—couldn't avoid walking past them if I wanted to see Ben—but I hadn't really looked at them and now I was curious. Now I wanted to look at faces and see if any were missing.

'Although two out of the three security guards were a dead give-away,' I said.

'Oh?'

I nodded. 'I never met a female werewolf.'

It was something I'd worried about when I'd been bitten myself but I'd survived and stayed human. A win-win situation.

'You never will,' said Conn.

The first captive was still furred up and rocking. The rocking got less as we spoke and two brown eyes cautiously looked up over knees.

'Alejandro?' I asked. Conn had told me the name before but there was an electronic name plate on the plastic that was obvious, now I knew what I was looking for.

Not-quite-dog-like ears twitched.

'The security don't know but Alejandro's always furred up?' I asked.

'We only have cameras at the ends of the corridors. They don't look into the... rooms.'

'A pretence at privacy. I assume someone who knows comes in to feed and water them, though?'

Conn didn't reply and I wondered what Alejandro would do, what he would be like if he were offered his freedom.

'Philip's next door, right?' I asked.

That one had sniffed at me as I walked past, snuffled and whimpered after me as if I were a treat just out of reach. He'd whined softly while I'd played chess with Ben. Today he was silent until Conn and I walked into view.

'Get another one. This one's no good any more, Conn,' he said with a boyish grin and a South Welsh accent, 'Not for another... two weeks or so.'

Philip, I decided, would end up dead if I ever met him outside. I looked at him carefully, cataloguing his pale features, before walking past. It wasn't until I was looking at Ben that I realised that it had been Philip's face I'd been looking for.

The woman in Conn's photos, the one who'd looked familiar, looked like Philip. Or he looked like her. This was way past a family resemblance and into identical twin territory. Except they were different genders and ages and different characters from the way the lines gathered at his eyes and mouth.

'*S'mae*, Elkie,' said Ben through his plastic wall.

'Shit,' I said. 'What? Wait. Sorry. I'll try that again. *Helo*, Ben.'

Ben was standing, had just stood up from being on his bed. He looked rumpled and sleepy and enthusiastic, like a child just woken up on Christmas day. Things must be really boring if I was the best thing that happened all day.

'Have you come to play?' Ben asked.

Conn stood tall and silent next to me. He hadn't talked to Philip, hadn't even looked in the older man's direction.

'Conn's just showing me the others,' I lied. I wanted to see the others but so far I'd only seen the ones I had to walk past to get to Ben.

I put a hand out and touched the air holes in the plastic wall briefly, as if I were reaching out and touching Ben's arm. Ben stepped forward with his hand out.

'We'll be right back,' I added, even though Ben would have been able to hear and smell us as we walked down the corridor.

'There are two more,' said Conn. He had the flat tones of someone who doesn't want to be there but can't be bothered to make a fuss or argue. 'Eric and Simon.'

'May I see them?' I asked.

The not making a fuss or arguing thing was a fake. He had no intention of giving in meekly. 'No.'

'But—'

'They're too dangerous.'

Maybe they weren't there to see. Did Conn know, either way?

'Really? In a high security cell?' I asked.

'They're both killers, Elkie,' said Conn. 'They're hunters.'

My hunters, probably. The ones that had killed another werewolf, who hadn't been kept on this corridor, in front of me. Secrets within secrets.

'And I am *not* prey,' I said.

Ben laughed. 'She's right. She's not.'

I couldn't stop myself from looking over at Ben and I caught a look of possessive pride. Not a sexual thing, just the look that children have when showing off a toy. Great.

'No,' said Conn, our parental authority.

'You don't think they're going to be worthy of a second chance?' I prodded.

Conn was unlocking Ben's door. 'Not yet.'

There was a fair chance that someone else had, though. And that would still leave one werewolf from the night before unaccounted for.

'They can't hurt me on the other side of the glass,' I said.

'Physically, no.'

'And I can't hurt them,' I added.

'Physically, no,' Conn said again. 'Ben, step back behind the bars.'

Ben stood still, watching me.

Conn waited. 'Ben. You know the rules.'

Ben stepped back towards his bed. This was enough for Conn to open the clear plastic door. If he could, I'm pretty sure he would have pushed me through, locked us in and forgotten us both. As it was, he only managed the middle one of those.

'Chess?' asked Ben as I stepped through the doorway.

I nodded, the sound of being locked in echoing in my ears, although the reality was little more than a muffled click. Part of me would have loved to know how it worked, plastic locking. The other part was sulking about being locked up.

'See you later, Conn,' Ben said and started setting up the cheap set I'd bought him.

Conn said nothing but I heard his footsteps as he turned and left the corridor, along with Philip's snorted 'stupid gogs' and Alejandro's almost base-line growl. There were no sounds I could identify as Eric or Simon, which suggested I was right about them not being here.

'They're not in,' said Ben.

He spoke Welsh, perhaps in response to Philip's dig at us but Welsh was as good as any other language for our games. Who else was going to understand us? Even if Philip did, would he bother to tell anyone what he heard?

'Who took them?' I asked.

'White or black?' Ben asked back. He wouldn't look at me.

'Whatever,' I said. I sat down in one of the basic office-type chairs. I watched Ben's hands moving. He put the black pieces nearest to me. Then, 'Do you know them?'

'I've met them in a couple of art sessions.'

I tried not to think about the canvasses they could have painted.

'You talked?' I asked.

A white pawn moved and Ben said nothing.

'Have you been practising or reading up on this?' I asked, a lump of sickly dread forming in my stomach.

I touched one and then another pawn, undecided what to do. I didn't really know what to do. I was good at tactics not strategy, reaction not forward thinking.

'Have you?' I asked, watching my chances of winning disappear.

'Now how would I do that?' Ben asked. 'Do you see any books in here? Any other people?'

'No.'

But that wasn't that reassuring. I flicked a glance over to where his computer had been plugged in to the Institute network before Conn had unplugged him. There was no replacement cable.

'No,' I said again and a black pawn mirrored the move he'd made already.

The next white move didn't take long and I was staring at the board trying not to get lost in possibilities again.

'If you were to be able to research chess, that's all you'd be doing, right?' I asked carefully.

'Hypothetical questions,' said Ben. 'Great.'

I made my answering move. I was fairly confident I'd reduced the number of ways he could attack me with his little white game pieces.

'Seeing as you didn't make it to GCSEs, how did you learn a long word like "hypothetical"?' I said with a bit of a smile to take the edge off.

He glared at me. 'When I've had nothing better to do but surf the Internet for the last six years? Bitch, please.'

'You weren't allowed Internet access all of that time,' I said, thinking of when he hadn't been playing his weird games and I'd had something remotely resembling peace.

'True.'

'So, you'd only have been looking up how to beat me at chess, right?' I prodded.

He looked at me with another smile and made his move. I wasn't sure whether the amusement was for my question or what his unfolding strategy was about to do to my army of little black plastic soldiers.

'I mean, you wouldn't be looking for more werewolves for me to fight, right?' I asked. 'Not after I asked you to stop?'

Ben frowned. 'I don't see why you'd want to stop—'

'You mean aside from the trauma and potential for injury?'

I moved a piece without really thinking. I was too focused on the conversation.

'But you're so good at it, Elkie!'

'I mean, what the fuck was it all for?' I stood up, unable to sit down while my body wanted to shake and pace and fight back. 'Did you want to kill me? Or did you want me to kill?'

'I just wanted to... play.'

'Play?'

Ben looked down at the board and there was pink creeping along his cheeks and neck. I wasn't sure if it was embarrassment or anger. All I could tell was that I wanted to pick things up and smash them. It hadn't been this hard to stay in control yesterday. But yesterday I hadn't talked to the police, or been hunted, or realised it was unlikely I was going home.

'You know,' said Ben, 'Like the computer games. Where you keep fighting and level your character up.'

'To do what?'

My screech was probably heard in Oslo, let alone the security room at the end of the corridor. Ben jumped but didn't look up, even though the pink was turning red. Another white piece was moved into a new position.

'I dunno. More fighting I guess.'

I clenched my fists and forced myself to sit back down again. Deep breath. Count to ten. Repeat until I can frame sentences.

'Thank you,' I said, 'But I think I'll pass on that.'

I didn't look at the board or Ben but up at the white ceiling. It was about as much stimulation as I could take in at that moment.

'I just want to go home,' I said. 'I just want to go back to the middle of nowhere—Welsh nowhere—and look after the animals. You know, farmer-y things.'

'You like it, then? You like the farm?'

'Yeah. Yeah, I do.'

I'd never expected to like being left behind in an underdeveloped, underfunded part of the UK but I wouldn't have been happy if I'd followed the assumed path from secondary school. And I wouldn't have known how to fix it, how to get back into what I really wanted. Every cloud has a silver lining and all that.

'Are you going to move or do you want me to move for you?' Ben asked.

'Don't you bloody dare.'

I took another couple of deep breaths and looked down at the board. I couldn't tell if he'd moved anything extra to the allowed moves. I couldn't even remember what my last move had been.

'Do you?' I asked.

I stared at the board and picked a sacrificial victim. Well, if things went wrong.

'Do I what?'

I chose a piece and moved it into its new position.

'Miss the farm. Do you miss the farm?'

It had been his. He'd put it in my name, perhaps as payment for playing his stupid game. Something I'd have to ask about when I could do it calmly.

'I dunno. Maybe.'

I thought about telling him he would be free soon. For the price of two puppies being hand delivered, Conn was going to get him out of here. But Conn was going to try, not necessarily achieve, and I hadn't really worked out what I was going to do with Ben when I had him free of Olsen's influence.

I spent the next morning—my second morning at Olsen's Institute—pacing my room, wishing I'd smuggled some jars of chocolate hazelnut spread with me and playing with my mobile phone. I should have had it turned off to save the battery but I had an idea that might become a plan in time so I was scribbling down all the stored phone numbers and erasing them from the SIM card.

I'd need to pick up a replacement but I was pretty sure I'd seen a phone shop at the airport. I'd have to tell the rescue team and the Williamses and my mum that I had a new phone number when I got the replacement.

I stared out of my window onto a snow covered, untended courtyard. I paced. I went to the canteen for breakfast. I missed the taste of chocolate and hazelnut. I picked up my phone again, turned it on to check it had charge, turned it off, put it down. I found the charger, unwound the cable, wound it up again, hid it back in my bag with the plug converter. I sat on the bed. I stood up. I stared out of the window. Captivity is boring.

I tried to do something about that, despite knowing that there were roaming werewolves. At least I had the sense not to go out in the Norwegian snow on my own.

I tried to find the plywood door, or what remained. I think I even got to the place where it used to be but the framework that had once blocked off the narrow corridor was gone. I couldn't even see signs of a framework having been attached. The stair-well smelt of fresh paint and bleach—and that was the closest I had to confirmation. Bleach covers smells better than it cleans, so something had happened that needed to be hidden from noses. Here that meant the blood.

I looked at the floor, trying to trace where I'd walked then run two days before. I knew I hadn't left any because my skin had remained, thankfully, unbroken but maybe—

'There,' I breathed.

A small, smeared spatter in a corner of the stair-well. More or less where wall met floor so it was probably easy for a lazy, bleach-wielding cleaner to overlook.

'Whose blood?'

I crouched over the spatter and thought about it. Trying to work out why this scenario didn't add up was better than thinking about mobile phone smuggling.

There were footsteps but they sounded like human footsteps. I assumed they were harmless—Olsen wouldn't come out this way, Conn would just ask me what I was doing—and continued to stare at the patch. Why would werewolves fight over me, here in their haven?

'Why don't you just run back to your room?'

A shiny black Doc Marten was on the edge of my vision. I looked up. He didn't carry anything that might be hiding his werewolf fur. This was a hunter who didn't mind what form he killed in.

'You must be Eric,' I said because Simons never looked like that.

The advert for Viking youth smiled at me. He may have been handsome but it was like being smiled at by a serial killer. That may have been because he was one.

'I'll give you a head start,' he offered.

He held out a hand to help me up and I took it without thinking. When I achieved full height, my nose was about level with his solar plexus.

'Thanks,' I said, instead of asking him what was going on like I should have.

'Go back to your room,' he said.

I opened my mouth to argue but I couldn't manage it. He'd knocked everything that should have been there out of my head. I did as I was told and walked away. I could feel him watching me, could hear his breath as he stalked me.

I closed myself back in my room and waited for lunch time. But, when I opened the door to leave for the canteen, I could still feel his eyes, hear his breath and, I'm pretty certain, hear him laugh. I slammed the door shut and waited for Conn to take me to see Ben.

Eventually, Conn came to get me.

I felt sweat forming as we walked through the security office—my body was suffering from the side effect of fear, both of discovery and of my stalkers. I had difficulty meeting the security guards eyes as I emptied my pockets but not one of them commented on the turned off mobile phone, not that they had before, either. It didn't matter. When it did matter, I'd have to find a way to get the charger and the converter through, as well. I would have to think about it.

Alejandro still rocked, Philip made comments I ignored, and I walked into Ben's pen without arguing with Conn about wanting to see Eric and Simon. Or mentioning I'd met them.

'I'll be back in a couple of hours,' said Conn.

I nodded but didn't look at him as he locked us in.

'Chess?' asked Ben in Welsh.

I shrugged and responded in the same language. 'Unless you want to play a console game.'

I was fed up of chess but I had to play some kind of game with Ben, the only way to stop him playing with my life was to join in with something safer.

'No. You never did like computer games,' he said.

At least in chess I lasted more than five minutes.

'What's it like?' I asked, watching him lay out the board. 'Being a werewolf?'

'Less colour, more smell, more sounds. Still boring.'

'Oh.'

He hid a couple of pawns, swapped them around behind his back and offered them out in closed fists. I tapped and chose white. I swore because I hate making the first move.

'You don't smell good, Elkie,' Ben said. 'Something wrong?'

I looked at him, hand hovering over the board without

any aim. Yet.

'Sharp,' he added. 'Fear. You were scared before you came in and now you're calming down. Like the day before yesterday, when you saw Olsen.'

Right then, for that ability, I might have been tempted to turn werewolf myself. But I couldn't because I'd already been bitten by a werewolf and stayed perfectly human. This wasn't a game for girls.

'I met Eric and Simon,' was all I said. 'They had a friend I didn't recognise.'

I'd known werewolves had a better sense of smell, I'd just never actually thought about what it meant.

Ben wrinkled his nose. 'You can have it. Outdoors and hunting was more you and the other dork's thing.'

'Dave isn't much of a woodsman these days,' was all I said.

I picked a white pawn and moved it. It seemed like an inoffensive decision.

'Where is he?' asked Ben, eyeing up the black pawns. 'Hiding out on his dad's farm in case I decide to play with him?'

'No. He's locked up somewhere around here waiting to hear what the Norwegian authorities are going to do about murder.'

Ben looked up.

'Did you meet Giovanni?' I asked.

Ben nodded.

'Well Dave was stupid enough to stab him in front of witnesses.' I sighed. 'Unlike with your dad or Diarmuid. At least he had the sense to keep that amongst ourselves.'

'He's not visited, the miserable bastard.'

A black pawn move that left me with a multitude of opportunities, most of which would probably end up in white piece suicide.

'He's not likely to. Not only will he have a similar room to yours but he hates your guts.'

'No change there, then,' Ben said with a snort.

I hmmed and then shifted another innocuous white pawn into a position that hopefully wouldn't get it killed for at least a couple more moves.

'Well, relationships do tend to go downhill after you flush

someone's head down the toilet,' I said.

'You were such a pair of dorks.'

I watched Ben touch first one black piece and then another. In his head, there were probably lines and probabilities. In mine there was just the belief that I would soon be outflanked and beaten.

'You never did anything to me,' I said. 'Well, aside from the odd insult.'

'That you used to send back right back,' Ben said with that proud smile. I wasn't sure what he was proud of.

Another black pawn moved forward.

'Williams, though, he just used to run to someone else or cry.'

'And that made it right?' I asked.

Ben frowned. 'I was hoping he'd fight. Make it interesting. After all, you used to play around with weapons away from school.'

'Basic staves and spears,' I said. 'And no technique.' Then, 'You saw that?'

'Once or twice.'

He didn't explain how. Chances were that he'd been helping out on his dad's farm and seen us mucking around in a neighbouring field, though.

'He doesn't fight back,' I said. 'He waits until you've turned your back and gets in while he can.'

It didn't sound any better. Smart, maybe, if you're smaller and less physical with no weapons but there's taking advantage of a weakness and there's heading right through the moral grey area into evil.

'Strike that. He'd wait until he had your trust and then he'd stab you. And turn the blade in your back a few times so you feel it as much as possible.'

I wasn't just talking about physical attacks.

'No change there, then,' Ben said again.

I almost dropped the piece I'd just decided to move.

'*Be*?' Whuh?

Ben shook his head and didn't explain; there was history between Ben and Dave that didn't include me and it felt a little weird.

'So the dork isn't going home with you.'

'It's nice to know what you think of us, but do you think you can broaden the vocabulary from "dork"?' I asked.

A white move that seemed to limit damage then Ben's finger did its pointing-touching thing over the black army and I wondered what went on in his head.

'No,' he said.

'So, there's not even a hypothetical connection with the outside world in here?' I asked.

'Didn't we sort that out yesterday?'

'Not really.'

He moved a knight and I frowned. It was time to break out the bigger pieces already?

'No,' he said. Then, 'I don't even know what's going on one corridor down. If that's where Dave is.'

I couldn't focus on the board. 'If I give you a phone—and the charger—would you like that?'

'Why?'

I had to pace again. I couldn't stay still and I couldn't work out what pattern the pieces on the board were trying to make.

'What for?' asked Ben when I didn't answer.

'So we can talk without Olsen being able to control the conversation,' I said.

Because that way Ben was playing with me and not listening to whatever game Olsen tried to play.

Ben said nothing.

'Not that I can afford proper conversation. It's a pay as you go and there's only about two quid left on it.'

It was still quiet. Too quiet for my nerves.

'So it's probably best to send texts.'

'About what?' Ben asked.

Anything that would keep him occupied until he got out of here. Anything that stopped him playing with my life or for Olsen.

'Games?' I asked.

Ben nodded slowly.

'Anything you want to talk about that you don't want Olsen to know,' I added.

Another nod.

'I just don't know how to get it all past the security. I mean, I can bring the phone through but it's going to be a bit obvious not taking it back through, right?'

Another nod.

'So?' I prodded.

'Are you going to make a move?' Ben pointed at the chessboard. 'Or do you want me to move for you?'

I made a hurried move without thinking it through. I paid for it by losing the game. I lost several in our two hours together and only won one to make up for it.

'You're useless at this,' said Ben.

'Don't spare my feelings, just say what you think.'

He laughed at me then looked over my shoulder to the other side of the plastic. I turned.

'Time to go,' Conn said, in English.

There was something about the tilt of his head that made me want to ask if he'd understood what we'd been talking about. I'd assumed he didn't but I'd assumed a lot of things. All things considered it was one of the saner things I've been paranoid about.

'Sure,' I said, back in my mother tongue, 'See you tomorrow, Ben.'

Ben stood up and backed away, towards his bed, as Conn unlocked the door. '*Hwyl*' Fun, but also see you later.

'Yeah,' I muttered, 'Like there's so much fun around here.'

Lie 5: I Don't Need Help

Conn took me to Olsen's office again the next day, my third full day at the Institute.

Conn and the rest of the world gave no sign of how important this might be but, for myself, there were the little rituals I used to keep my breathing even and my hands steady. I would have appreciated something to indicate whether this was the passage from guest to in-mate or a walk to freedom. Instead, there was just the mental soundtrack, the snap of teeth, as I felt the jaws of the imaginary big, bad wolf closing around my throat.

'Go on in,' said Conn.

I looked at the open door. It opened in such a way that I couldn't see Olsen or his desk without stepping into the room. Who designs their inner sanctum so they can't see people approaching?

A deep breath. Another. There was no-one out here but me and Conn, no-one in the room but Olsen and Marie. Eric and the other one, Simon, might have been around somewhere but they wouldn't be obvious. They wouldn't show themselves around Marie. Maybe not Conn, if he weren't in on it.

'He won't bite,' added Conn with a slanted smile.

He meant Olsen, who wouldn't do anything in front of someone like Marie, and I nodded slowly before I walked through the doorway into whatever happened next.

'Hello, Elkie,' said Marie with a smile.

She was sitting in front of a window, an ocean of desk between her and the rigid Olsen.

'Hello,' I forced a smile back and checked the room, basically counting possible exits. 'How are Løvlien and Nygård?' I asked, stumbling over the Norwegian names.

'On another case, I expect,' she replied.

I nodded.

'I'm just here discussing the basic findings with Olsen,' Marie said.

I glanced at Olsen a few times but he didn't acknowledge me. He either looked at Marie, his computer or something by his desk. 'You mean you've worked out what to do with the three of us present at Giovanni's... murder?'

'Well, ordinarily, the prosecution service would be inviting you back to see the inside of a court-room in a month,' she said. 'But the evidence and statements suggest that your friend will not be making it to a proper trial. He's not mentally fit to stand and will need to be put under secure supervision.'

'Oh,' I said.

'Although he has to stand before the judge in about a week for the judge to actually declare that,' added Marie.

I nodded. I wouldn't be here. Not if she could talk about inviting me back. If the officials said I was free to go, Olsen would really have to work on the situation to come up with a way to force me to stay. As Conn had said, in not so many words, Olsen still had to fit in with the legal framework if he didn't want to get shut down or exposed. Eric and Simon, or any other strange werewolves he was hiding, on the other hand...

'Will Dave have to stay here or could he be moved to a place nearer home?' I asked.

Marie shrugged. 'That depends on the judge. And whether there's a secure facility near enough to your home to make the risk of moving him acceptable.'

'But he won't be on the plane with me in two days' time,' I said.

'No,' said Olsen. 'It takes a little more time than that, I'm afraid, Elkie. And the police certainly won't be letting your young friend on a plane with innocent people.'

It was a mixed blessing. I didn't particularly want Dave sat next to me in a confined space for several hours, anyway. His presence had been far from calming for years.

'Has—' I swallowed to wet a suddenly dry throat. 'Has anyone contacted his parents? I probably should have rung them but I didn't want to talk about... you know. Not before it was okay to talk about it.'

'Not yet,' said Olsen.

'Oh.'

There really wasn't much to say to that.

'You joined us when we were debating the wisdom of

allowing Williams to contact his family,' said Olsen.

I held on to a snort of disbelief. They hadn't been discussing anything when I came in. They had been silent when Conn opened the door and there was nothing to indicate they had been mid-conversation before that.

'Someone official should talk to them, surely,' I said. With luck I'd only have to hug his crying mother, pat his father on the back and say something meaningless.

Olsen gave a thin, insincere smile. 'It isn't really anything to do with you, Elkie.'

I considered. To all intents and purposes, Dave was just an old friend and the son of my business partner. Family news was supposed to come to me second hand, not in meetings with Dave's new psychologist.

'True,' I said. 'So what meeting am I here for?'

Olsen steepled his hands and leant forward on his desk. He'd done that last time, too. All he needed was a fluffy white cat to complete the image—although I suspect he probably would have eaten it with relish as soon as the normal, human psychologist was out of the room.

'I want to ensure that your return to England will go as easily as possible,' he said smoothly. 'There's no point letting you catch your flight if it means you'll need to be back a couple of days later.'

Marie looked like she'd just eaten something sour. 'It's unlikely that Elkie or Conn's presence will be necessary at the hearing.'

I frowned. This appeared to be something they had talked about before. I recognised the 'you're not listening to me so I'll say it again' expression.

'I'd prefer it if anything like that could be moved forward to fit in before my flight,' I said.

Olsen chuckled, a disturbing little rumble of amusement at my expense. 'I don't think we can organise the Norwegian legal system to run at your convenience.'

'Then you'll have to put up with me going home and then returning when I've had time to put my business interests back into some order so that I *can* attend any hearings,' I said.

'Again, the legal system doesn't run at your convenience, Miss Bernstein.'

'No,' I said, 'But I assume they give people at least twenty-four hours notice before asking for them to turn up in court. And I'm only— What? A day's travel away.'

Give or take.

Olsen linked his fingers and he looked a little less evil mastermind. 'Still—'

'Are you even listening to me?' I interrupted.

My heartbeat was going pretty fast and I tried not to start breathing any faster and louder than I already was. I was scared—but Marie's presence meant I had a chance to hit back without worrying too much about the result. Just about every form of reprisal had also been blocked by her paying attention. Coming in, sitting in on my supposed interview with Olsen, meant she was the kind of person who would notice if I wasn't on a plane out of Norway.

'I run a farm,' I said. 'I have animals to look after. If nothing else, I'd rather not end up in a court in Wales over their welfare just because you thought I should spend another couple of days sat on my fat arse watching it get fatter.'

From the corner of my eye, I caught a twitch of Marie's lips, quickly hidden behind a hand.

Olsen frowned. 'Your business partner—'

'Is semi-retired and can't handle the whole spread on his own. That's why we're business partners.'

Like most of the neighbours said, farming was a young man's game. Or mine.

Olsen was going red but he had the grace not to explode. 'But you're here—'

'Because we made arrangements for a week of extra help.'

We couldn't really afford it and it was only for the early feed and checks to save Mr Williams going out at half five in the morning. The week would be up the day after my flight. If I were expected to come back... Well, financially, it didn't bear thinking about. Maybe we could do some bartering with the neighbours.

But that wasn't what I was really telling Olsen, or trying to, anyway. What I really wanted to get across was 'I will be missed', something I probably hadn't made clear in our previous meetings because I was so damned scared of getting stuck here. With him and his hunters.

‘Of course,’ Olsen said eventually, ‘We can’t have animals being mistreated.’

There was gentle emphasis to the word ‘animals’ that, combined with the flat and emotionless tone, made me want to run and hide. Who did he think of as animal? As I’m pretty sure he considered himself better than a mere human, that would be me—and Dave.

‘No,’ I said.

‘So,’ he said, ‘I’ll make sure that Conn takes you to the airport. Let him know what time the flight is so he can get you there in plenty of time.’

I nodded.

‘Don’t worry,’ said Marie with calm confidence, ‘The preliminary hearing won’t need you or Conn. If witness statements are considered at that time, Conn’s near enough that he can be called on.’

‘Thank you,’ I said.

She shrugged. ‘It’s just the way the system works.’

And she was making sure it *did* work. I made a mental note to tell Ben about the new playing piece on the board. It was the kind of thing he would be interested in. Although I hadn’t exactly explained about Olsen and Conn, yet. Which reminded me...

‘What about Ben?’ I asked Olsen.

He raised his eyebrows at me. ‘Hmm?’

‘Ben Lloyd? The apparently family-less friend of mine you have in a secure cell?’

Marie almost leant forward. There was a little twitch that I’m pretty sure a predator like Olsen saw if I did.

‘He’s just addicted to game-playing,’ I said. ‘It’s a bit harsh to keep him so isolated, surely?’

Carefully ignoring the fact that Ben’s games usually involved trying to get me killed by werewolves and that he probably wasn’t safe to be allowed out. The reasons why were reasons Olsen would want kept quiet and I didn’t want Ben left here.

Olsen smiled, another thin and humourless parody. ‘Again, I’m not sure that’s any of your business.’

‘If this Ben is safe to return home,’ said Marie, ‘And his doctors agree, he just needs a hearing in front of the board, surely?'

'I hadn't considered recommending him for release,' said Olsen.

Marie and I just looked at him, Marie presumably expecting more information and me just waiting to see what lies he spread.

'Lloyd has no known family. We've been unable to find his mother and his father passed away shortly before he was taken into care in England. There's nowhere to release him to.'

I felt the need to protest. 'I'm basically the closest he has to family. He signed his property over to me so I could keep the farm going.'

Well, half of the overall business, now, seeing as I'd decided to join forces with Dave's parents. It might have been a sound business decision but my personal life remained screwed up.

'Well, the closest to family unless his mother crawls out of the woodwork,' I added, remembering that local rumour at least had always assumed that Mrs Lloyd had run off with a more interesting man than Mr Lloyd.

'Is that likely?' asked Olsen, which meant he knew better.

There was always the possibility that her remains might turn up in my septic tank, but I shrugged. 'I have no idea.'

'Maybe there's some way to get you listed as a recognised next of kin,' suggested Marie.

Olsen pursed his lips. There were reasons why he wouldn't want to but it didn't mean they would be acceptable.

'So he could come home to the farm?' I asked, suitably wide-eyed and hopeful. And trying not to curse over potentially ending up sharing a house with a game-playing maniac who probably still didn't clean up after himself.

I did, however, enjoy how much it must have hurt Olsen to say, 'That's certainly something I could look into.'

I turned my wide eyes on him. 'Could we sort it out tomorrow?' I asked, 'Before I go home?'

Olsen's attention dipped to his side of the desk again and then me. I was willing to bet that whatever held his attention held his fur-skin, the thing that made him a pretend wolf.

I felt like coming out of Olsen's office singing. I didn't. I had to bite the inside of my lip to hold in a grin. It felt like I'd achieved something, like I'd fought and beaten a dragon rather than just an office-bound werewolf.

'Elkie?'

Marie had come out right behind me so no victory skip, leap or run down the corridor while no-one was watching. Which then reminded me that I shouldn't have been considering doing it, anyway. There were likely to be an Eric or a Simon watching if nothing else.

'Marie,' I said back, keeping my voice flat and the grin from my face.

She smiled and held out a white business card. 'In case you need anything.'

'Like what?' I asked.

It's hard not to sound like a sullen teenager with a question like that.

'To talk,' she said, 'You've obviously been through a lot and I don't think you're getting the support you need. Conn said you might need an ear.'

That made me smile. What support is there for someone who has been hunted by werewolves? But I took the card because it was obviously part of Conn's plan to get me out of there in one piece.

There was almost nothing on the card. On one side a stylised bear, maybe a polar bear, and on the other there was Marie's name, a job title, an email address and a phone number. The only thing I understood about the job title was the word 'psykolog' and the email address, 'imbakken@vale-monogeftf.no', made even less sense than the rest.

'Thank you,' I said.

She nodded and folded her hands around a small, neat briefcase that could have doubled as a leather document folder. 'I would quite like your contact details.'

'I gave them in my interview,' I said.

'For my use, not police-related.'

Of course. I should have seen this coming. It was Conn's plan, after all. 'Oh.'

'I think your case fits in with my own... interests.'

I looked away and one of the canvases near Olsen's office

door caught my eye, painted in what looked like paint spills and splatters. The paint was different shades of red, some of which clashed, and one shade of dark green that definitely didn't fit. This close to Olsen that meant it was a werewolf, one of his patients. I hoped it wasn't Ben who'd painted what suddenly looked like the aftermath of a violent attack.

'I'm not a case,' I said to Marie.

I wasn't the kind of person who painted pools of blood, although I had made them on occasion.

'I suppose not,' she said, 'But I would like to discuss... things.'

I was pretty certain the odd choice of green had happened because the painter had assumed it was red. In this Institute, it probably meant his red-green sight had gone the way of his humanity.

'You mean how I'm coping with Giovanni's murder?' I asked.

'Among other things, yes.'

I looked at her, attention finally caught from the sickly green paint. 'Other things?'

Marie smiled again. Serene, calm, centred. 'Other things,' she agreed.

'Have you got something to write on and with?' I asked. 'I can give you my address and email but my phone's broken. I need to sort out a replacement so I don't have a number at the moment.'

'Well that explains why I haven't seen you playing with a phone. You young people never seem to stop playing!'

There was something about the emphasis on 'young people' that softened it and made it a joke at her expense, rather than someone complaining that I was one of those youth of today who seemed to be doing something she couldn't or wouldn't at her hardly advanced age. I didn't have the heart to tell her that I couldn't and wouldn't, either. I couldn't afford a contract or a smart phone, just the brick and enough credit to be able to check in with the mountain rescue team.

'If you've broken the handset, surely you'll have the same number?' Marie fished for pen and paper in her case.

'I need a new SIM card,' I said.

Ben needed mine to make phone calls or send texts.

Marie raised her eyebrows at me. I wasn't sure if it was because Norwegians used another phrase for it or if she found my cover story questionable. I know I did.

'Okay,' was all she said, though, 'I'd like your address and email, then.'

She held out a small notebook and a ballpoint pen. I hesitated despite having been the one to ask for pen and paper. Why was she determined to stay in touch with me? What was so important about me? What had Conn said? I should have been happy. Her attention meant someone would notice if Olsen got rid of me. Her current presence probably meant I'd get off this corridor in one piece.

'How about I send you an email with it in,' I said.

I held up the card she'd just given me with her business email address carefully on display. She didn't withdraw the pen and notebook.

'How important is this?' I asked.

'Trying to put me off?' Marie asked with a smile. 'And how important it is depends completely on you. You shouldn't have to cope with this alone.'

'I'm not,' I lied.

If I found a way to explain Dave's incarceration to his parents, to talk around this with my own mother, and to concentrate Ben's game playing on something constructive. With those four people, I had something vaguely resembling a family—or a pack.

'And I'd like to know that your friend gets home.'

I blinked. 'Ben or Dave?'

'Not Dave,' she said. 'He deserves justice.'

There was an edge of 'And I'll see that he gets it'. Whether her idea of justice was the same as the police or Olsen's, I couldn't tell.

'I'll email you if Ben comes home,' I said.

I couldn't quite bring myself to say 'when' because there was still a chance for Olsen to block it.

'I'd like to know if he doesn't, too.'

Did this make her an ally or another opponent, intent on political moves that could potentially take me out of the game. I suppose my confusion showed.

'It's okay,' Marie said. 'Actually, it's probably better if you just email me so I know you got home okay.'

'You distrust Olsen that much?' I asked, knowing that I did regardless of her answer.

Her attention shifted to a point over my shoulder, and I turned to look. It was another canvas, this one with a bright red werewolf paw print in the middle.

'I suppose so,' Marie said.

I barely noticed. I was staring at what looked like the Red Hand of Ulster, if the Red Hand had actually belonged to badger the size of a man. With the dog-like shape, there was no way it could be human but, with the five digits, there was no way it could be canine.

'Interesting painting,' I said.

'Yes.'

I was still stuck on the Irish symbolism. I couldn't think that anyone here would purposely paint a Red Hand of Ulster. It had to be one of those coincidences, right? A werewolf inmate asked to paint a picture who got fed up and made a paw print instead. In red, like blood, that they might not have been able to identify as anything other than grey.

'This place is weird,' I said.

'Yes.'

I looked back at Marie and she was putting the pen and notebook back in her neat leather folder. She knew that a paw print was more than an interesting painting, and she didn't trust Olsen. Was she worth staying in touch with?

'I'll email,' I said. 'When I get to an Internet connection.'

'You don't have your own?'

Something told me she found that weirder than Olsen's Institute.

'No,' I said. 'Land lines and internet connections can be expensive. When you have no money in the first place.'

The eyebrows seemed to edge higher. I wondered what it would take to push them off her face altogether and almost giggled on the surreal thought. I coughed.

'Farmers,' I said, pretending I'd been clearing my throat. 'Asset rich, capital poor.'

Marie nodded slowly.

I put her card in my back pocket. Maybe I'd remember it was there when Conn took me back to my room. Maybe I'd send her an email after I got home. Assuming Conn showed up to lead me around like he usually did. Assuming Olsen honoured everything that had just been foisted on him. Assuming there weren't still werewolves stalking me. My happy buzz was gone.

'I'll email,' I said, only half sincere.

'Please,' she said, 'Do.'

She turned and walked away and I watched. She knew her way out of here and knew how to get where ever she was going next. She had the firm step of someone who expects the ground to stay level beneath her feet and no surprises hiding around corners. I knew where my guest room was by now, of course, I just preferred to have Conn's company when there were other werewolves out there.

I looked at the Red Paw again. I still saw overtones of the Ulster loyalism I associated it with but I was too young to remember the Troubles first hand—and not Irish, so I doubt I grasped all the connotations of the Red Hand it resembled.

'So who are you proclaiming loyalty for?' I asked aloud.

The answer was probably the one werewolf still in his office.

'No-one,' said Conn from behind me.

I jumped. I didn't ask how he managed to turn up without me noticing. The answer would most likely be a combination of his being light of foot and my subconscious starting to relax and stop paying that sort of attention to him. My brain kept telling me 'parent' and 'safe'. I wanted to shout back, 'not mine' and, 'how can you be so sure?'

Conn waved a casual hand towards the canvas. 'That one's Alejandro's.'

Which explained it all. Every time I walked past his room, he was in his fur and rocking like a disturbed child. Whoever the therapist or art teacher was, they were lucky Alejandro had paid any attention to paint and canvas at all. Possibly also lucky he hadn't tried to eat them. The Red Paw, then, meant 'I am here, can I go now?'

It also meant that the therapist had seen a furred up werewolf. Somehow I doubted Alejandro had been allowed out, so had it been Olsen playing with paints or another trusted employee?

'Do you know which picture is Ben's?' I asked.

Conn walked off. I felt it more than I saw it, a sudden loss of authority figure. I considered being rebellious then hurried after. Obedience was an acceptable price for not being eaten by Simon or Eric.

'Here,' said Conn, not far from the bend I'd disappeared around my first day here.

'This?' I asked, pointing.

'He's been here long enough to do more than one,' said Conn, 'But apparently he always draws or paints the same thing. More or less.'

'He needs some lessons in life drawing.'

Conn snorted. 'Enrol him at your local college.'

I leant my head to one side. It was kind of obvious what he was trying to get across, I just wasn't sure if I was supposed to recognise the who. There were three figures in golden yellows standing back to back. I say 'standing' but I think they were supposed to be in combat stances. One of them may have been me. They were almost spot lit in a white circle, then there were swirling blacks and greys and browns. I could see some red eyes, maybe teeth and claws, in the shadows.

'Kicking ass,' I said.

'About to get eaten,' said Conn.

I tried not to think about Eric and Simon. 'Ben saved my life once.'

Conn said nothing.

'Have you ever done any of this?' I asked waving at the canvases on the wall.

Conn laughed. 'I've never been a patient. Only a guest and an employee.'

'Why?' I asked.

'Where else was I goin' to go? Home wasn't home anymore.'

Lie 6: It's You And Me Against The World

'*Felly,*' I said to Ben as we were left alone, So...

'So what?'

I shrugged, momentarily distracted because it had just occurred to me that I wouldn't have left a man in what amounted to a secure cell alone with anyone, let alone me. Only four days late. I looked back at the door and wondered if I could claw my way out.

'Chess?' Ben prodded.

I turned back to him. 'Fine.'

This time I was the black pieces. A relief. I might be able to get away with just reacting instead of having to work out a plan. I watched the first white pawn move purposefully towards my battle line.

'The guys down the hall,' I said, finally getting around to finishing off my 'so' sentence.

Ben paused, hand hovering instead of returning back to his side. This might delay my outright defeat a little longer than I'd hoped.

'What about them?'

I looked Ben in the eye and asked, carefully, in Welsh, 'Are they back yet?'

He looked away. 'I don't know what you're talking about.'

'Eric and Simon,' I said.

That was still a missing third, the attacker Eric and Simon had killed, who hadn't been on this corridor. Maybe he had escaped from a secret corridor behind the plywood door. But the door had gone and Eric and Simon were still around so I didn't dare look at what Olsen was hiding from Conn.

'No,' Ben whispered.

He still wouldn't look me in the eye and now he'd sat on his hands. He didn't like this conversation and something scared him.

'Does Conn know?' I asked.

'Only if next door told him. He talks to the *hwntw*, sometimes, but he doesn't speak to any of us much.'

Because something about the werewolves upset him, probably. Like the fact that most of them were killers.

'So who took them?' I asked.

Ben rubbed at his nose. 'Olsen,' he said flatly. Then, 'Are you going to move?'

I looked down at the board and tried to focus. Only one move in and I was already lost because I was thinking about Eric and Simon chasing me around the Institute. After umming and ahing a bit, I took my finger off the pawn I could have used in an exact mirror of Ben's move and moved another one instead. I couldn't make it too obvious I wasn't planning even one move ahead.

'Oh,' I said, 'I've seen your painting, too.'

Ben looked around. 'I have a painting?'

His show made me check the room out, too. For a change, I ignored all the stuff that was here and finally noticed what wasn't. Again, four days late.

'The therapy thing,' I said.

'Oh. Those paintings. You've seen them?'

'One of them. Olsen has them in the corridors.'

'It's just a thing we have to do,' he said.

'Do you go to another room or do the paintings here?' I asked.

He moved another pawn and then said, 'Usually in the cells with Olsen watching.'

'Oh.'

'It isn't important,' he added.

'I don't know... Being immortalised in—' I tapped my head, trying to think. 'What did you use?'

'Paint.'

I glared at him.

He grinned. 'Acrylics.'

'Being immortalised in acrylics is a pretty big deal,' I said.

I looked away to focus on moving another little black soldier, obediently going to its doom as it mirrored Ben's first move.

'You got it? You understood?'

'You, me and your dad against the world?' I asked.

Ben stood up and threw his arms out in a wide, angry gesture. I'll never be sure if he meant to take the board with it or not. It was too early in the game to be throwing it around like that in frustration, not that he'd done that before.

'Da? Hell, no. Not that bastard!'

'You, me and Dave, then?' I guessed.

Ben paced, and ran hands through hair, and took deep breaths, and—

'Ben,' I said.

He ignored me.

I stood up and got in the way of his pacing, despite the fact that my instincts were telling me to run and hide. I could feel my heart pounding and wondered if his anger was making his beat just as hard as fear made mine.

'Ben.'

He turned away from him and I touched his arm, the one raised as he ran his hand through his hair. I figured that one was safer because it was occupied, moving. Lashing out would take time for reaction, thought and change of direction.

He froze.

'You might as well stop drawing Dave,' I said. 'He's never going to be on the same side as you ever again.'

The arm came down slowly to Ben's side.

'He's not that important,' he said.

But he was still angry. I could see the twitch of eyes that wanted to narrow. I could feel the muscles in his arms bunch and flex. I could see his hands clench and unclench. He'd had some kind of game plan, something long term that had the three of us against the world.

'Dave really doesn't like you. He blames you for being attacked the first time and everything that's gone wrong since. He hates werewolves.'

Ben snorted and looked away from me with a smirk. I'd missed something important but then I always did when it came to strategy. Even so, I was certain Dave would never have my back again, let alone Ben's.

'It's just the two of us,' I said.

Ben looked at me. 'Really?'

'Yes,' I said.

After all, I'd hopefully set things in motion that would have Ben coming back to the house he'd grown up in. I wasn't going to release him on an unsuspecting world and I wasn't likely to leave him undefended against the prying eyes of the general public.

He smiled. A beatific, golden smile that reminded me of him as a kid, when I'd had a crush and my biting back had been as much my way of flirting as it had been fighting against his bullying. The muscles under my hand finally stopped bunching and clenching. I looked down and his hands were loose and still. He was calming, even if he wasn't totally rid of the anger.

'*Iawn,*' I said.

A deep breath of my own. I let my hand drop away.

'Ben?'

'Yeah?'

He was still stood there, so close my mere human nose could smell musky young male. I stepped back to my chair and sat down.

'Where's your... you know... fur?'

I couldn't see it in the room—no folded fur in a corner, no skin laying out on the bed—and I couldn't remember having seen it before. Which is odd, because there weren't many werewolves I hadn't met wearing their fur-skins or carrying them. At a guess, Olsen's was in or near his desk, the thing he kept looking at. Only Conn and Ben—and, previously, Ben's dad—never seemed to have one around.

'Da burnt them,' he said. Clipped, short words that gave nothing more than the basic truth. There was no more explanation.

'Oh.'

Ben picked up the board and put it back in the space he'd made among the computer and games consoles. It had some scratches in the surface paper from being pushed against hard edges when he'd thrown his hands around. He fingered the damage and huffed. Nothing good ever stays undamaged.

'It's just a cheap set,' I said. 'I'll buy you another set when I can afford it.'

Although we might not need it. I'd originally planned for us to be playing long distance with him here and me in North Wales, so I'd bought a second set for me. If he was going to be there in person, instead of email, we only needed one set.

'Na. Don't bother,' he said.

He concentrated on putting the pieces in place, both the ones that hadn't moved yet in their ranks and the four that had moved into what I could only assume were the right squares. I couldn't even remember the last move I'd made and we were only four steps in.

He looked at me. 'That look right to you?'

I looked down. I couldn't afford to admit I didn't know and barely cared.

'Sure.'

I looked up in time to see an odd look, his head cocked to one side like one of Conn's pups. I'd missed something again.

'My move,' Ben said.

For a moment, I thought maybe I'd miscounted or something because of the way he said it. I had to check how many pieces had moved from their starting places before I could say 'sure' again.

'You haven't got a clue, have you?' he asked.

I stalled. 'I'm just distracted.'

I couldn't afford to have him think I wasn't involved. Finding a game that would involve us both was usually bad for my health.

'Anyone would be distracted by an upset werewolf,' I added.

Ben's hand hovered over his small white army again but he didn't make a move. 'You're scared of me.'

Terrified, part of me said. My mouth went with, 'intimidated,' if only to downplay the weakness.

But 'intimidated' was what I'd been when we were both teenagers and he'd been the golden boy with a tendency to making fun, not this. It was a reasonable fear, wasn't it? Being a werewolf made him that bit faster and stronger than me. He could smell my emotions and, combined with his obsessive game-play, manipulate me.

'Werewolves bother me,' I said.

I'd been hunted. Repeatedly. It didn't pay to forget how they—he—could be.

Ben shook his head. 'I don't want to be a werewolf.'

He moved another piece and I barely noticed. Did it matter what he wanted? He was a werewolf. That was it, the end of his story, regardless of what had happened to his fur-skin.

'I'm no different than I used to be,' he said. 'Were you scared of me then?'

'You're different,' I said, not answering his question.

He shrugged. 'Well, I have no family. I never got my GCSEs. I can't *do* anything. But I'm me.'

There was the small matter of being obsessed with games but I knew better than to say that. He'd always needed to be doing something, had enjoyed competing and winning just a little too much. It might have become an ugly personality trait with natural development but now...

'You're bigger and stronger and faster,' I said.

All of which meant 'more dangerous' to me.

'I've always been bigger and stronger and faster than you,' Ben said.

He'd been the star athlete while I'd been someone that had to be forced into PE although I loved being outdoors. On the other hand, these days my work was physical and I knew that technique could beat raw power hands down. In a controlled situation. My problem was that werewolves didn't make for controlled or easily managed situations.

'You work outdoors, Elkie,' Ben said. 'You're probably fitter than I've ever been. And you've fought werewolves and won.'

But the raw strength was still there, the potential, even if he'd not left this room in what? Six months?

'You're twenty-two,' I said. 'Not middle aged and tending to fat.'

'You remember when my birthday is.'

I caught the exact date before it tripped off my tongue. We'd gone to the same tiny primary school and been in many of the same classes at secondary school. I'd lived through his birthday enough times to have an excuse for knowing the date. But I didn't want to admit that weakness, either.

Ben grinned at my silence.

'I remember it's early in the school year,' I said, keeping my tone level.

I forced a shrug. If I pretended it wasn't important maybe he'd believe it. Although that might have been the source of our original problems, pre-werewolf bite. Ben was one of the oldest in the year, I was somewhere in the middle as usual and Dave was one of the youngest, his birthday falling in the school holidays. At almost a full calendar year younger than the school golden boy, Dave must have felt like he had a lot of ground to make up.

'If I scare you, why do you want to stay in touch with me?' Ben asked.

Again, there was nothing I could do but remain silent, this time even if he pressed or pushed or otherwise manipulated me. There was no way I could tell him what I knew and what I felt. That Olsen's plans meant Ben would be put to bad use, that Ben's obsession meant both I and others would be in danger if I had no influence or control, that I still wanted to preserve what remained of the golden boy.

'Are you going to move or not?' Ben asked.

I didn't sleep that night. I hadn't exactly been sleeping well in Olsen's Institute, anyway, but I could usually persuade my body that there were no threats nearby. This was different. This was me too wired to fall asleep in the first place.

After the first hour of trying, I got up and checked the charge on my phone. At about three quarters left, there was an argument for plugging it in. I did. I watched the little battery symbol do its charging thing.

I paced. I wasn't quite brave enough to push my luck by pacing in the corridor or prowling around the building. My mind replayed Eric's laugh whenever I approached the door. I lay down and tried to sleep again. I got up and checked the mobile and then paced some more. Rinse and repeat.

About four in the morning, I gave up and got dressed. The phone was fully charged and I started working out where to put it so the lump wasn't obvious. I considered trying to hide it in my bra or pants. I giggled at the idea of Ben having to use it afterwards. I decided to try putting it in other places, inside my clothes and pocketed against falling out without being in an actual pocket.

I practised pacing my room with the hidden phone.

The charger remained beyond me, too ungainly to be anything but an obvious lump of metal and plastic hidden under fabric. I hoped it wouldn't matter. If Ben only turned it on once a day for maybe fifteen minutes to receive any texts and reply, it could last a couple of weeks, at least. We'd work out what came after that... well, after that.

As soon as I thought the canteen would be open, I disappeared for lunch, trying to act normal—or as close as I could get when I was smuggling a mobile phone under my clothes. I concentrated on my breathing and thinking about my flight home rather than everything that was about to come in between.

I was so busy concentrating, I barely noticed that everyone pointedly spoke Norwegian around me unless I spoke to them directly. The other days it had felt impolite, as if they might be talking about me. That day, it was just background noise. If they knew what I was doing, they wouldn't have been talking about me, they would have been calling security.

I dawdled back from the canteen to my guest room because I had nothing to do but pace or lie on the bed, both of which I managed to do without jumping at slight noises, breaking into a cold sweat, or dropping my phone.

When Conn knocked on the door about mid-morning, I was careful not to be too eager or too abrupt.

'Morning,' I said with just the right amount of attention.

He looked me up and down with narrowed eyes and then shrugged. 'Mornin'.'

I didn't demand 'What?' as it would have made me looked guilty.

'Am I going to see Olsen or Ben?' I asked.

I'd only seen Ben in the afternoons but that didn't mean there was a set time. Olsen I'd seen at more random intervals, when he could be bothered to fit me into his schedule.

'Ben,' Conn answered.

'Okay.'

There was a pause and then Conn asked, 'Is there a reason Olsen would want to see you?'

I opened and then shut my mouth, trying to think of what to say. I didn't say anything about paperwork or Ben going before some board or other to be allowed out for good. I hadn't mentioned it to Conn the day before. I couldn't explain it without mentioning Marie and I didn't want to mention her interest in me, despite him having set us up. The interest of mental health professionals is not necessarily a good thing, particularly when folkloric creatures like werewolves are involved.

'Never mind,' said Conn with a noise halfway between a sigh and a chuckle. 'It's not like you know what's goin' on in his head at the best of times.'

He turned and walked off. I had to jog a few steps to catch up.

'Do you?' I couldn't resist asking.

'Do I what?'

'Know what's going on in Olsen's head,' I said.

'No.'

Final, firm and cutting off all other avenues of conversation. But I was beginning to realise that Olsen didn't share everything with Conn, anyway. I was pretty certain that even if Conn knew about Eric and Simon roaming, he had no idea about the werewolf attacker.

'Fine,' I muttered.

But I guess I wasn't the actual source of his annoyance that day because he was surprisingly helpful with the security team between us and Ben's corridor. As I prepared to not-quite-lie about having nothing in my pockets he ran his hands through his greying hair.

'Look,' he said. It was the kind of tone that had all of us turning to look at him, waiting for the next instruction. It must have been his dog-training voice. 'We've been through this every day for the last four days. She's not a threat and the boy she's visitin' is under lock and key. What could she possibly have in her pockets that would be dangerous?'

'But I don't have anything in my pockets,' I said.

I mean, I was carrying something but not in my actual pockets. I'd spent an hour or so working out how to put it there, after all.

The security guards—three men today, two of whom I'd seen before—looked at me and then at Conn. Conn just looked at them, eyebrows raised. There was the possibility that this could change from me trying to sneak a mobile phone passed the guards to the guards and Conn having a pissing contest.

'I've only seen her one of those days,' said the one who'd been on duty yesterday.

The other guard I recognised shrugged. He'd been here the day I arrived and the day after. 'Well, she was well behaved enough the two days I saw her.'

'I haven't seen her at all,' said the one I didn't know.

'I'm not carrying anything in my pockets today,' I said and I patted my jeans to prove it. 'See? No noise, no bulges.'

The guards ignored me and stared at Conn.

'Would you like me to pull them inside out to prove it?' I asked.

'It's procedure,' said the one I'd seen yesterday.

'Procedure I set up. Yes, I know,' said Conn. 'I'm just gettin' fed up of being subjected to it.'

Yesterday's guard nodded and the one I'd never met almost smiled sympathetically. They might have been tall but they weren't exactly winning any awards for being intimidating. Just determined to follow procedure.

'So, in order to save time, you decided to argue about it instead?' I asked sharply.

Conn didn't bother to look angry with me. He just held the bridge of his nose for a moment, then said, 'Fine. Pull out your pockets, prove there's nothing there, so I can get on with my day.'

'I didn't realise you were that busy,' I said, pulling my pockets out like I'd practised.

Of course, the fact that he was basically babysitting me for the duration of my visit had led me to assume there wasn't much else for him to do. I suppose I should have turned that on its head and assumed that I was important enough for him to babysit seeing as I was a werewolf killer.

'Clear,' said the guard I'd seen twice before.

It was as if the guards parted like the Red Sea or something. One second they were obviously between us and Ben's corridor, the next they... weren't.

'They're just human,' said Conn as the door closed behind us. 'But they're very annoyin'.'

'Trained them yourself,' I added.

'I've told you before, Elkie, use your in-head voice for the smart-arse stuff.'

'Sorry.'

He looked at me and growled, 'Yeah, right.'

'Pot,' I said, 'I'd like you to meet kettle. I think you'll find you have a lot in common.'

Conn all but pushed me into Ben's run and the only reason I can't describe his exit as hurried is because I didn't see it, just heard it.

'*S'mae*,' I said to Ben.

'Bad mood?' Ben asked, carrying on our use of Welsh.

'Mine or Conn's?'

Ben laughed. 'Chess?'

He'd already got the board out and the two plastic armies were facing each other over the divide. The answer I wanted to give was 'Do I have a choice?' but the answer would have been 'about as much as the pieces'. Sure, I could have said 'no' but then I probably wouldn't like the consequences.

'In a minute,' I said.

I shuffled my clothes around, reaching for my mobile phone. I couldn't reach it properly. I had to take my sweater off.

'Elkie,' Ben said, 'I'm sorry to tell you this but—'

I threw my sweater to one side and started to shuffle the phone about under the remaining shirt and t-shirt.

'I'mreallynotinterestedinyouinthatkindofway!' Ben squeaked.

I paused, barely touching the warm plastic I was aiming for. 'What did you just say?'

He was bright red and looking everywhere but at me. 'I'msorrybutIjustdon'tfindyouattractive.'

If he'd said it back when we were kids I would have been crushed. There was a certain amount of dented pride, even now, enough to mean that the only thing I could reasonably do was keep looking for my phone. It wasn't until I had it firmly held in my hand that I managed a response that wasn't too defensive.

'I'll do my best to live with the disappointment,' I said.

The phone, best described as brick-like as I'd owned it for a couple of years now, was thrust out between us.

'I brought you this,' I added.

Ben was still red-faced and staring at me like I'd turned

into something dangerous. Well, dangerous to him.

'My phone?' I prompted. 'Like we discussed?'

I put it down in the middle of the chess board. I had to step forward to do it and Ben scuttled back a couple of steps to avoid me, almost falling over his chair. He was still very red but not as brightly as he had been.

'I guess I'll put my sweater back on,' I said.

He nodded. The lips started to move and then he stopped himself. It would probably have been something I didn't want to hear.

He didn't come back to his desk until the sweater was on and he stayed flushed pink for some time. He didn't meet my eyes at all for the rest of my visit.

'I think this is my last visit,' I told him but it didn't bring his eyes up. 'I'm catching a flight to Oslo tomorrow morning.'

'Oh.'

'I'll need to get another phone before I can text you. I'll try to pick one up when I land in Gatwick tomorrow afternoon.'

'Okay.'

'And I couldn't work out how to get the charger in, so you probably only have a fortnight at best,' I added.

'Okay.'

'I'd suggest only turning it on once a day to check if I've texted to make the battery last.'

'Okay.'

'And you're going to need to find a place to hide it. Just in case they decide to search this place.'

'Okay.'

I felt like copying Conn's earlier fingers-on-the-bridge-of-nose gesture. 'Are you going to say anything other than "okay"?'

'Maybe.'

Make that a desire to bag my head on Ben's desk or possibly the wall. 'Just find a place to put the bloody thing and let's get on with the chess, shall we?'

'Okay.'

'Oh, for f—'

An Honest Bit, or: Intermission

Conn's mood didn't improve by the next day, and nor did mine.

'Are you ready?' were his first words when I opened the door.

I'd been packed and ready since shortly after midnight and had spent the rest of the time pacing the room, so the answer was a grumpy 'yeah'.

'Then let's go.'

I already had my back-pack in hand but wanting to do something didn't stop me wanting to bare my teeth and growl at being told to do it. I managed to hold it in, though.

'Great,' I said, 'But it would be easier if you weren't looming in the doorway.'

After a couple of heartbeats, Conn stepped back and sideways. 'Sorry.'

The shock of an apology, even though I wasn't sure what it was for, had me standing still. Eventually I managed, 'That's okay.'

After an uncomfortable moment's pause, Conn walked off. I ran to catch up. If he could have picked me up and run down the corridor with me over his shoulder, he would have done.

'Eager to be rid of me?' I asked.

'Eager to get things sorted,' he said, the words short and snappy.

I nodded but he couldn't see me and I couldn't be bothered to talk in case I sounded just as short-tempered as he did. I could do without those kind of misunderstandings with someone who was, probably, an ally.

'There're some papers for you to sign at reception,' he said.

Again, the tone was abrupt but there was also a pause at the end before his attention was back on his mental list of things to do, the kind of pause that implies 'What haven't you told me?' I had a feeling I'd be getting a lot of that at home, too, when I arrived without Dave.

My response was 'Oh.'

Why bother trying to explain myself. In the mood we were both in, we'd end up fighting—because he was trying to control the outcomes as much as possible and I was feeling unnecessarily rebellious after several days hiding from the werewolves that stalked the hallways.

His tone was marginally better with the receptionists. I got the impression that he understood, if not spoke, Norwegian from the sharp look they got but he spoke English with a relaxed curl to his mouth. 'Olsen sent some papers for Miss Bernstein to sign before she left?'

The two receptionists—one man, one woman—hustled as if Conn's expression meant bad things in their very near future. I almost asked how he managed it.

'Here they are.'

'*Takk*,' said Conn.

Yeah, he understood Norwegian all right and those two had been saying something he didn't find amusing. Paranoia suggested it was about me but, considering that their employer was heading for Mad Scientist territory, it could have been anything.

I said, 'Thank you.' Then, 'Do you have a pen?'

I flipped through the form. There were a few pages of what I guess was Norwegian and a few pages of English. My signature was required on both and I could only assume that the English was a translation.

'Can you read Norwegian?' I asked Conn.

'Not well enough to advise you on a legal form,' he replied.

I bit back on a 'But I bet you want to look at it, anyway'. I would in his shoes so why should he be any different?

I put down the Norwegian language version—Olsen must have realised I'd disregard it, right?—and tried to get my head around the English. On second read, I changed my mind about the language being English. It was obviously only meant to be understandable to people who studied law. However, Ben's full name was in there, along with mine, and a few words that implied I was to be considered Ben's next of kin.

'Thanks,' I said when I realised a pen had materialised on top of the Norwegian form.

Then I signed the English version.

'If I don't bother to sign the Norwegian copy, will it invalidate the agreement?' I asked.

'I have no idea,' said Conn.

The receptionists simply watched. I wondered if it was Conn holding them off or whether they just didn't care.

'I would have thought one of the copies was yours, though,' he added.

Movement caught my eye and both of the receptionists were nodding. One of them bothered to say, 'That is what I was told.'

I signed the Norwegian copy with a shrug and left the pen on top of it. The English copy got folded up and stowed in the back-pack.

'Let's go,' I said.

I shouldered the back-pack again and headed for the big doors.

'*Takk*,' Conn said again to the receptionists and he followed at his own pace.

I stared out into snow and grey skies. At least that was snow resting on the ground and not snow falling. The steps and the drive were cleared, Conn's estate car parked neatly right in the middle. I couldn't see his pack of assorted mongrels in the car.

'The car's unlocked,' he said and I was gone, out into the real world for the first time in days.

I put my pack on a back seat and looked into the boot to see two travel crates with some panting coming from inside. Out of curiosity, I walked around to the boot door and peered in. Moll and Sadie looked back at me as if I were still an idiot. Their crates were currently doorless and there was a large but only partially filled water bowl, one of those that isn't supposed to spill, in front of them.

'What did you tell Olsen about them?' I asked when Conn's reflection joined me in the rear window.

'I didn't. Get in.'

I could have sworn the larger pup, Moll, smirked at me. Dogs didn't do things like that. Grin and smile, yes. Smirk, not usually. But I did as I was told and the drive to the local airport passed in restful silence right up until we parked.

'Here,' Conn said, fishing in the driver's door, 'This is for you.'

He held out a mobile phone, a little worse for wear but certainly no worse than the one I'd handed over to Ben the day before.

'To replace the one you've given to Ben,' Conn said, as if he could read my mind. Maybe he could.

He thrust the phone at me and, once I'd taken it, held out a charger, its cable coiled tightly round it. 'There's a charger here, too.'

'Thank you.'

'I need the one that fits the phone you snuck in to Ben.'

I looked at him. 'Why?'

'So I can get it to him.'

'No. I meant why are you doing this?'

Conn just looked at me. 'So his phone doesn't run out of charge.'

I looked back.

'This is part of what we agreed. Once you get home, we can work on getting your friends out of the Institute. Just let me know that the... the pups made it to their new home okay,' Conn said.

'OK. Thank you.'

I couldn't do much more than stare at the phone and the charger in my hands. Why was he providing me with a phone and charger? How?

'Is this on a contract or—'

'Pay as you go,' Conn said, cutting me off. When I stayed quiet for too long, he added, 'I've had reason to need an independent phone number myself.'

'I'll... Thank you.'

'You're welcome.'

I got out of the car and opened up the back door to get to my bag. 'So what gave it away?'

Conn had his hands on the steering wheel and he was staring forwards. I'm not sure he heard me. I tried again, louder.

'How did you know about the phone?'

'What? Oh, Philip told me.'

I wondered why the werewolf had bothered. I also wondered why Ben, who must have been able to hear the conversation in the room next to him, hadn't told me.

'He understands Welsh, then,' I said with forced lightness.

'"If you can call what those two speak Welsh."'

'Bloody *hwntw*. Did he tell you about Eric and Simon being on the loose, too?'

'Yes,' said Conn.

'Did Olsen?' I asked.

'No.' Conn shook his head. 'And things are too fragile for me to ask what he's doing. He's never trusted me absolutely.'

I fished my own charger out of my pack and put the new-to-me phone and charger in its place. The pack was just small enough to go on as hand luggage, so I didn't need to worry about either of them getting lost in the baggage handling.

'You're his security chief.'

'I'm the person he trusts not to try to give werewolves a second chance,' said Conn.

He was all about the second chances and protecting people. So Olsen was up to something he thought Conn wouldn't approve of.

'How about Philip? Does he trust you with everything?' I asked.

Conn's shoulders stiffened.

I changed the subject. 'Are you going to help me get the pups through?'

Conn looked at me, although the shoulders didn't loosen. 'I already have.' He held out a small pile of cards, paper, a map and a couple of small booklets. 'Their paperwork.'

I put the dogs' paperwork in the plastic wallet that held my own in a pocket that could only be accessed when I wasn't wearing the pack.

'I meant getting the travel crates to... Actually, where do I take the crates?'

'Just take them to the check-in. The airline should do the rest,' Conn said.

The puppies whined, as if they knew we were talking about them. I felt like joining in because I wasn't convinced they weren't about to tossed into a baggage hold.

'Hush,' said Conn, 'I'm comin'.'

He was opening the boot before I got my next questions out. 'But what about food and water? And toilet breaks?'

'They've got water and food containers inside. You can get to them from the outside, see?' He showed me how to get to them. 'Required by most airlines. You should be in airports and planes for, what, five hours, tops? Give them a break at Gatwick before you travel on.'

He was fitting the doors back on the crates so I shouldered my pack and held on to the charger while I waited.

'And I've given you the address and directions for their new home in the paperwork. Along with a map with the route marked on.'

'Organised,' I said.

'Tryin' to make everything idiot proof,' he replied.

I said nothing.

'I've organised a hire car for you at the other end. Well, that there's one booked. I couldn't sort out everything because they need your driver's licence. You have it with you, right?'

'With my tickets and passport,' I said.

I hadn't known for sure that Dave and I would be met at the airport coming in and I'd prepared for that just in case.

'Put the... pups' paperwork with them and try not to lose anything.'

I felt the need to argue again but, as he was basically telling me to do what I'd already done, I didn't bother.

'I've worked out where the nearest place to your home is to drop off the rental,' Conn said, 'It's in the paperwork somewhere.'

There was a pause and then he said, 'You're only on the same local flight. They're on a different cargo flight to Gatwick. I managed to shuffle around the flights agreed with Giovanni but everything's now in your name and they should turn up at Gatwick within half an hour of you.'

'You're jumping around the conversation a lot,' I said.

'I'm telling you things as I remember.'

He didn't look at me. He was too busy lifting one of the crates out. Moll's, I think. He set it down on four castor wheels I hadn't noticed and pulled up a handle. The crate was basically a box on wheels with enough holes for the pup to breathe but not enough to see clearly what was inside.

'Have you remembered everything?' I asked.

The second crate joined the first on the car park. There

were tiny whimpers still from inside. The pups weren't happy, although whether it was a response to Conn's mood or because they had some idea that they were leaving, I wasn't sure.

'I'm tryin' to,' said Conn.

'Except the charger?' I asked.

I held it out. He blinked at me, mentally side tracked, before taking it. 'Ta.'

He put the charger down in the boot without really looking. I wasn't a hundred percent sure he'd remember to hand it over to Ben but it was no longer my problem.

'The dog food and bowls?' I asked.

'In with the... pups.'

That was the third or fourth time he'd paused before saying 'pups', like he wanted to say something else. What else was there to call them, except maybe 'Moll and Sadie'?

'Let's get you all checked in.'

Lie 7: Life Doesn't Have To Be Complicated

Conn had done just about everything in his power to make my detour from Gatwick to home as easy as he could short of doing it for me. However, he hadn't actually thought out the toileting the pups part of the deal. Gatwick, it turns out, is not a suitable place for pets. I gritted my teeth against the whining and kept them in their crates.

'Sorry,' I whispered in English, 'But I'm not allowed to let you out here.'

The whimpering quieted as if they understood me. I didn't think about it much, except to be grateful that the sound wasn't ringing in my ears any more. I was not so grateful when I got into the estate car Conn had hired and the two started whining and, well, sobbing for real.

'Okay, okay,' I said. 'I'll find somewhere for you to get out as soon as I can.'

They didn't stop and it took a lot of concentration to read their new address and Conn's route marking over the top of it. This was my first time driving this car and my first time driving on a motorway. I wasn't exactly happy about it. The only thing that kept me going was picturing the jar of chocolate hazelnut spread I had waiting for me when I got home.

'For Deity's sake, shut up!' I screamed.

People on the car park turned and looked, even those several hundred metres away, but my outdoor voice just seemed to make the pups more determined to whine, and howl, and cry, and basically make my ears ring. I may have sworn and abused their parentage more than once, particularly as they kept making noise until the exact moment I opened the door of Moll's crate to let her out on a patch of service station grass.

'Shit,' I said.

The big brown eyes blinked at me. That shouldn't have been odd but it was. Because there wasn't an eight month old—I checked the paperwork—Japanese Akita looking at me. There was a naked eight year old child with short, wispy, chestnut coloured hair.

'Shit,' I said again.

I should maybe have seen this one coming, what with werewolves being real, but it was not what I expected.

'If I open Sadie's crate, will she be... human, too?' I asked.

The big eyed girl nodded.

'Shit.' Then, 'I really have to stop swearing in front of you two.'

Moll's too human eyes didn't get any smaller or less round. There was a large ring of white showing and with the way she huddled in the crate, even if I hadn't heard the noise they'd been making, I would have known she was terrified.

'Could you, erm, change back?' I asked.

I felt bad asking about something that was mainly for my convenience but, hey, there was a reason it was more convenient.

Moll shook her head in response and whispered something too quiet for me to hear. At a guess, something to the effect of being scared and dog form being hard to hold on to under the circumstances.

'I need to leave you two in here for a few minutes, then,' I said. Again, for my convenience. 'I'm going to see if I can pick up some clothes or something for you and then you can go use the human facilities. Okay?'

Moll nodded. I tried not to think about what would happen if anyone realised I had two young girls in my boot. In dog crates, no less.

'Shit,' I said again when I had the boot lid closed.

Then I had to open it again. 'Er, what size shoes do you two wear?'

Moll stared at me still. If she had a clue what size her feet were in the UK, she wasn't in a fit state to tell me.

There wasn't even a t-shirt for sale.

I forced a polite smile at the woman behind the till who spoke in an accent that only reminded me of Eastenders and looked at me like I was an illegal alien. 'Could you tell me if there's a shopping centre nearby? Near the next junction?'

She continued to look at me as if I'd just landed in a space craft.

'I've had a spillage and I need some new clothes,' I explained, falsely.

'If you go back to junction nine, there's the Swan centre in town,' she said.

Great. Town driving and parking with two nude girls in the back of a rental car. How much more interesting can life get?

'And the other way?' I asked. Conn had my route marked along the A3, off at the next junction.

She shrugged. 'Go to Guildford. If you can get there before six.'

It was about two in the afternoon but she said it with the cynical tones of someone who ends up stuck in traffic on a regular basis. Bearing in mind that my typical experience of a traffic jam was being in the slow old tractor at the front, I was inclined to ignore her.

'Thanks.'

'Are you actually going to buy anything?' she asked.

I shrugged. 'You're not selling what I want to buy. But thanks again for your help.'

'Bitch,' she muttered as I left.

I bit my lip so I didn't giggle hysterically and tell her the actual bitches were in my car. And I had to dress them in my dirty clothes to give them a crack at going to the human toilets. Their being bare foot and drowning in adult clothes got some funny looks but I couldn't leave the services without letting them empty their bladders.

'There's no clothes for sale here,' I explained when we got back to the car. I watched in disbelief as they got back in the crates of their own accord. 'But we'll be driving past a town in an hour or so.'

There was silence.

'That's a "we want to go shopping for clothes", is it?'

There was a squeak that may have been 'yes' from Moll's crate. Sadie's managed a more audible 'Do we have to?'

'She's human and not-family even if she smells like it,' I heard Moll hiss back. 'Not-family humans don't like naked.'

That was one way of putting it, I thought.

We made it to Guildford in a couple of hours. The slow

moving traffic had made me swear at Conn for getting me into this. Trying to find my way around a town that was basically bigger than anywhere else I'd ever been, discounting airports, just made me want to run away and hide.

'Are you coming or staying?' I asked as I got out the car.

More silence.

'I'm going to find some clothes. If you're staying here, stay out of sight. I'll be back as soon as I've found something and then we'll find you a toilet again,' I said just before I shut the door.

With luck, there wouldn't be police, social services or any werewolves waiting for me when I got back.

The nearest open shop turned out to be a charity shop and, for that, my wallet was grateful. With a bit of help from the well-spoken retiree behind the till, I managed to come away with two sets of clothes 'to fit a seven and an eight year old' along with a couple of pairs of shoes that would hopefully fit.

Neither of the girls was particularly impressed.

'They smell funny,' said Moll as soon as I opened the boot lid.

Sadie was still in her crate.

'Is everything okay, Sadie?'

Moll shook her head at me.

I dumped the clothes in front of her and sorted into two piles. One for her and one for her sister.

'These are yours,' I said, pushing clothes at Moll, 'And don't worry about the smell. I'm sure you'll have something better to replace them today or tomorrow.'

'Sadie?'

The little girl was huddled at the far end of her crate. There was liquid settling nearer the door. I'd kind of expected it. Kids always need breaks in car journeys. I was only surprised they'd made it from Norway to the services.

'Hey,' I said quietly, 'Why don't you come out?'

She looked at me and all I could really tell about her in the crate's shade was that she was still smaller than Moll, with lighter hair but equally big eyes.

'I have a towel in my bag if you give me a minute to get it out,' I said.

She said nothing but her focus dropped from me to the

pool of pee then jumped back up again.

'You can dry yourself off and then come sit on the back seat like kids should.'

Sadie remained unconvinced but Moll was already struggling into clothes—that didn't quite fit right but close enough.

'If I'd known,' I said, 'You wouldn't have been in the crates.'

'Huh,' said Moll. 'Dad said it was the best way for us to travel.'

'You're people, not animals.'

Although someone—somebody—in their family tree presumably was. I tried not to think about it. Maybe there was another explanation. I'd probably have to strangle Conn to get it.

Moll pushed me out of the way and clambered out of the boot, clothed and relatively presentable. Everything looked as it should, aside from the whole wrinkled, mismatched approach. She was hurrying around the car and letting herself in as a passenger before I could tell my paranoia to stop worrying about child care.

'The back seat, Moll,' I said.

She paused long enough to stick her tongue out at me but she did, at least, close the front passenger door and get in the back, like I'd wanted.

'I'll wait in the driver's seat,' I said to Sadie. 'Would you like me to close the door so no-one can see you?'

She nodded.

There were no family humans here, of course. After being reminded by Moll, Sadie was too scared to do anything. Moll, on the other hand, had effectively ignored her own advice and got on with it. This was not the way I would have expected it to pan out based on Sadie trying to chew Moll's ear off back in Conn's kitchen.

I got the towel out of my back-pack first and put the back-pack in Moll's crate out of the way.

'I'll put the towel over your clothes so you can get that first,' I said.

Then I went to sit in the front, staring out at the multi-storey car-park's walls while I heard little shuffling movements from the boot.

A minute later a very young and very quiet voice asked, 'How do I get out of the boot?'

Well, I know it asked something but I didn't hear the words properly. What I actually heard and understood was Moll replying, 'The human comes and lets you out.'

Something about the tone almost gave me a shiver and I looked at Moll in the rear view mirror. I could almost see Conn staring back at me but there was something about the shape of the face and the you're-not-quite-a-real-person look that she was giving me that made me think of... Philip. I did a double take and it was gone. Moll was almost exclusively Conn—aside from the red in her hair, the colour of her eyes and the ability to turn into a dog.

'Shit,' I whispered.

The bastard had put his own kids in crates and shipped them like freight. What was he thinking? But I knew the answer to that almost as soon as I thought the question. Olsen would have had these two locked up and experimented on before they could say 'non-family human' if he knew they existed. The only way to hide them properly was to send them as canines rather than humans.

'I'll come and let you out,' I said more loudly. 'Just give me a minute.'

I opened the boot to another miniature Conn in a badly cared for and uncoordinated outfit in shoes that were obviously too big. Closer to strawberry blonde with hazel eyes, there were a few differences from Moll but they were clearly related to Conn. Sadie's mouth pursed as she looked back at me gravely. I could see Philip again, only not as sickening.

Moll and Sadie were very quiet in the back seat. I didn't expect that. People always talk about kids fighting on long journeys, and watching them play in Conn's kitchen would suggest that they were inclined to being playful. But maybe being shipped to live with total strangers took that kind of behaviour out of them. They both watched me driving, still and wide-eyed.

I could see them in the rear view mirror. They had the look

of two young rabbits cornered by something they expected to turn out to be dangerous. A snake, maybe. I felt like... No, I wanted to be just a passing human being, totally unaware of their existence and with no effect on their lives. Too late for that now but I would soon be handing them over to someone else.

It made me feel guilty because, while I was wondering what kind of man could ship his responsibilities off to someone else, I was busy trying to shed my own share of said responsibilities. The only way to avoid thinking about it was to ignore the big eyes watching me in the mirror and focus on driving. Deal with life one step at a time or, in this case, one mile at a time. When you look in the rear view mirror, look at the road, not the children. Concentrate on getting there, not on what happens next.

Which, of course, only lasts as long as it takes to get to the destination. In this case, a large gate on wheels set in a palisade fence with an electronic radio interface intercom thing on the driver's side. There was even barbed wire fencing.

'"Greywolf's Conservation Sanctuary",' I read out. 'I still think Greywolf is a bloody ridiculous name.'

I reached for the paperwork Conn had given me and checked the notes against the sign. This was definitely it. Conn's map had brought me straight here—discounting my own diversions.

'We're here,' I said to the two girls.

They said nothing and continued to watch me with that scared stillness. Despite the tickle between the shoulder blades that had told me they were watching as I drove, it was hard to believe they'd been doing nothing but looking at me for a couple of hours.

I pressed the button on the intercom. 'Hello. I'm Elkie Bernstein. Conn sent me.'

I let the button go. There was a pause and then the hiss of a connection from the other end.

'Conn who?' A male voice, deep and dark and almost sexy, given the quality of the connection.

I looked round at Moll and Sadie. If they knew their father's surname, they weren't telling. I turned back to the Intercom and pressed the button again. 'Buggered if I know.'

There was a brief hiss and then laughter as the gate groaned into action, wheeling back from the lane. I was clearly meant to hear it, otherwise the operator wouldn't have bothered to press the button. The hiss and laughter were gone before the gate had finished opening, though, and there was nothing more to say or do but drive up the lane as soon as the gate had stopped.

The gate, however, was the most impressive thing about the place. Even by my hill farm standards, the land inside the palisade was fairly obviously a smallholding. Divided by eight foot high chain link fencing into otherwise traditional fields; to the untrained eye, it would be easy to assume pastures but there were signs of being lived in by something without hoofed feet. Along with the high fencing, this meant 'exotic'. The unbelievable surname simply meant 'wolves'. Had Moll and Sadie actually been dogs, I would have assumed they bred wolf-dogs as well.

'Weird people in the English Home Counties,' I said, unabashedly tarring everyone within a hundred mile radius—if not more—with the same brush.

The short drive to a quaint looking red brick and tile farm house with a couple of wooden barns and a red brick stable had me working out land area. I suspected that the Greywolf land could have fitted several times over just into my place, never mind the whole partnership with the Williamses. And we were both small holders, small fry, in comparison to most of our neighbours.

'But land's expensive round here,' I said aloud. 'I'll bet my spread's worth a quarter of theirs at best.'

'What's a spread?' asked Sadie.

I looked at her in the rear view mirror. She was starting to shuffle in her seat, though it could be more nerves, not less.

'A farm, *cariad*,' I said, 'A parcel of land owned or run by someone.'

She wrinkled her nose. The explanation wasn't good enough but I couldn't be bothered to give another one. I concentrated on pulling in beside another couple of older vehicles. A midrange estate and a battered Landie. Farm vehicles.

'What's a carry-add?' asked Moll.

'It's Welsh,' I said. 'It means "beloved". Like "sweetheart" or "darling".'

'What's Welsh?' asked Sadie.

I turned to look at them both. 'What the f—'

They were looking suspiciously innocent.

'A language. Used in Wales.'

'Do you speak Welsh?' asked Moll.

'No,' I lied.

I was aiming for sarcasm but I think it went right over her head because she only blinked at me.

'Oh.'

There was a moment's peace as I wound the windows down.

'So why did you use a Welsh word?' Moll asked.

'Because I can,' I replied.

Moll's eyebrows gathered over her nose like grey clouds ready to thunder.

'I'm going to talk to whomever was on the other end of the Intercom,' I said, ignoring the coming temper tantrum. 'The two of you stay in the car. Don't get out unless I come for you.'

Moll glared. Sadie looked at her sister.

'Please. It could be dangerous. I don't want strangers taking you away and not bringing you back.' I remembered I was technically a stranger and added, 'Other strangers.'

Moll's response was to turn to her sister and say something in Norwegian that I didn't understand. I could have laughed. If nothing else, it meant that Conn had allowed his two daughters out and about, to speak to human beings local to where they lived. Well, at least in that country. Hiding them from Olsen kind of required that they didn't get to run around the Institute. I got out of the car hoping Moll's language rebellion was enough to keep her entertained and in the vehicle.

'Hello?' I called.

The farm house door was open—despite this being mid-December. At least it wasn't raining.

'So Conn sent you with the pups,' said the voice from the gate without the crude corruption of the Intercom in the way.

A grey haired man sat at the kitchen table, watching me

through the doorway, his hand on what was presumably the other end of the Intercom. He had skin tanned dark brown—and the loose pony tail, complete with feather, and the broad checked shirt he was wearing could have been out of a bad western. The broad, flat face was... boring. A disappointment but the voice was still easy on my ears. I had no idea if the Native American thing was just an image or a reality.

Well, not entirely true. I knew he didn't spell his name the American way, so that much at least was false.

'There are no pups,' I said.

A bark of surprise and he was sat back in the wooden kitchen chair. 'What?'

I stayed in the doorway, unwilling to enter unknown territory. What kind of people would Conn send his daughters to? I'd had enough of people that shouldn't exist. There ought to be no such thing as werewolves and no such thing as children who can turn into dogs.

'There are two scared young girls in my car,' I said evenly. 'No pups.'

'You know, then.'

I should have asked 'Know what?' but I kept my mouth shut.

The Greywolf, assuming that's who he was, took a deep breath. 'You're not a werewolf. You don't smell like one.'

He didn't know werewolves were men only but he had a non-human sense of smell? That was... starting to make alarm bells ring.

'Conn was going to send them by werewolf.'

'Change of plan,' I said, trying not to think of hot red blood on cold white snow, or Olsen, or Eric, or Simon, or the unknown third.

'You're not staying.'

An order that made me laugh. 'I have a farm to run. I couldn't stay here even if you wanted me to.'

Although parts of me kind of wanted to; my curiosity was piqued by wondering what Conn had got me into now and I had a protective urge to stand between this man's plans and two young girls.

'I'm not leaving the girls here,' I said.

I hadn't meant to. It just came out, as if something had

taken control of my mouth and out the words popped.

'What?'

It wasn't a bark this time, it was a growl. More alarm bells in my head.

'You aren't here on your own,' I said. I stepped back from the doorway so I was technically outside. 'Where's your family?'

'Visiting the wolf packs,' he said.

There was a touch of smile to his lips but the growl was in his voice. The smile was the sort that spoke of confidence in success. Success, unfortunately, could just as easily be some Home Counties' answer to a hill-billy pinning me down while their cousin-sibling-parent pulled Conn's daughters from the car. Or I could just be imagining things.

'How do you know Conn?' I asked.

'We've done each other... favours.'

The old man said the word 'favours' as if it was something alien and unknown, like he never or rarely used it, as if he wasn't entirely sure he understood it.

'That doesn't explain why he would put his daughters in your care,' I said.

The Greywolf stared at me and I stared back. The eyes were a sort of golden hazel that scratched at memories in the back of my head.

'I don't know you,' I said, ignoring the whispering voice in my head that reminded me I didn't know Conn, either. 'I don't know I can trust you with two young girls.'

I heard light footsteps on the drive or in the yard. I wasn't sure which and I stepped clear of the door and turned so I could look both into the kitchen and where I thought the sound had come from.

'And I'm not going to,' I said loudly, to make sure the old man heard me with the increased distance.

There were two newcomers. Both women, both tall and rangy with cropped short hair, both about my age. The nearest one had a strong resemblance to the old man that marked them as family. Oddly enough, she was also wearing a checked shirt. The other, however, was virtually identical to him—given the different age and gender. That she was standing there naked did nothing to make me feel calmer and less creeped out. The only other time I'd noticed that strong a resemblance was when I identified Conn's woman with Philip. Those alarm bells were making sense. These people were both wolves and humans, like Conn's girls were both girls and pups.

'Everything okay, Dad?' the nearest woman asked, the same growl in her voice.

The old man stood, so slowly and uncomfortably, I could almost feel an answering ache in my own joints. I had a moment of both shame and relief—this old man wasn't capable of attacking me, let alone winning—but werewolf-trained paranoia soon sent those emotions skittering away. He had a family and I was in the middle of a wolf sanctuary. There was a distinct possibility that I could be dog food before the end of the day. Could I make it to the gate with the girls before some member of this pack or another got me?

'Nothing I can't handle, May.'

May shook her head as if to say 'old fool' but didn't actually say it.

'I'll call the packs,' said the naked one.

I blinked and... and then... there was a large grey wolf galloping across the drive. They had even more in common with Conn's woman than I wanted to think about.

The Intercom crackled and a voice I recognised said, 'Hello, Elkie. Who are your new friends?'

The old man pressed a button, glaring at me all the while. 'Go away. You're not welcome here.'

'I'll give you a head start,' the familiar voice offered.

'Shit,' I said. Yet again.

Lie 8: The Enemy of My Enemy Is My Ally

'You know who that is,' the old man said.

I looked at him and he looked at me. Lying wasn't really an option around humans that may or may not be able to turn into wolves. While they weren't what I would call werewolves, they were bound to have that sense of smell. Like Moll and Sadie.

'Sort of,' I said. 'He's Olsen's.'

'Who's Olsen?' someone asked from behind.

I turned to find my escape route blocked.

There were sixteen of them in human shape, of varying ages, differing amounts of clothing and mostly so similar to the old man it was horrifying. There were maybe three in wolf shape including, I think, the young woman who had run off to get them. They didn't bother to cram themselves into the kitchen and nobody commented on the cold December weather. That said, it wasn't snowing, blowing or even raining, so that was pretty good weather by my standards.

'Greywolf,' I said. 'Grey wolf. I see what you did there.'

One or two of the other human shaped gave teeth-baring smiles. One of the wolf-shaped huffed through a canine grin. The effect was far from comforting.

The old man practically spat at me. 'You've brought that... scientist's men with you?'

'Not on purpose!'

A woman, greying like the old man and maybe his sister, exchanged a look with him. 'That freak can't know about us.'

I could guess why—because he would want to find out how they worked and what they could do for him, whether they wanted it or not. I had to hide Moll and Sadie from him for much the same reason.

'I doubt he's told Olsen yet if he just followed me,' I said.

Olsen would have given Eric means of contacting the Institute but I was pretty sure he had only been sent to follow me, to follow whatever tracker they'd managed to plant in my things, and make sure I stopped being a threat—well away from Marie's prying eyes. Olsen probably didn't know about the Greywolves, yet. If I was lucky, he still had no idea who or what Moll and Sadie were, either.

'You can hide whatever it is you need to from him,' I said. 'Just be quick. Your gate isn't going to hold him for long.'

And, even as I said it, I could hear an approaching car, driven a bit faster that was healthy on a country lane. Bloody townie.

The Greywolves just stared at me. They weren't quite... human and I doubted they were really all that wolf. How does a wolf learn to act naturally in an enclosure, never mind when they can become human at will.

'I'm going,' I said. 'I'm not letting this bastard take Moll and Sadie. And I'm not leaving them with you when I don't know what your plans for them are.'

'Why do you feel the need to protect two pups that aren't your pack?' asked a middle-aged male.

This was Giovanni's knowledge, that Conn had shared over dinner. Pack is family, usually immediate family only, and the one who'd run off had said 'packs'. This was an extended family, human-like. The resemblance was too strong for them not to be related but there were probably cousins and multiple generations. Several smaller families and packs making up one settlement.

'Because they were given to me to look after,' I said.

The old man snorted. 'Not only do you smell like Conn, you act like him.'

'I smell like Conn?'

I didn't understand and the old man didn't explain.

'We can take them from you, regardless of what you want.' said May, the woman who'd stayed.

I smiled. The numbers were in their favour—provided we all survived Eric—and the only thing I was confident about was that I would go down fighting.

'I eat werewolves for breakfast,' I said, putting all that certainty into my voice, 'You're not a werewolf and you don't stand a chance.'

Although May gathered herself in to leap at me, she never really got the chance. The car pulling to a halt in the farm yard took away everyone's attention, the sleek, executive vehicle out of place in the mud. The damaged front, though, proved that it had been driven straight through the oh-so-secure gates. The engine cut off and we stared at it, expectant.

Eric got out of the passenger side, long slender legs unfolding, his shit-kicking boots shining in the afternoon sun. His sunglasses hid some of his expression but there was a lot of amusement and anticipation.

'Simon!'

OK. I made a mistake. He was a Simon, after all. He turned to look at the driver I could just make out behind tinted windows. Whatever the driver said after calling Simon's name, though, I have no idea.

Simon nodded. Then he turned to look at me. 'Don't expect these fools to help you, Elkie.'

I looked around for something I could use. He was coming for me and I didn't have anything to fight with but bare hands and Greywolves. I did have something else, though. I took the silver cross from my pocket, wrapping the chain around my hand so the pendant lay against my palm. With luck neither Simon nor Eric knew what silver did to their kind.

'What's going on?' I asked, trying for innocent and slightly bewildered.

My nineteen potential weapons stepped back, clearing a path from the werewolf to me. Simon obviously didn't care about them, at least for the moment, so they chose not to care about him or me.

'Olsen wants you gone,' he said simply.

I'd already guessed that. I cast a last look around the kitchen—not even a knife on handy display—and walked into the gap the Greywolves had made. Maybe I could throw one of them. One of the two obviously pregnant ones would probably get the packs upset enough to fight anybody. Shame I wasn't strong enough to actually do it.

At least the werewolves hadn't parked between me and the estate car. I tried not to look in that direction, in case I gave away my intention of making a run for it.

'Could we hurry this along?' I asked.

Simon leapt.

I ducked and rolled, winding myself in the process so that I lay on the ground for longer than I should. I got to my feet and ran for the estate. The passenger side was nearest and I opened it.

'Don't say anything,' I hissed. 'Lie down, cover your ears and close your eyes.'

I didn't even dare look to see if Moll and Sadie were doing as they were told in case the movement attracted attention. Conn would kill me for having them this near a fight but it was too late for that.

'Where you going, Elkie?' Simon called. 'Don't you want to play?'

He was right there, his hand on my leg and pulling me down, even as I tried to climb into the car. I slammed the door shut, knowing it would buffet me but hurt him more.

'That's not going to do anything, Elkie.'

'You're right,' I said.

I sat down in the passenger seat and grabbed at him, careful to touch the cross to the bare skin of his temple. He started screaming as soon as the silver made contact.

I pulled him closer and I held the door so he couldn't get away. Simon didn't know it but he was already dead. I thought I heard the sound of a car door closing but it wasn't mine—there was a werewolf in the way.

'How about now?' I asked.

I opened and then slammed the door again.

'So much for your "great promise", eh?' I asked.

I was trying to hold the door shut but it was dragged open, the mysterious driver looming over us. He had taken the time to put his fur-skin on and it was difficult to see anything other than a big, misshapen humanoid. And lots of thick, grey fur.

'Hello, Eric,' I said.

The real Eric grabbed hold of Simon with both hands and pulled. The screaming werewolf was flung across the yard and landed like an overgrown rag doll. I winced. I could see a black mark spreading on his face and I knew the silver poisoning would get him. At least I knew Olsen had never tried putting silver to skin before. Otherwise this would have been more difficult.

Eric reached in and grabbed me. I tried to bat his hands away but wasn't strong enough or fast enough. Then it was my turn to fly through the air. I got to lay on the floor counting potentially broken ribs while waiting for my lungs to work again. I looked around while I tried to struggle up, a bit too woozy from the fall to hold myself steady.

The Greywolves had withdrawn. Bared teeth and raised hackles, at least on those in wolf form, but they also didn't look eager to do anything—to me or the werewolves.

Eric stood over the estate car, looking in at Sadie and Moll, neither of whom were visible to me.

Simon continued to lie like a rag doll. It was unclear whether he was conscious or even alive because the screaming had stopped. The black was slowly spreading and soon parts of it would begin to flake off.

'Hey! Hey, Eric!' I shouted, desperate to get him away from the car. 'I think your pretty boy's dead.'

The furred up werewolf turned his head to look at Simon, then turned everything to look at me. He charged with a growl.

I hobbled for the house.

May sneered at me. 'You eat werewolves for breakfast, remember?'

I was hit from behind before I could come up with a decent answer. All I could do was lash out with my silver cross and hope I managed to land it on Eric—and that it would make enough of a difference to get away. At least I could land it anywhere on a furred up werewolf. In human form it only worked in contact with bare skin.

However, I was pinned from behind and could barely move my arms. Teeth closed around my right shoulder, a near miss because I managed to tuck my chin and save my neck.

'Get off me,' I screamed.

Well, I screamed and that's what I meant to say.

Eric growled, releasing my shoulder but not letting me go. 'What did you do to Simon?'

The Greywolves did nothing.

I flailed.

Eric growled some more. 'What did you do to him?'

I managed to get my cross hand to his arm and held it there for a couple of panicked heartbeats.

His grip loosened as he gasped in pain. It was too soon

and too easy a place for it to cause major problems. Yet.

I dropped my weight and hit backwards with a hand, aiming for the groin. He gasped again, weakened already by the silver, and his grip loosened enough for me to make a quick dodge for freedom. I ran for the estate on shaky legs, holding the bitten shoulder. He'd just about torn through the clothes and there was blood. It was too early to tell what damage had been done but I probably only had a few minutes before shock set in to the wound and I couldn't use my arm for a while.

I got into the driver's seat of the estate, started the car and put my foot down. Eric ran for the car and I pushed the accelerator down.

There was a slight bump but it wasn't Eric.

A look in the rear-view mirror told me I'd just driven through Simon's head. Everything below his neck was still there but the head was crumbling into black lumps that the car wheels had kicked up. The rot would spread under his clothes and the body would be gone in twenty minutes or so. Eric stopped running, clutching at his own right arm, and looked down at his former partner.

The same look in the rear-view mirror also told me I had a Greywolf in wolf form on the back seat, lying over Moll and Sadie. The Greywolf bared teeth.

'No way,' I said. 'I'm not going back.'

The Greywolf growled.

I put my foot down a little more and drove up the lane almost as recklessly as Eric and Simon had driven down it.

'Fine. If you want to cause an accident and kill us all, get it over with.'

It wasn't until Moll, Sadie and I returned from using the facilities in another motorway services that I got to see who my new plus one was.

'Ready to go,' said a young Greywolf woman from the front passenger seat.

It was the one who'd turned into a wolf, who looked like she could be a female clone of the old man or the old woman. She was wearing my clothes, some of which Moll and Sadie had been wearing earlier.

'So what do I call you?' I asked.

She looked at me with a steady gaze. 'May.'

Like the one who hadn't changed into wolf form and run to get the Greywolf packs. I shrugged and helped the two girls into the car. Home and my jars of chocolate hazelnut spread were calling me. Everything else could go hang.

'I'm not taking you back to the sanctuary,' I said. 'It's not safe for me or the girls.'

It wasn't exactly safe being anywhere if Eric worked out a way to deal with the silver poisoning or was determined to chase me before it killed him. He should be dead within a few hours of contact but I couldn't guarantee it.

'Well, someone has to look after the Greywolf interests,' the alleged May said, her head tilted towards the girls.

They were squirming into back seats, with movements scarily similar to those they'd used to indicate needing the toilet. I wondered if we'd make it to another service station before they were asking to stop again. Part of the problem is letting people drink when they're thirsty, I suppose.

I shoved my bloodied and torn clothes back into the boot, alongside the remains of my back-pack, and adjusted the last set of dirty clothes I'd had to put on to hide my stiffening right shoulder. I wasn't sure it was technically legal for me to drive. Never mind, I needed to get home.

'At least I've got rid of that gadget somebody managed to get into my luggage,' I sighed.

I'd flushed the non-descript bit of plastic and wiring I'd found in the lining of my ex-back-pack. I had no idea who had got it in there or how it had got through the airport security teams, but it obviously had.

I took my time seating myself and strapping in comfortably, checking whether my shoulder still had the full range of movement. It didn't but I could work with that. My grip wasn't what it should be, though. Maybe it wasn't a problem as long as I remembered to keep both hands on the wheel.

I got out the mobile phone Conn had given me and texted Ben while I remembered. 'Tell Conn I'm taking his girls back to the farm with me.'

There were long drawn out sniffs from the back while I

did, as if the two girls were grabbing this alternative May's scent. It almost covered her more discreet, quiet little sniff when she looked over her shoulder at them to do the same.

'You smell funny,' said Sadie.

The Greywolf bared her teeth in something only a naive human would consider a smile. 'Says the puppy dog.'

Both Moll and Sadie shrank back in their seats.

'Scare those two again,' I said, 'And I'll leave you by the side of the road. You won't be able to look after pack interests from there.'

She didn't look at me but her canine teeth flickered into longer fangs and then back to human-normal again. It was accompanied by a snarl that made me wonder if the quick change had hurt.

'My pack will hunt you down and kill you.'

'Maybe,' I replied, 'But you won't be alive to see it.'

This May turned to face forward, removing the snarl from her face. Moll and Sadie didn't unshrink. Still, we had a few hundred miles to work on that.

Some time later I asked, 'Can you drive, May?'

'Why?'

Because I'm not safe to drive.

'Because this is a long journey and I wouldn't mind a break.'

'So we aren't there yet?' asked Moll.

'No, Moll,' I said. 'Probably another three or four hours.'

'Yes,' said May.

I managed to get out a response although I was busy trying to control the wheel why watching the road and two kids in the back poke at each other. 'Good. I'll stop at the next services and you can drive for a couple of hours.'

'Why should I?' asked May.

I repeated the earlier threat, 'Because otherwise I'll leave you there.'

We had a break so that Conn's girls could be hustled to the toilets as well as Greywolf and Bernstein legs stretched although tempers didn't improve.

'Where are we going?' asked May as she adjusted the driving seat.

'Home,' I said, 'Just follow signs to the West and Wales.

We'll change over before we leave the motorways behind.'

'Where's home?' asked Sadie.

'Llados,' I said, naming the small village nearest to the farm house.

Sadie tried to sing-song the name and failed. Something like 'Lad-oss. Lad-oss. Lad-oss.'

It was enough to make May bunch her shoulders and grip as if the steering wheel was the only thing preventing her committing infanticide. Considering she, as well as the kids, were displaced from the only place and people she had known, it was understandable.

'Where's that?' asked Moll.

'North Wales.'

'What's there?' asked Moll.

I smiled. 'Sod all.'

But I had to work out how I was going to explain two children suddenly turning up in my household. May could be glossed away as a friend. Two kids without a parent to watch over them was going to be tough.

'Have you ever met Conn?' I asked May.

'No.'

'I have,' said Sadie.

Moll snorted at her. 'Of course you have, he's our father.'

'How do you know him, then?' I asked.

'I don't,' said May. 'Will does. And the aunt.'

Will must be the old man. The aunt must be the old woman. Or they could have been almost any member of the Greywolf packs. They'd looked like some combination of clones and very close relatives.

'So there's no point asking you why Will said I smelt like Conn,' I said.

'You smell as if you're related to the pups,' she said.

'She's not,' said Moll. 'She's just a human.'

I didn't know what to say to that. Maybe it was time to talk to my mother about my own family tree instead of wondering about everyone else's.

'They look a bit like you, too,' May added.

I looked back at them. All I could see was a mix of Conn and Philip. Which made sense if their mysterious mother had been Philip's daughter. Which meant that Philip was a danger to females of several species not just humans. I hoped the inner disgust didn't show because it was the last thing Moll and Sadie needed to pick up from me.

'Coincidence,' I said.

We swapped back when the motorway ran out. One of the first signs that the modern, urban lifestyle had been left behind. I was tired but happy, moving the driver's seat back into position, because my arm was working properly again. We probably should have got something to eat but Moll and Sadie had fallen asleep and I was anxious to get home.

May was less than impressed. 'You weren't kidding about there being sod all out here, were you?'

I checked that the girls were still asleep in the back before I replied with a certain amount of sarcasm.

'Like you were living in the middle of a city. So, what? Did you go up to London every weekend?'

She bared her teeth. 'What the hell do you people do for entertainment? Play pooh sticks?'

'It's been known,' I said.

The bared teeth turned from growl to sneer and her canines did that growth spurt thing again. 'I bet you don't even have a tv.'

'I can't afford one. Does that hurt?'

'And you probably think you're better for it. You can be such a sanctimonious shit.'

I stared at the road. I wasn't entirely sure what she meant and I didn't know why she was saying it. What had I done to her?

'Where the hell do you get off, telling us we're not good enough to look after two of our own?' she demanded.

I flicked a look in the rear view mirror. Despite their inquisitiveness, the girls remained asleep. If they could sleep through this, then they would probably be able to sleep through bombs dropping and several forms of apocalypse. This was a good thing.

'They're not yours,' I said firmly. 'Although you can babysit if you really want.'

'We need the new blood,' said May.

I felt a sneer form on my own face in answer. 'What are you talking about? They're, what, seven and eight? They'll probably not be capable of bearing children for at least another six years. They're not legally adults for another two or three after that. And if they're not mature enough or don't want to—'

'The pack comes first.'

'The Greywolves are not a pack. They're a group of packs. There's more than one breeding couple there.'

I'd seen a couple of rounding bellies, after all, and there may have been less obvious pregnancies among them.

'And the best thing,' she continued, 'Is you get to run away to your little bolt hole in the middle of nowhere where no-one can bother you.'

Like that had worked before. Werewolves had this tendency to hunt me down anyway, making the middle of nowhere less than idyllic.

May was still going. 'You think you can just waltz in and waltz out again without getting involved? It doesn't work like that.'

'You think I'm not involved?' I asked.

'You ran away, leaving my family to cope with two werewolves.'

'So did you,' I said. 'And those two are already dead from silver poisoning. Eric just doesn't know it yet. And I have a farm to run. And I'm trying to look out for those two.'

I waved a hand backwards to indicate the two girls.

'You didn't want to leave them with us because you think we're freaks,' said May.

'It isn't like that.'

'It isn't? Really? So tell me that you don't find the idea of me fucking a wolf repugnant and make me believe it.'

My stomach churned and not in a pleasant way.

'Their mother was half dog,' May said.

'So?'

'So can you tell me that doesn't disgust you?'

I tried not to think about Philip and his slimy talk of whether I was useful or not. I swallowed. 'Actually, I'm more disgusted by the man I think is their grandfather.'

That would be about right. If a dog-human hybrid aged slower than a dog and faster than a human, then the mysterious mother figure could have looked older than Philip when she was actually much younger—like in the photo of her in human form in Conn's kitchen.

'As if that isn't the same thing.'

I checked for cars behind us and pulled over to the side of the road. Moll and Sadie stirred but didn't wake.

'Look,' I said as evenly as I could manage. 'I find rape disgusting and I'm pretty certain that your superhero origins include non-consensual sex—bestiality, in fact—at some point in the family history. It doesn't mean I find the resulting people disgusting.'

May snorted. Perhaps, to her, there was no difference between the Greywolves' origins and how they lived. Maybe she wasn't a first generation—in which case...

'You're... What's the right word? Two-natured? And that's great. I have no idea how two totally different species can have viable offspring but obviously it's been managed at least a few times.'

That seemed to upset May even more. '"Viable offspring" she says, like she can make it something neat and tidy and easy to put away.'

'As someone who's only human and only into humans, I can't understand finding a dog or a wolf attractive—'

I was pretty certain the first generation of Greywolves wasn't about attraction, any more than any other rape was, but the offspring could go either way, right?

'You're right,' said May. 'You're just a human. You know nothing about anything.'

'I know you ought to have a choice,' I said.

Nothing I'd seen at the sanctuary suggested there was really a choice. If the two-natured were being raised as wolves, if they had the paperwork that said they were captive wolves, then they were pretty much destined to be... livestock. At least they weren't livestock that end up as part of the food chain like my sheep and cows.

'Shut up and drive,' said May. 'Or don't you want to get back to your little wilderness paradise this decade?'

I spent a few heartbeats staring at my hands on the steering wheel, thinking about livestock, before I did as I was told and started the car again. If I'd brought Moll and Sadie into the country as dogs, did that mean they didn't have a human identity? Did they have no choice about being treated like dumb animals?

Lie 9: Business Partners Are For life, Not Just For Christmas

We drove through the town my mum lived in.

'Great, another place with sweet fuck all in it and an unpronounceable name,' May muttered.

'You invited yourself along,' I muttered back.

I thought about calling in with Mum on the way through but really couldn't cope with it, having done so much travelling and picked up three extras on my way home. I still had Dave's parents to call in with, explain their son's absence if Olsen hadn't already and beg for the farm Landie so that I had something to drive once I handed the hire car back. All while my shoulder ached with the imprint of yet another werewolf's teeth and I tried not to fall asleep. It had been a long day.

'Oh, shit,' I said.

And I just realised I had to figure out how to get a hire car back to Sweet, while not leaving two young children unattended. Mum must have had a really constricted life being a single parent with me in the middle of nowhere.

'Are we there yet?' Moll and Sadie asked in chorus.

I swore again as I checked the rear-view mirror. Moll and Sadie were no longer asleep but watching me with barely open eyes.

'Almost. We have to call in on some friends before we get home and you can sleep properly,' I said.

Although with my luck they'd be wide awake from sleeping too much in the car and I'd have to find a way to entertain them. I needed some motherly advice. I shouldn't have driven past.

'Do we have to?' Sadie asked.

There was a pause before I managed my 'yes'. There wasn't any decent way I could get out of it.

We drove through the overgrown village I needed to call in sometime when the library was open to send a couple of emails—

'I thought you were joking about the sod all,' said May.

'I'm not and this isn't it. Llados is smaller than this,' I replied.

She raised her eyebrows. 'So how do you pronounce this bundle of nothing, then?'

'Llareggub,' I said, only with the real name. 'We'll probably be back here tomorrow after we've dropped the car off in Sweet.'

'We?' asked May.

'Why?' asked Sadie.

'Unless the three of you want to stay on the farm,' I said.

May looked horrified, despite apparently being here to make sure Moll and Sadie were never totally lost to the Greywolves. I knew exactly how she felt, if only because being left in charge of two young girls I didn't know was a terrifying prospect. The only thing I was certain of was that May couldn't run off with them without a vehicle. There was no way Moll and Sadie would follow her the hundreds of miles back to Surrey.

Then there was the fact that there might still be some Institute werewolves out there. Having one of Olsen's inmates come across the girls while they were in May's care was... The idea of not being there, of not being able to protect people from my hunters was almost enough to make me gasp in pain. The three of them would become Olsen's lab rats and I wouldn't be able to do anything to stop him.

When we got to Llados I pointed at the sign and said, 'Now we're in Llados.'

'How the hell do you get "Llados" from all of those consonants?' May asked.

I winced at the casual blasphemy—despite not being especially religious. 'And now we're out of it.'

And driving up the single track lane past the remains of the cottage I grew up in—

'That wall has a tree on top,' said Sadie, pointing.

'So it has,' I said.

In spring, the ruin looked lush and green. In winter minimalism, it looked grey and desolate. However, at eight o'clock on a night with drizzle, that tree shouldn't have been visible, even with the moon sneaking out from behind a cloud.

'Could you not mention what it looks like when we get to

the Williamses?' I asked.

'Why?' asked Sadie.

Moll got there first. 'Because they can't see in the dark.'

'Stupid humans,' said Sadie.

Both May and Moll made agreeing noises.

'Yeah,' I said. 'Stupid humans with our lack of super powers.'

They remained unimpressed when they met Dave's parents, the Williamses. I was lucky enough that they managed to keep it to themselves. I wasn't so lucky with the actual humans.

'What the hell are you doing here?'

Again, I winced at the cursing, as much because I'd ever known Mr Williams to use language like that before. 'I just thought I'd let you know I was ba—'

'Why would I need to know?' he asked. He got up from the kitchen table and stalked out into the yard, pushing past May and the girls. 'Why would I care about you being back, you Jewish slut?'

His wife just sat at the table looking away.

'What's a "Jew—" "Jewish sl—"' Sadie tried to ask.

'"Jewish slut",' May said. 'Her, apparently.'

In the little Welsh hill farm kitchen, her Home Counties accent—that kind heard on films made for an American market, or at least approximated by them—seemed totally out of place.

'So Olsen told you then,' I said.

Lying bastard, playing a game of his own. His behaviour reminded me of at least two other people in the Institute.

'Yes,' said Dave's mum. She still didn't look at me.

'When?' I asked.

'The day you got there,' Mrs Williams said and I felt the air rush from my lungs as if I'd just jumped into an ice cold lake.

With no intention of leaving without at least finding out what work I was supposed to do the next day, I sat down in the chair Mr Williams had left pushed out. 'Olsen made it sound like he didn't want to give you the bad news himself.'

Dave's mother gave one of those squeaky acknowledgements that's just a couple more things going wrong from a hysterical giggle.

'So...' I said, not entirely sure how to put the questions that I wanted to ask.

Mrs Williams finally looked at me and she looked at me as if I was worse than the stuff in the septic tank. 'How could you leave him?'

'I didn't exactly have a choice,' I said. Strictly speaking, the answer should have been 'easily'.

'It's not true. I know Dave's done some silly things...'

She tailed off and I wondered if she was thinking about him cheating on me with a university girlfriend, or avoiding coming home, or any one of a million less hurtful things children do while growing up.

'He's not a killer,' she said firmly.

I didn't bother disagreeing. Disagreeing with her meant explaining about werewolves, and how both Dave and I had seen off quite a number in our time. That way also led to conversations about my being a bad influence because my count was a lot higher than Dave's.

'You should have stayed and waited while he appealed,' Mrs Williams said.

May sighed and took the chair next to mine. Sadie, too tired to be wary of me, pushed her way on to my knee. Moll leant against my chair. Weirdly, Mrs Williams didn't seem to notice.

'If you'd just rung and talked to us, we would have told you to stay,' she said.

I couldn't stop myself saying, 'I can't afford to make phone calls from Norway on my mobile. And we can't afford to keep hiring help.'

It had been a struggle to organise the help we'd had and today was their last day. I was supposed to be taking over from them tomorrow.

'There is no "we" in this,' said Mrs Williams and her expression went from looking at the cesspit to enraged. 'You left him behind. Alone.'

I could have said the same of him but they never reacted like that when we found out he'd had another girlfriend. But then I suppose they wouldn't. He was their son and I was just the business partner.

'We're dissolving the partnership,' she said as if she could read my mind, 'And we're selling the farm to raise funds.'

'Convenient,' muttered May but I doubt Mrs Williams heard her.

I didn't say anything. I was too busy turning over the business side of things. I'd been working for them before Ben wrote his farm over to me. I hadn't owned the ex-Lloyd's place long enough for the official grant paperwork to be filled in and filed and paying. The business's existing government funding was for the Williamses' land. Dissolving the partnership didn't leave me with a lot of paperwork, just a lack of stock and a lack of funds. And maybe a need to sell my own farm.

'Then we're going over to Norway to help Dave,' Mrs Williams said with an evangelical certainty.

'Have all the cousins agreed to sell?' I asked.

Not that it was any of my business any more, if I were no longer a business partner.

'Of course,' Mrs Williams said. 'They're family. They help in times of need.'

And no longer cared about the actual farm, just its value. I'd never met any of Mr Williams' cousins and was highly unlikely to now. But, then, I wasn't family and never really had been.

'What time do I need to get out to the animals tomorrow?' I asked.

'They're all back on Williams land. You don't have anything to do with them anymore.'

Almost a relief. I could have as much of a lie-in as caring for a seven and an eight year old would allow.

'Did you arrange this?' asked May, quietly.

'Arrange what?' I asked.

I turned my head to look at her and my shift of focus caught Mrs Williams' attention.

'Who is this?' Dave's mum asked. 'Who are these strangers you brought into my house uninvited?'

She was usually more hospitable than this but my presence was unwanted and, as they were with me, May and the girls got the same lack of welcome. I was more surprised when Mrs Williams did a double take at the scowling Moll.

'You have sisters,' Mrs Williams said.

I didn't bother to correct her. If nothing else, it was a decent explanation for how I ended up with two little girls. Although I'd have to explain myself to Mum before anyone else thought to mention it to her.

'This is May Greywolf,' I said.

May held her hand out over the table, very human but more polite than anyone around her was likely to be. 'My family are friends of Elkie's dad.'

She put heavy emphasis on 'dad', and gave me a sly sideways look. She'd already noted my similarity to Conn and his daughters based on scent but she hadn't thought I was that closely related. Now someone with a poorer sense of smell saw some similarity that I didn't.

Mrs Williams, of course, didn't take the extended hand. 'Oh. I didn't realise Elkie even knew who her father was.'

'I didn't,' I said.

I really would have to get around to asking Mum about him. I'd never asked before because it seemed like the kind of thing to break a woman who worked hard just to stay on the poverty line—even when I'd been too young to recognise the cause of her fragility. Now I just wanted to be sure it wasn't Conn. Despite the odd thoughts I had about whether he'd be a good dad or not.

'I'm sorry for calling in so late,' I said. Belatedly. 'I just wanted to be sure what work needed to be done tomorrow.'

'None, as far as you're concerned,' said Mrs Williams.

I tried to put myself in her place, to consider how hard it must be to even look at the woman I held responsible for abandoning my son to the Norwegian legal system. It only gave me so much patience.

'Sorry,' I said and managed to stand up still holding Sadie. All things considered, she was about as heavy as a feed sack and considerably easier to manoeuvre. 'Come on, Moll. Time to get you two to bed.'

'Do I have to?' asked Moll. 'Daddy lets me stay up as late as I want.'

I snorted my disbelief and started walking.

'What about me?' asked May, close behind.

'You're big enough to tuck yourself in.'

Habit woke me up for a five o'clock start. I slept better than I had in Norway, with less waking to defend myself from nightmares, but that didn't mean my body could get over routines I'd been subject to for years. So I got up and nursed my shoulder wound before I did what chores I could do, like getting the emergency loaf, butter and milk out of the freezer, and checking on the guests in the stable—the three horses and ponies on basic livery that were currently my only source of income.

'I should have done this last night,' I said to them as I checked all the locks, and their food and water supplies. 'Sorry.'

It looked like Mr Williams had taken away about half of the haylage. It wasn't a massive deal. There was plenty here and, assuming some of the stack had been left for me, there was enough feed to see them through until next cutting season but it grated. Couldn't they have waited until I got back and we could sort this out? Did they expect me to refuse to hand it over and leave their livestock to starve?

Breakfast was black tea with plenty of sugar in it and chocolate hazelnut spread right out of the jar. I could have broken off a couple of frozen bread slices and defrosted it in the toaster but I prefer my spread unadulterated anyway. Especially when the first sign that life was returning to my non-equine guests was a growl that could only come from an upset wolf or a woman who needed an IV drip full of caffeine to function. In May's case, she was apparently both.

There was giggling and play growling as a small herd of elephants found the stairs, and then the kitchen. Then they became a puppy Moll and a naked girl Sadie.

'*Bore da*,' I said. 'Could you keep it human?'

I didn't want to explain to any horse owners how I had two pups and two girls who couldn't be in the same room at the same time. Or, for that matter, two creatures who couldn't decide which they were this morning.

'It's easier being human, anyway,' said Sadie.

Moll, though, looked sulky once she'd change into naked girl form but first there was a lips drawn back in pain stage that I, thankfully, had never seen before. I'd suspected but not seen it.

'It hurts to change?' I asked.

Moll sulked some more and Sadie asked, 'Can we have breakfast?'

'That depends on what you want,' I said.

They both looked at my open jar of spread.

'Bad for dogs,' I said, wanting to growl like May had.

'We're only a quarter dog,' Moll said and the sulky look turned to big brown eyes.

'Yeah,' said Sadie and another pair of big brown eyes stared at me.

I didn't reply but made them some toast with as little spread on as my conscience would let me get away with.

'Sit down at the table,' I said when I realised they were still standing around.

They bit into their toast with the kind of enthusiasm that dogs do when they manage to get their jaws around human food—not sure what it is but sure it must be worth wolfing down because the humans eat it. Then there were blissed out looks that proved it wasn't a bad choice.

'You've never had chocolate spread before,' I said.

Moll's sulky look returned. 'Daddy never let us.'

'We have to go shopping in a bit,' I said. 'We need to get you some more clothes and we need to buy some food in.'

'More spread?' Sadie asked hopefully.

'Not yet,' I said. There was just enough left for me to scoop out a couple more spoonfuls. 'We need to buy some more at the supermarket.'

Which meant a run to Sweet. Might as well do it while we still had the rental car, which meant I'd have to drive there twice, once to do the shopping and once to hand the car over. If I could persuade May to look after the girls the second time, maybe I could call in at the library in Llareggub and send that email to Marie Bakken who was presumably interested in hearing that I made it out of the Institute. But nothing else. Wolf-women and dog-girls weren't her area of interest, any more than real werewolves were.

'You already bought us some clothes,' Moll said around a her breakfast.

'One set of clothing each isn't enough,' I said. 'They get dirty and need washing. And don't speak with your mouth full.'

She stuck her tongue out at me and it was brown and grey with chewed up toast and spread.

'Lovely,' I said and turned away.

Sadie swallowed loudly and asked, 'Can I have some milky tea?'

'We haven't got any milk at the moment. I forgot to get it out of the freezer last night. Do you drink black tea or would you rather have water?'

She pulled my mug towards her before I stopped her and sniffed it suspiciously. I was about to comment about her caution but then she lifted it up—smearing it with the spread-covered toast held in one hand—and virtually poured the contents straight down her neck.

'What was that?' she asked when she put it down. 'I'll have a bowl of that, please.'

There was a mouth-shaped smear of half-chewed toast and spread on the lip of the mug and the dregs of my drink in the bottom.

'Black tea. And how about a fresh mug?'

I picked up my grubby mug and washed it down in the sink and found two more for my guests. Three teas in the amount of time it took the kettle to boil. I made sure theirs was watered down and weak so I wouldn't have them bouncing off the ceiling or burning their mouths. Mine I made so strong the spoon almost stood up in it.

'What about May?' asked Moll.

'She can have hers when she's ready to come downstairs.'

'Can we go get her?' asked Sadie.

'No.'

'Can we watch TV?' asked Moll.

'Does your dad let you watch a lot of TV?' I asked back.

The two of them looked at each other before Moll said, tentatively, 'Yes, we watch it all the time.'

Sadie giggled.

'I don't have a TV,' I said.

They both deflated. 'Oh.'

'You said we'd finally find out what TV was like,' Sadie hissed.

Moll shushed her.

'Why don't you just sit and have your teas?' I asked. 'Then you can go play in the sitting room.'

'Playing's no fun as humans,' said Moll.

There wasn't really an answer to that. There also wasn't much I could do to distract them. Mum used to bake with me but I didn't have enough ingredients in the house. I couldn't take them outdoors with normal human beings or Greywolves or Olsen's henchmen—the ones that were still alive—possibly showing up at any time. There was no way I was introducing them to chess this early in the morning.

'How long have you lived here?' asked Moll.

Now I knew why Conn had found ways of leaving them on their own as if they were a hundred percent dog. Before, I'd thought that was down to having no-one to leave them with and not wanting to raise Olsen's suspicions. Now, I was having a rethink.

'About six months,' I said.

'Where did you live before?' asked Sadie.

'With the Williamses.'

'Why? They're not your family?' asked Moll.

'No,' I agreed.

I heard a car come up the drive. One of the horse-owners was coming. Maybe I should have run out and ask them to rescue me.

'Do you have a family?' asked Moll.

'My mum lives in Sweet.'

'Our mum died,' said Sadie. 'I don't remember her.'

'What about your dad?' asked Moll.

I shrugged, and heard a car door shut firmly.

'Don't you know who your dad is?' asked Moll.

Firm steps from car to house door. There was no knock as it was thrust open. 'Hello?'

My horse-owner sounded combative in her no-nonsense middle-class country woman kind of way.

'Hello,' Sadie said back and then flushed into embarrassed silence.

'*Bore da*,' I said, standing and turning to face my horse-owner.

'Elkie! You're back. I'm sorry, I just saw a strange car on the drive and I thought I'd better check who it was. What with that Williams fellow taking all that haylage without asking.'

'You saw him?' I asked, curious.

'Oh, yes. He tried to take it while I was here one morning and I told him he couldn't, not while you were away. He must have come back after I left because it was gone by the evening.'

'He has livestock to feed and it is partly his,' I said with a shrug and a smile.

No point talking business, yet. I needed to make sure I had a plan.

'Yes, but he shouldn't take things without letting you know,' was my horse-owner's response. 'Anyway, now I know where you've been and you've brought your little sisters back with you! I must say there's a strong family resemblance.'

Neither Sadie nor Moll said anything to deny the relationship and I didn't correct the assumption. The customer is always right, and all that. Not to mention that it seemed the sensible thing to pass Moll and Sadie off as my sisters for not-getting-arrested-for-kidnapping purposes. I made a mental note to call in on Mum on one of the trips to Sweet to make sure she didn't hear it from anyone else first, though.

'Yeah,' I said, 'We get that a lot.'

'Was it a good family visit?' my horse-owner asked.

I stared at the mug of tea I'd left on the table and decided it would be rude to pick it up and drink. 'Quiet. Would you like a cup of tea?'

She smiled. 'No, thank you. I'll just see to the horses. As you're here, though, I'd better pay you. I rounded up last week's rent from the other girls.'

She was rooting around in a big leather handbag that didn't really go with the jodhpurs and muckers, but who was I to give fashion advice? Moll and Sadie watched with interest and I realised how few people they must have even seen.

'Here!'

A fistful of paper money that should pay for new-to-us clothes and a major food shop. Maybe with some left over to put towards buying a cheap car in a couple of months. Without the farm—no, the Williamses'—Landie, we were reliant on public transport and that just wouldn't work with me and two young girls. Nor May, who I was hoping to get rid of some time. When I told Mum about her two new 'step-daughters', I'd have to ask her how she managed to raise me in the middle of nowhere with no money.

'Thank you,' I said, thinking of how to split the money this week so that everything I'd promised would be available for the livery could exist and my household could survive. And the next week. And the week after.

'No bother,' said my horse-owner.

She was gone before I could think of anything else to say, striding towards the stable and her beloved 'hack'.

'Who was that?' asked Moll.

'One of our customers,' I said. 'I let out the stables.'

'What's a stables?' asked Sadie.

'Where people put horses.'

'We have horses?' asked Moll and both she and Sadie were crowding the doorway, staring out after our visitor.

'Not ours,' I replied.

'Oh.'

I managed to get them back in the kitchen and shut the door.

'So we can't ride them?' asked Moll.

'No.'

Although my customers had already asked if I knew how and if I would be interested—to help them exercise their animals—I didn't think teaching children to ride was in their plan.

'There's nothing to do here,' Moll said.

I agreed but didn't admit it. 'If you've finished your tea, why don't you go and play in the sitting room until May gets up?'

'Humans aren't as much fun,' Sadie said.

I bit down on my lip before I asked, 'Do you mean being with them or as one of them?'

Lie 10: Families Make Sense

May refused to come with us and somehow my trip into Sweet with the girls became me standing in the rain on my mother's doorstep desperately hoping she could fix my life. This wasn't what I planned. I'd intended to go into the town centre, park up and drag Moll and Sadie around the charity shops—just the way my mother had done with me when I was their age. Only she'd had to bring me in on the bus, not drive a two year old hire car. Instead, I was staring at a door painted in green gloss, hoping she was on the other side of it and not at work.

'Can't we wait in the car?' asked Moll. 'Dad would have let us wait in the car.'

'I'm cold and wet,' said Sadie.

I managed not to growl or shout. 'No. And we all are.'

I tried to work out when the last time I'd seen Mum was. Probably about the time Ben had signed over the farm to me. She hadn't approved. Probably thought it was for services rendered, even though I'd said Ben and I'd never been together. All that effort and time she'd given me and I'd just... let her walk off.

'Please be in,' I whispered.

I didn't realise the words had escaped me until I got more questions.

'Why wouldn't they be in?' asked Sadie.

'Who are we waiting for, anyway?' asked Moll.

At least I managed not to kneel on the floor and beg her to take them off me. I banged on the door again.

'Someone's coming,' said Moll, 'I can hear footsteps.'

I heard nothing until the lock turned.

'I hope they're nice,' said Sadie.

The door started to open.

'Hi, Mum,' I said.

She looked at me, and then at the two girls huddled close to me as if I could provide shelter from the rain. I saw a moment of calculation pass across her face, as if she also saw the possible family resemblance that everyone else had commented on but knew better and discarded the idea.

'Hello, Elkie. You'd better come in from the rain.'

I opened my mouth. I'd been mentally rehearsing later in the conversation, that 'Mum, you know how we never talk? Well I have something I need to tell you...' leading in to 'I'm telling everyone that these two strange girls are my sisters'. What I actually said was 'Mum, who's my dad?'

I covered my mouth. Although it was something I felt I ought to ask before announcing that I'd apparently adopted a totally different male parent and his offspring, it really wasn't something I had intended to ask straight out, first thing.

'Elkie,' she replied. 'Come in and bring those two in with you before you all catch colds.'

I did as I was told, and Moll and Sadie followed me in. Well, their hands were curled up in my coat, so I don't suppose they really put much thought into the matter.

'Shut the door behind you. Cup of tea?'

Mum was turning and gone before the three of us had escaped the rain. I'd upset her, I guess.

'Yes, please,' I called out. 'But none for these two, they've already had a cup this morning.'

I helped Moll and Sadie get out of the oversized coats they'd borrowed from my coat rack and hung them, dripping, out of the way before taking off my own. I almost missed the sound of Mum putting something down too heavily but the flinch from Conn's daughters was obvious.

'It'll be fine,' I said to them.

'She's muttering about giving caffeine to children,' said Moll. 'What's caffeine?'

'Something that's in tea, coffee and a few other things,' I said, not entirely sure.

'Is it bad?' asked Sadie.

'Only if you have too much of it.'

Maybe not a good time to mention to Mum that these two were part dog and I'd fed them chocolate hazelnut spread. Although I'm not sure she'd believe that I'd actually shared my spread without coercion.

'Kitchen,' I added. 'Now.'

They weren't happy to go—the pushing me in front as if I were a human shield was a giveaway—but they knew where it was just by following the noises I couldn't hear properly.

'Would you two girls like cordial?' my mum asked.

Moll and Sadie looked at me.

'Squash?' I tried.

They still looked at me, this time with a head tilt that implied I wasn't all there.

'Could you make up a glass for them to try?' I asked.

'What do you ordinarily drink?' Mum asked them, ignoring me.

'Dad gives us tea,' said Moll.

'With lots of yummy milk in,' said Sadie.

'Elkie didn't have any milk this morning,' Moll added.

Mum glared at me. Black tea, it seemed, was a bad choice for children.

'It's still defrosting,' I said. 'We've only just got back from Norway and I forgot to take it out of the freezer last night.'

Mum's only response was to put two mugs of tea on the table. So heavily they almost spilled.

'Thanks,' I said, taking one.

She turned her back and I shifted the other mug further away from Moll and Sadie who were sniffing in its general direction.

'Maybe we should just give Moll and Sadie a mug of milk each,' I suggested.

Mum covered whatever she was thinking with the general moving about kitchen that meant she was busy. 'So, what brings you see me today?'

'Erm... Happy Chanukah?' I guessed.

It was supposed to be about the same time the Gentiles celebrated Christmas, right?

Mum froze. 'That was in November this year and we don't celebrate.'

'Oh,' I said. Then, 'Did you get anything from your sister in Oxford?'

'Yes.'

I nodded but she had her back to me. She kept busy at the kitchen counter.

'Sorry,' I said.

Two glasses of milk—complete with curly straws I would have never expected Mum to have in the house—were placed in front of Moll and Sadie. They looked at the straws and looked at me. Conn's parenting skills, it seemed, weren't that much better than mine. I stole a sip from Moll's glass to show them how straws worked. Moll pulled her glass away and drank out of it, leaving the straw in my mouth. Sadie giggled and tried to copy me.

'For what?' Mum asked.

I looked at her, straw dangling from my mouth.

'For which one of the things that you've done are you sorry for?' she clarified.

I pulled the straw out of my mouth and found it was the most interesting thing in the world. 'Erm... All of it?'

'Really? So why don't you tell me what you did wrong?'

Sadie made a slurping sound through her straw and giggled. Moll was watching with big eyes. I was finally grateful that May hadn't come with us. The thing I hated most was that each item came out more like a question.

'Going to Norway without telling you. Turning up on your doorstep unannounced. Turning up with two young girls in tow. Giving them black tea to drink this morning—even though it was very weak and watered down. Asking who my father is.'

Mum flinched on the word 'father' but didn't acknowledge it. Instead, she asked, 'What was in Norway?'

'We were,' said Moll.

'Ben Lloyd,' I said. 'I wanted to talk to him.'

'You couldn't pick up a phone?' Mum asked.

I said, 'The air fare was almost cheaper than an international phone call on a pay-as-you-go mobile.'

The corner of Mum's mouth tucked, briefly. 'How is he?'

'Might be coming back to the farm,' I said.

If things worked out. And maybe, one day, he'd be okay to leave it again, this time of his own free will.

'Oh,' said Mum.

'Is he going to sleep in the fourth bedroom?' asked Moll.

'Erm,' was as good as I could mange with my mum watching me for a while. Then I added, 'Well, it was his bedroom before.'

'Oh,' said Moll. 'But what about Dad?'

Sadie, in the meantime, had stopped sucking on her straw. She fixed my mum with big, brown eyes and asked, 'Is our daddy Elkie's daddy?'

'Everyone's been assuming they're my sisters,' I said to Mum, smoothing the question over a bit. Now was not the time to mention I hadn't disabused anyone of the notion.

'There's a certain resemblance,' Mum agreed, 'But unless their father is a Jewish banker, I doubt you're even related.'

Conn wasn't exactly banker material, and probably not Jewish.

'A Jewish banker?' I asked. 'You mean like your sister's husband?'

Mum flinched again.

'Shit,' I said. Then, 'Sorry for swearing.'

'What's a Jewish?' asked Moll.

'What's a banker?' asked Sadie.

At least neither of them asked what shit was.

'Their father's called Conn,' I said.

Mum shook her head. 'Conn what?'

Moll said, 'Connor MacLochlann.' She pointed at herself. 'I'm Moll. That's short for Margaret.' Then she pointed at her sister, 'She's Sadie. That's short for Sarah.'

Sadie wrinkled her nose. I guess she didn't like being called Sarah.

'Nice to meet you, Margaret MacLochlann,' Mum said gravely.

'Oh, we're not MacLochlanns,' said Moll. 'We're Joneses. Like our mum.'

Mum looked at me and I shrugged. The woman who ran away from home pregnant by her sister's husband wasn't exactly in a position to judge.

'Nice to meet you, Margaret Jones,' said Mum.

'And me,' Sadie said, like a puppy yapping for attention.

Mum smiled. 'And nice to meet you, Sarah Jones.'

'What's your name?' asked Moll.

'I'm Rebecca Bernstein,' said Mum.

'Is Elkie a Bernstein like you or is she like her dad?' asked Sadie.

I didn't know whether to bang my head on the kitchen table. It had never seemed a good idea to talk about the parent missing from my life, as if it would upset or offend her. At least for as long as I could remember. Now I knew why.

'Elkie's a Bernstein, too.'

'What's her daddy's name?' asked Sadie.

I tried to remember the aunt's married name and failed.

'So, Elkie,' my mum said, 'What brings you to Sweet this morning?'

'I need to buy some more clothes for Moll and Sadie. And some food. And drop the hire car off, maybe on another trip. I need to call in the Llareggub library on the way back.'

Mum's eyebrows hitched up. 'Hire car?'

'Conn arranged it so I could transport these two,' I said.

'We went to a wolf sanctuary,' said Sadie.

'May came back with us,' said Moll.

I wondered if there were any gestures subtle enough for Mum not to notice that an eight and a seven year old could understand for 'shut up'. Probably not.

'May?' asked Mum.

'Another guest at the farm,' I said.

Was it a good thing or a bad thing that the one thing Mum and I could have actually had a decent conversation about—the Williamses deciding to sell up and move away, leaving me without an actual farm as such to run—was unlikely to be interesting to Moll and Sadie? On the other hand, if they mentioned it, I would have to explain why Dave was still in Norway.

'Have you nearly finished your milk, you two?' I asked. 'We should probably get on with that shopping.'

'I'm not at work today,' said Mum.

'Oh,' I said. Did this mean she was inviting herself along?

'How about I take the girls clothes shopping and we stop by the supermarket to buy you some child friendly food—'

'And some more chocolate spread,' said Moll. 'Elkie needs lots more chocolate spread.'

I flushed.

'—And you can go and drop off the hire car and meet us back at yours?' asked Mum.

I was torn. Did I bite her hand off accepting freedom from a never-ending game of twenty questions or did I get Moll and Sadie away before they told her everything she didn't need to know?

'You'll probably be there before me,' I said.

'So give me the house keys and we'll let ourselves in.'

'You really want to take two young children and a load of shopping on the bus?' I asked.

'It wouldn't be the first time,' she reminded me. 'But I have a car.'

'You do?'

That was new. Well, new to me. The last little car I'd known about had died a couple of years ago and wasn't replaced at the time due to lack of funds.

'Yes,' she said, and held out her hand.

The relief at no longer being the adult responsible for Moll and Sadie lasted about as long as it took Mum's front door to shut on me. Because I was still responsible for whatever they put my mum through, because I was still responsible for a number of other things, and because there was still the possibility of being attacked. Somehow, somewhere, somewhen.

'Right. Car first.'

Considering how small Sweet was compared to driving through Guildford with the girls just the day before, it took me a long time to find the hire car firm. The time it took to explain that the car had been hired at an English airport and wouldn't be driven back took longer. They were a little sharper on who was paying, which was worrying because I'd just given up all my cash to my mother—except for the money to get back home.

'What name did you say it was all arranged in?' the woman at the desk asked.

'I'm Elkie Bernstein,' I said. 'But the car was booked by Connor MacLochlann on his credit card.'

I hoped. At least I knew his full name now that Moll and Sadie had said it.

'And you don't have that credit card with you?'

I sighed and rested against the desk. 'He's in Norway and I assume he needs it himself.'

'Do you know the number?'

'No,' I said. 'Isn't all this on the computer?'

'I need to verify the details.'

I looked out of the window at the hire car and considered

telling the poor woman that if she didn't want it, I'd keep it. The company's name was on both of the number plates and the logo was not so tastefully stuck on the windscreen, though.

'It's definitely yours,' I said.

She hmphed at me and started again. We repeated the same conversation three or four times before I was allowed to leave.

'Rescue service,' I muttered to myself as I walked out of the hire car office. 'I should have written a list.'

There wasn't an office to go to for the Mountain Rescue team I worked with. The organisation's registered address was the treasurer's and the person to contact about my change of circumstances was the organisation's secretary. He lived in Sweet so I figured I might as well call in as ring him.

His response to me turning up on his doorstep in the rain was not particularly enthusiastic. 'Elkie. I thought you were still away?'

'Nah,' I said, 'I'm just not on the rota for another few days.'

He looked at me and I could feel rain water turning into a drip on my nose. My hair had long ago given up a pretence of dryness.

'Well, I asked not to be put on the rota for a few more days so I assume I'm not.'

He continued to stand and look at me.

'I have a new mobile,' I said, 'With a new number, so I need to change my contact details.'

'Oh, okay. Let me just get a pen and a piece of paper.'

I couldn't quite contain the eye roll when he closed the door in my face and went off. Was he worried that I'd leave permanent water marks on the floor?

'Okay,' he said when he came back, and he leant against his hall wall, pen poised to take my phone number, 'I'm ready.'

Conn had been nice or dumb enough to put an entry in the phone's address book labelled 'Me' and I'd checked it several times so I was able to pull the number out of my head instead of pulling the phone out of my pocket and into the rain. The secretary quoted it back.

'That's it,' I said.

'Good.'

I stood and stared at him, willing him to make a comment about how uncomfortable I looked or how bad the weather was.

He paused with his hand on the door handle. 'Was there anything else?'

'Yeah,' I said. 'I have my little sisters staying with me indefinitely. I can't be on call all hours anymore because I'll have difficulty arranging baby-sitting.'

He nodded but he thought he was too polite to say 'this isn't my problem'.

'I'd rather set it down to definite days of the week. Regular, you know?' I said.

'Aren't they supposed to be at school?' he asked.

Mentally, I cursed. Outwardly, I just went with, 'They're not starting at the local school until after the Christmas holidays. And that'll only be from nine to three.'

At least, I thought that was the school times. I had no idea. I also had no idea how to go about enrolling a couple of girls without human identities and the paperwork to prove it—that I knew of—into primary school.

The secretary's pen came out again and he scribbled something I couldn't see on the piece of paper. Maybe something like 'never put Elkie on the rota again', which I'd hate because I loved the training and the activity.

'I'll give you a ring when I'm organising the next rota,' he said. 'See what days are available. Do you still want to be down for the training days?'

I nodded to keep from venting some frustration.

'Okay. Talk to you soon.'

The door closed in my face and the rain continued to fall.

'At least it's not horizontal.' I squinted at the grey sky. 'Yet.'

Then it was time to catch a train to Llareggub so I could walk to the library in the rain. As I didn't have a land line, I had no phone or email at home so I had to go to the library to send that promised email to Ida Marie Bakken. I would have sat and moped about it on the train but the mobile phone went off with a text message alert.

'What the hell have you done now? C'

There was a moment of confusion. Other things had happened since I'd sent a text the evening before, things that kind of pushed it out of my head. Then I remembered I'd texted about bringing Sadie and Moll home.

'I didn't think the Greywolves were suitable guardians,' I texted back.

In almost no time at all, there was a reply. 'And you are?'

I put the phone away and rested my forehead against the cold carriage window. I wasn't ready to answer. The phone made the text alert sound once more as if demanding I reconsider and then was silent.

I had to get out into the rain again at Llareggub and leave behind a puddle where I'd been on the train. Of the handful of people who got on at the small station, no-one took my place. I squelched all the way to the library, the rainwater having soaked through my clothes to sting the shoulder bite and pool in my walking boots.

'*Bore da*, Elkie. Bit wet,' the librarian behind the counter said when I walked in.

I looked down at the puddle already forming at my feet.

'You could say that. Is there a computer free?' I asked.

Maybe it was time I got that land line so I didn't have to have days like these. Or have days when I had to bring Moll and Sadie through on public transport and attempt to entertain them while also sending emails. I didn't even know if they had enough education to read. They can't have always been kept like dogs at Conn's cottage, right? I could see how he would have to leave them on their own as he had to hide their presence from Olsen, but they couldn't have spent their whole childhood to date like that, could they?

'Not at the moment,' replied the librarian. 'Should be one free in twenty minutes or so.'

'I'll wait,' I replied.

I turned to drip dry in front of some bookshelves then stopped.

'Can I register my sisters to use the library?' I found myself asking.

Even if they couldn't read, coming to the library couldn't be a bad thing for them. It was another source of entertainment, something to do in the middle of nowhere.

'I guess so. Same address as you?' asked the librarian and she started to get out forms.

'Yes,' I said, and then because it seemed expected, 'They've just moved in with me for a while.'

The librarian smiled. 'Will they be going to the Llados primary school?'

'After Christmas, if I can get them enrolled.'

She nodded. 'They'll have to be enrolled somewhere or you need to let the council know they're being home-schooled—'

At that point, my mind started to panic and wheel-spin. There was no way I was good enough to home-school them.

'—as the law requires them to be in education.'

'Oh,' I said.

'I didn't realise your mum had... erm... married when she moved away.'

I started to wonder about the sanity of even mentioning Moll and Sadie here and now. It would be all around the area by the end of the day. 'She didn't. She's still on her own in Sweet as far as I know. They're my dad's kids.'

The librarian was too polite to say what Mrs Williams had the night before, that she hadn't realised I knew who my father was, let alone know him well enough to end up in charge of his children.

'So... erm... what names shall I put?'

'Margaret and Sarah Jones.'

The librarian nodded and I could practically hear the 'Elkie's father's Welsh?' running through her head.

'Actually, maybe I should get a card for my dad,' I bluffed, 'As he's bound to turn up some time. Same address but for Connor MacLochlann.'

The librarian looked at me and, again, I could see the thoughts in her head. This time it was the stability of the known universe reasserting itself. Elkie Bernstein was still white, if lapsed Jewish, trash and she got it from her father. After all, he now had three daughters with different surnames. Well, she was half-right, I was just lying about who my father was.

'Okay,' she said.

Someone else walked up to the counter and there was an exchange of looks that meant gossip was on its way.

'That computer's free now, Elkie. I'll have the forms filled in for you to sign when you get down. It'll take another few days for the cards to come through.'

'*Diolch*,' I said and managed not to run for the Internet connection.

I was in so much shit if Conn heard about this.

Logging into my email account, though, wasn't a good way of getting away from it all. There was nothing there but spam and no excuses not to draft that email to Marie. I got her business card, now floppy and wet, out of my pocket and placed it carefully on the desk. The ink hadn't run, thankfully, but the thin card was just looking for an excuse to part company with itself.

I typed her email address in and stared at it for a while. It was the first time I'd questioned why she was so interested in hearing from me. More precisely, why was she so interested in the things surrounding Olsen. This was surely more than professional interest.

I'd accepted her just being a shoulder to lean on talk while I was still in Norway but however many miles away I now was made it seem, well, distant. It was amazing how that and my current distraction seemed to have taken away the threat. Well, that and killing a werewolf or two.

It was hard to consider something that far away a problem anymore now there were no direct assaults. There was nothing Olsen could do to me from this distance, without more recruits, and Ben would soon be out of his power because I'd signed the paperwork. I still had the nagging feeling that I was about to be attacked at any moment, but that wasn't rational.

That only left Dave to worry about but if his parents were running off to look after their little precious, I didn't have to worry about leaving him behind, did I? They were adults and they could protect him. Even if they didn't know about werewolves.

I just had to let Marie know I'd got back okay and that I was now Ben's official next of kin. Then I texted Conn and Ben. For Conn, 'I need the girls' information so I can enrol them at school.' For Ben, I imagined a chess board set up in front of me, worked out a move and texted the result. I'd have to remember to set the board up when I got home.

Lie 11: We Can Work It Out

I walked past the neat little car parked where the farm Landie used to sit and ignored the noises coming from my kitchen for running straight up to my room. It was like being a teenager again.

I stripped off the wet clothes, dabbed at the shoulder wound, then dried and dressed in almost identical fresh clothes. I dug out the second cheap chess set I'd bought and set it up on the window sill. I checked the text messages—nothing new—and made Ben's opening move and then my response. I would have to come up with something more creative than echoing his move for the next one.

Given the hours we'd already put in to playing chess, I should probably have been able to guess what the next three or four moves were going to be. If I concentrated and thought about it. But I hadn't been good at that while we were locked in a glorified kennel, let alone now that we were however many miles apart. Playing chess with Ben was an idea I was finding it hard to hold on to.

Just like it was difficult to hold on to the idea of a white winter while outside was grey with horizontal rain. Just like it was hard to hold on to the idea of Olsen being threatening when he was also so many miles away and I didn't have to see him. All I had left was general paranoia that made me count exits and plan escape.

'He's still a problem,' I reminded myself. 'He can still hurt Ben or Dave. He can still hurt you.'

'Who can hurt me?' asked May.

I twisted to look over my bitten shoulder, away from the chess board. She was standing in the doorway, obviously not willing to come in from the way her nose wrinkled. She hadn't been quite so choosy when she came in to borrow some clothes—and we still needed to get her to the shops to buy some of her own.

'Olsen,' was all I said.

Or someone working for him. Eric was probably dead from silver poisoning but there might be others he could send. And it counted just as much for May and the girls. I didn't need to be told that Olsen would love to know that there were actual shape-shifters in the world, not just men who put on fur to become something like a deformed dog. He'd probably have them locked up in cells and prepared for lab tests in no time. If he ever found out about them.

'That's Conn's boss,' May said and her lip curled to show canine teeth. Which only went to show that Olsen's reputation proceeded him. 'You know him?'

'Well, I was at his place. How else do you think I met Conn? And ended up with Eric and Simon following me?'

Not entirely true. I'd met Conn not far from here when he delivered the deeds for the farm to me. Olsen had signed them on Ben's behalf—a guardian for a mentally unfit young man who now had a new guardian. Me.

'He doesn't know about Moll and Sadie,' said May.

A statement of fact. The two girls wouldn't be here if Olsen had wanted to keep them.

'No,' I agreed. 'Not so far.'

May nodded. 'Your mum wants you downstairs. To help with the mess they're making.'

She left.

I followed her across the landing, down the stairs, to the kitchen. She was right about the mess, but people learning to bake generally do make mess. I have strong memories of leaving floury hand prints behind when Mum was teaching me. This time it was Moll and Sadie up to their armpits in white powder while Mum half-taught, half-tidied up after.

'These two are almost as bad as you,' Mum said to me.

She didn't look up and I hadn't said anything. I had that moment of childhood irrationality, wondering if she could see everything whether she was looking or not.

'You know,' I said, 'I spend my life feeling like I never see another woman around the place then suddenly I'm surrounded.'

She ignored me. 'They wanted to buy a whole crate of chocolate spread. If I didn't know better, I'd be saying you were sisters, too.'

'Yeah,' I said. 'About that.'

She looked up at me and there was a hint of 'I'm not finished' to the way her stare seemed to pin me to the door I'd just closed behind me.

'However,' she said, ' *My* daughter doesn't change into dog when she's bored in the car.'

I looked at May and she shrugged. Moll and Sadie deciding playtime was better in canine form had nothing to do with her and she wasn't going to come clean about Greywolves any time soon. She also wasn't going to help me out with explaining that they got it from their mother, not our allegedly shared father.

'Yeah,' I said again. 'About that.'

I was pinned down with another look, the kind that says 'whatever you're about to say is a load of bollocks, so don't bother'. So I didn't.

'I need to talk to you in the living room,' Mum said.

Somehow that was enough to make the scenery change to another room. I have no memory of leaving the kitchen and, yet, there I was in another room with only my mother for company. I was going to need something to use as a shield.

'What exactly is going on?' Mum asked.

I could see the door. If I just shuffled around a little more and moved my hand, I could turn the handle and—

'Elkie? At least tell me you're not in any kind of trouble.'

'Trouble,' I echoed.

The word was enough to set off mental images of Olsen behind his large wooden desk. Imaginary Olsen had his fingers steepled like a super-villain from a film. He'd done that a couple of times in real life.

'No trouble,' I said. 'Not anymore.'

'Not anymore?' Mum asked.

I opened and closed my mouth a couple of times but nothing found its way out.

'And you still haven't told me why you're babysitting—why I'm babysitting two girls that aren't related to us,' Mum said.

'Conn's a friend,' I said. 'He helped Ben out and brought the papers when he gave me the farm. I'm just... returning the favour.' I paused and then added quietly, 'Indefinitely.'

'By what? Becoming their guardian?'

'I guess...'

More like pretending to be their big sister until Conn came up with a better plan.

'You're letting people think Moll and Sadie are your sisters, aren't you?'

'Erm... Maybe...'

'Why would you do that?'

'So they don't ask questions about why I've been left in charge of two children?' I suggested.

'Why shouldn't they ask questions about it?' Mum said.

I didn't say anything. I wasn't entirely sure I could come up with a good answer.

'I'm not lying for you, Elkie. I'm not telling people they're your sisters and that some man I never met is your father.'

'You don't have to,' I fired back. 'You just have to not talk about who *is* my father. Just like you've been doing for all of my life.'

Mum froze, except for the opening and closing of her mouth, like a landed fish. There may have been a squeak.

I swallowed and wished I could take the hurt back, even if I'd meant every one of the words I'd said. I bluffed away my guilt and gave her back one of her looks. 'Have you considered what would happen if they ended up in social services?'

'Surely they would just take them back to their father. It would be the obvious thing.'

I snorted. 'Yeah, right. Assuming there are records for them being human, they'd get sent back to the man who arranged their being imported to the UK as dogs. So, yeah.'

Plus the small matter of them turning into dogs when they decided they were bored and wanted to play. They'd be on a lab table quicker than we could say 'What the fu—'. It wouldn't matter whether it was Olsen or the Social Service's choice of lab table.

'Then maybe he shouldn't be the one responsible for them,' Mum said.

It was hard to remain certain Conn was good father material. Distance made everything look vaguer and greyer. With distance I was realising that I'd been in Olsen's Institute for five days and had spent an awful lot of that time with Conn—without his daughters. Who'd been looking after them while he'd been looking after me?

'And their mother?'

She'd always been referred to in past tense, that was all I

knew. 'Dead.'

Mum nodded slowly. That was the bit where people traditionally said things like 'I'm sorry' but Conn's mate had nothing to do with me. There was nothing for either of us to say to mark the unknown woman's passing.

'You're going to have trouble doing the farm chores and looking after those two,' Mum said. 'Unless this May is here to help as well?'

I shrugged. 'The farm isn't so much of a problem.'

'What? The partnership fell through, didn't it? What did Dave do now?'

I couldn't do anything but watch her pace up and down. Something made me freeze with my jaw hanging down like some mouth-breathing idiot.

'I knew this would happen. As soon as he went away to university.' She was waving arms and shaking her head in the wild gesturing that probably should have come with the whole 'these two girls change into dogs' phase of the conversation but hadn't. 'He's always been one to act first and apologise later. If he thinks he has to.'

'Pardon?' I asked.

'I'm sorry, Elkie, but it was obvious he was going to cheat on you when he left. He was going out into the big wide world to new adventure. And you weren't.'

'And you tell me this now?'

She paused.

'You couldn't have suggested this— oh, I don't know, four years ago?'

'Would you have listened?'

'Yes,' I said immediately. Then, 'I probably wouldn't have done anything about it, though.'

Mum laughed, a bitter-sweet sound. 'You always were stubborn.'

'Determined,' I corrected.

'That, too.'

I finally sat down. It seemed appropriate now that she wasn't glaring at me or pacing any more.

'It was a mistake going into business with your ex's parents,' Mum said. 'Better to make a clean break.'

'It's not like there was work to walk into. Then Ben gave

me all this,' I indicated our surroundings, 'And I didn't have the resources to do anything with it. What else was I going to do?'

Mum sighed. 'So what did ex-lover boy do this time?'

I looked at my hands. I folded them neatly in my lap and adjusted my position so that the rest of me was arranged as ladylike as I could manage.

'Elkie?'

'He killed someone.'

'He what? What does this have to with going to Norway?'

Rubbing my temples suddenly became more important than keeping my hands still. 'Dave and I went to Norway to visit Ben. He's in care at a special Institute there. Conn picked us up from the airport. We stopped when the car blew a tyre. A stranger approached us and Dave killed him. Dave is now incarcerated in the same Institute awaiting trial for murder.'

Mum's mouth opened and closed again.

'His parents are selling up and going to support him,' I said.

Maybe it was time to switch focus from farming to livery. If anyone was willing to leave their horses and ponies out in all weathers, I had plenty of grazing land to rent out.

'On the plus side,' I said. 'it looks like Ben might be able to come home. The Institute just haven't had anywhere to send him until I signed the forms to become like his official next of kin.'

'Elkie, do you think before you do these things or do they just... happen?'

I thought about the chessboard upstairs.

'They pretty much just happen,' I said.

She closed her eyes and took a couple of deep breaths. She was probably counting to ten.

'You still haven't told me how those two children can turn into dogs,' she said.

'You didn't ask,' I replied.

'You're not going to tell me, are you?'

I shrugged. 'It's a kind of magic.'

It's not like I knew *how* Moll, Sadie and the Greywolves changed shape. I just knew that they did—and it was something to do with werewolf fathers and canine mothers.

'I thought I was going insane,' Mum said.

'It's always a possibility.'

I wasn't sure if I counted as sane or not but at least I hadn't killed anyone. Well, nobody who was all human, and no werewolves within twenty-four hours. Another couple of days of dealing with Moll and Sadie, though, and killing might become more attractive thing to do.

'I told them not to,' I said.

It sounded a little more plaintive than I intended; the child I would always be telling her mother it wasn't fair.

'They said. They also said they were very, very sorry and wouldn't do it again if I didn't tell you.'

'Great,' I said. 'Now they think they have no reason not to turn into dogs around you.'

She looked at me. 'They would have changed again anyway. They're children. That's what children are like.'

'Huh.'

'They said you wouldn't let them have any chocolate spread,' she said with a curl to her lips that spoke of amusement at my expense.

'They'll be lucky if they get to sniff the bloody jar.'

'That's the problem with some children,' my mum said with a light tone that almost hid a bitter tone I'd never noticed before, 'You never learn to share.'

She wasn't an only child, she had a sister. A sister who had decided to take away the man who then became her husband? Had there been actual sharing going on as well? This just got worse.

'Some parents never seem to, either,' I said.

I meant that sharing more information would have been better but I didn't make it clear enough. The good humoured indulgence we'd been working towards disappeared and I didn't get to find out what exactly had put the bitterness there.

'We'd better go back to the kitchen,' Mum said, tight lipped.

At least she didn't press further about Conn coming to pick up his daughters, why Dave would murder anyone, or how two young girls were also two Akita puppies.

May, Moll and Sadie looked up when we walked back into

the kitchen. Moll and Sadie were covered in flour and if it had been possible to tuck tails between their legs, they would have done. May had that bored look that comes with practice and a preference for not being in farmhouse kitchens. Weirdly, they were all looking at me, waiting for my reaction, as if I were the one in charge.

'Everything OK?' May asked.

I made a non-committal noise.

'Well, I need to make a phone call and you haven't got a phone,' she continued.

She flicked through the magazine she was holding—she must have been into the Llados village shop, at least, while I was out—and put it down. I have no idea where she got the money, though.

'There's not even a public phone in the quaint collection of cottages you call a village.'

'Taken down a while ago,' I said. 'No-one used it. I guess you don't you have a mobile with you.'

Wolves and naked women don't have pockets for such things.

'No.'

Mum wasn't involving herself in this side conversation. She wasn't even watching us, too busy cleaning up the flour Moll and Sadie had spread across the kitchen table. I had a flashback to her cleaning up like that after me in the cottage I'd grown up in. The memories of all those times was almost stronger than the present and I barely heard May. But I did.

'I need to call home,' said May.

'Here.' I held out the mobile that Conn had given me. I'd had chance, while being subjected to multiple times twenty questions that morning, to check the signal. 'The signal's best just in the doorway.'

May took the phone and looked at the door. On the other side was a lot of grey weather. There was an air of performance art about the movement, as if she wanted everybody to watch her but I was the only one paying attention. Moll and Sadie were whispering at Mum, words I couldn't quite make out and wasn't sure I wanted to hear in case it involved more questions.

'It might actually work better outside,' I said. 'I haven't

tried it out by the stable.'

It took her a whole minute to work her way from her seat to the door. She kept her eyes on the phone screen, watching the signal bars. She started pressing buttons when she was next to the door and stopped half way through.

'The number's already in here,' she said.

Her look at me was accusing, as if it was something I'd hidden. I shrugged. It wasn't really my phone and I had no idea what Conn had used it for, except for keeping secrets from Olsen. Although it made sense. He'd kept the Greywolves secret from Olsen so it stood to reason that his secret phone would have been the method for contacting them. A conclusion supported by the clearly audible greeting May got when the phone at the other end was picked up.

'Conn? What the hell are you doing ringing me now? And who the hell was that bitch you sent to see me?'

The old Greywolf man's voice was loud enough that my mother froze and looked up. 'The bitch' must obviously be me—if only because the phone had been in my possession.

'Will?' May asked.

She was flushed and it was the first time I'd ever seen her out of sorts, despite the obvious dislike of the Welsh countryside.

'May? I thought you went with that bitch. What are you doing with Conn?'

'I did,' she said. 'I am.'

And she fled, running across the yard in the rain, leaving the kitchen door flapping behind her.

'So what else did you do, Elkie?' Mum asked.

I shrugged. 'Nothing.'

Mum looked at the girls and then at me, undecided for a moment, and then, '"Bitch"?'

I didn't have to tell her what I'd done to upset the Greywolves. I could keep it to myself and she would never know. It wasn't like it made any difference.

'And that wasn't your phone, was it? Whose phone is it?'

'Conn's,' I said.

'So yours is...?'

I sat down in the seat May had left and picked up her magazine. It was one of those fashion things that made me feel lumpy and a failure at being a woman. I had no idea where she'd got it.

'With Ben,' I said.

'Why didn't this Conn just give his phone to Ben and you give Ben your phone number?'

I flicked through various pages and wondered if I'd ever wear spindly high heels. I'd spent too much time learning to run away or fight to trust that there would ever be a safe time to wear them, even if Ben had stopped playing the more violent games with me.

'Things got a bit odd,' I said.

It was kind of weird that May was reading it. The clothes she'd been wearing before she turned wolf were much more casual. The stuff in the magazine didn't fit her apparent style at all.

'They still are, by the sounds of it,' Mum said.

Sadie giggled and watched me to see if I reacted. Moll's mouth had become a grim little line that reminded me of her father.

'Less than they were,' I said, putting aside the magazine.

All the things I probably would never tell her about how Ben and then Dave ended up in Olsen's Institute, the werewolf hub of Norway if not the world. All the things that made me go bump in the night at the slightest noise. Maybe Marie was right and I could use someone to talk to—but who do you talk to about werewolves and their magical offspring? I rubbed at the bite Eric had given me and let my mind drift a little.

'Is there any chance I could persuade you to come around and babysit once a week?' I asked.

Mum looked as if she was concentrating on the mixing bowl, which was finally more of a liquid mix than a powder but still got everywhere.

'Oh?' she asked, a return of fire.

'I'd like to continue with the mountain rescue stuff,' I said, 'And I can't attend the training without someone to look after Moll and Sadie.'

Or get there without the use of a vehicle. Or be on call without both.

'You could just leave us on our own,' said Moll. 'Dad used

to do it all the time.'

Mum sucked in her breath and shot me a look. I ignored it. Well, I guess I already knew Conn had left them on their own with the pack of mongrels while babysitting me, or dealing with Olsen, or whatever else his job entailed.

Mum accepted my silence and moved back to the matter in hand. 'You still need a car. And once a week won't be enough if you're on call.'

'I guess.'

'Can you afford a car?'

I was going to have to. I could probably afford a cheap old banger, eventually, from the livery fees. Although committing to the rescue work was more dependent on how much said banger would cost to run.

'Probably,' I said.

'So "no", then.'

I shrugged.

'Sadie and Moll are lovely girls,' she continued, 'But I don't have time to look after them.'

I remembered when I was full time at school and old enough to be on my own in the afternoon afterwards. Mum had worked two jobs—despite the way tax ate into the second income—just to keep us homed, fed and watered. I suppose things weren't that much better except she didn't have me to keep and now she could afford a car. A fine trade off.

Moll growled a little. I looked and she was watching me while Sadie splattered the cake mix all over the kitchen table. I rubbed at the spot between my eyebrows trying to ease out the frown that must have sat there since the two of them got up this morning.

'Although I think maybe we should start having family dinners. Maybe once a week,' Mum said, as if the only thing happening was baking. 'We should alternate who hosts.'

She showed Moll how to pour the cake mix into a tin and put the tin in the stove.

'Sure,' I said.

Halfway there, I thought. If the four of us were under the same roof, I had a responsible adult to leave the girls with if I were called away. Now all I needed was a vehicle and another free day for the training days.

'Can you cook?' asked Sadie.

'Who are you asking?' I asked back.

She laughed. 'You, silly.'

'Mum taught me,' I said.

I used to cook while she was out working.

May clattered back in, wet and unimpressed. Conn's phone was almost thrown onto the kitchen table, sliding through cake mix and flour.

'Everything okay?' I asked.

She curled her lip at me. 'The dust you kicked up has settled and we have our own problems to deal with.'

Which I took to mean that Eric and Simon had both crumbled to dust and the Greywolves weren't going to pursue me. That said, I already had one here with me. I could only hope she was going to give up on whatever she was planning—unless it was going home without Moll and Sadie.

'Will May be coming for dinner, too?' asked Moll.

The look she gave May—and had returned—was not good. The puppy had already decided that wolves weren't allowed on her territory. At some point, baking with my mum had persuaded Moll that we were her territory, her pack.

'I think May will probably have better things to do than visit Mum,' I said in an even tone as possible. 'But she'll be eating with us while she's staying on the farm.'

Lie 12: The Outcome Hasn't Already Been Decided

I got the letter from Olsen the next day. Strictly speaking, it was a letter from the Institute, signed by someone whose name I didn't recognise on Olsen's behalf. Even before I opened it and learnt that little nugget, I knew something was wrong.

'This isn't right,' I said.

'Why?' asked Moll.

It'd only been two days since I left Norway. There was nothing they would contact me about so soon—or I couldn't think of anything that they had to tell me so soon after my leaving. Not unless it was a set-up. But these were things I couldn't tell children. Which didn't stop Moll swinging on my arm enough to bring the envelope to her nose.

'Ugh,' she said. 'It smells of that place Dad works.'

'Let me smell it!' Sadie demanded and Moll was pulling my hand down again.

I didn't resist, although I could have picked her up, or at least kept the letter away from them both, with the one arm if I'd tried hard enough. I found it hard to believe that the smell of the Institute still clung to it after at least two days in the postal system.

'What does it say?' asked Moll.

'I don't know until I open it,' I said.

Sadie sniffed but was unimpressed. 'Daddy didn't touch it.'

It finally occurred to me that I could just ask them. I could ask about the care their father—our purported father—had given them while also working at the Institute and babysitting me. I would have had the truth, if I'd asked. I didn't. I wasn't sure I wanted to hear the answer.

'Open it,' said Moll.

'It's nothing to do with you,' I said.

She hmphed and sat down at the kitchen table.

'You said we should get lunch,' she said.

Where I had meant 'we' as a group, she obviously thought I meant 'we' as in 'me'.

Sadie nodded and rubbed her tummy. 'I'm hungry.'

'We could have chased those rabbits and eaten them. Then we wouldn't be hungry,' said Moll.

'You're not supposed to change in to dog form outside,' I reminded them. 'And we're using the rabbits to learn about tracking paw prints not as a source of food.'

Well, up until things got so tight that our only source of meat turned out to be the furry critters lolloping around our pastures uninvited.

'We don't need to track rabbit paw prints,' said Sadie, 'We can smell them.'

'Yeah, you said.' I kept an even tone. I'd had difficulty keeping up and had had to do a lot of bluffing. 'But the basics of tracking animals can be applied to things that don't leave smells that are so easy to follow. Like vehicles.'

'So why don't we track vehicles?' asked Moll.

'Because we start with the easy stuff and work our way up,' I said.

I put the letter down and fixed a lunch from the food Mum had bought the day before. There were things in my kitchen cupboards I didn't remember eating since I was Moll's age.

'Besides,' I added as an afterthought, 'It rains too much around here to be sure of smells. We've been lucky this morning.'

I had a vague memory of someone saying that rain killed scents for dogs. I couldn't remember properly and hoped it was true. It meant I might stand a chance of keeping up.

'Cup of tea?' Sadie asked as I put the kettle on.

'Only for me. You've had your mug for the day and Mum will kill me if I let you have any more caffeine.'

Sadie protested. 'Daddy lets us have more than one.'

'You don't have to tell her,' said Moll with a sly look, taking a different angle.

'She'll know,' I said with certainty I hadn't felt in a long time. 'Mums always know these things.'

They just missed the big things like checking where the doors were, sleeping in a defensible position, and other signs of predation by werewolves. She hadn't even asked about the sore shoulder I kept rubbing.

I waited until Moll and Sadie were in bed to open the letter—assuming that being undisturbed would be more important than being in a position to act on anything it contained. I was wrong. My roar of frustration had all three of my guests thundering down the stairs to ask me what was wrong.

'The stuffed up, overbearing, —'

'*Awr*?' May asked.

I looked up and there was a wolf standing in the doorway, watching me. Behind her, Moll and Sadie cowered in girl form, using her like a shield. Nice to know they were happy to do that even though they didn't seem to like her. Maybe that was why they used her.

'Olsen's a manipulative bastard,' I replied.

May raised canine eyebrows, sighed and shook her head. This was neither new nor important enough to pull her from her bed. She turned and climbed the stairs, stiff-limbed. I stared after her for a moment, wondering if she always slept in wolf form. I didn't dare ask, if only because it seemed a weirdly private thing to talk about.

'Sorry,' I said to Moll and Sadie, 'I shouldn't have shouted. Or sworn. You can go back to bed.'

'What happened?' asked Moll.

'It's not a big deal,' I lied.

Olsen's minion had sent a letter explaining that the Institute didn't think Ben was ready to leave, given the recent incident that had resulted in removal of his Internet privileges. Which would have been fair if he was coming home to somewhere that actually had an Internet connection.

'Really?' asked Sadie, her eyes wide, as if she could hear what was going on in my head.

I nodded. It wasn't like I hadn't been told to internalise dialogue before. I should have known better than to shout in the middle of the night with guests here.

'G'night,' Sadie said with that solemn tone that only children can manage.

'*Nos da, cariad*' I said back in Welsh.

Moll sniffed. 'Good night,' she said with emphasis.

She still didn't approve of me using Welsh, which served me right for yanking her chain.

I rubbed at my eyes and the bridge of my nose and, by the

time I'd finished, Moll and Sadie were gone. Which left me alone to mouth curses against Olsen and his Institute, who must have organised this letter within minutes of Marie suggesting Ben ought to be considered for release.

What did I do now?

More precisely, what could I do in the wee small hours without any form of communication but a borrowed pay as you go mobile phone?

Nothing but wait. If sleeping, breathing, eating, drinking, and weathering the enthusiasms of two young girls can be considered waiting.

I managed to herd them on to a bus in Llados—after waiting in the rain for a good fifteen minutes—and then on to the library in Llareggub.

The instant recognition by the librarian on duty did not amuse me, particularly as he kept the 'Your sisters are so like you' until they started rampaging their way through the children's section, laying books about them with abandon once they'd looked them over and declared them 'boring'.

'May I use a computer?' I asked, pretending there was no impropriety in Moll and Sadie's behaviour.

The librarian eyed Moll and Sadie. 'Now might not be a good time.'

We were the only three people, other than the librarian, in the place. It was clearly not because there was someone else desperate to send emails.

'Moll! Sadie!'

They froze.

'If you don't like the books, you should put them back exactly where you picked them up from,' I said in an even tone. I didn't exactly expect them to take the suggestion but it was worth a shot. 'And if you come over here and talk to the librarian about what sort of things you *do* like, he should be able to find you something you might want to borrow.'

'We can take books home?' said Moll, suddenly at my elbow.

'I have a library card,' I said.

I held out my card and Moll grabbed it.

'You'll have your own in a few days. It'll come in the post. I sorted it out the other day.'

'Why?' asked Moll.

The librarian looked horrified. Given his employment, it was a sure thing that he thought reading was the greatest way to pastime ever invented.

'So then you can read more,' I said.

'Why?' asked Moll.

I looked at her. 'Just how many other things do you think there are to do on the farm?'

'Oh.'

'Yeah,' I said. 'Now clean up the books you've left lying around.'

She was gone in a heartbeat, sniffing at the books she and Sadie had pulled out.

'Now would probably be a good time to explain what order the books are supposed to be in,' I said to the librarian.

He looked at me.

'They'll have forgotten which ones came from where,' I said.

'Oh. Yes.'

'May I go on a computer now?'

He blinked at me.

I added a 'Please?'

Moll and Sadie had started to potter around the bookshelves again, holding several books they'd picked up before. They looked determined but the books weren't going anywhere. They were too stubborn to ask for help working out where the books were supposed to go.

'Sure,' the librarian said and I was gone even faster than Moll.

I was back seconds later to interrupt him explaining how the children's books were organised by both alphabet and intended age group.

'Is there a scanner?' I asked in a pause.

I waved the Institute letter quickly, slow enough to show it was official, fast enough that he didn't get any details.

'Yeah,' he said. He looked a little dazed and I guess Moll and Sadie had been peppering him with what, where, when, why, how and who. It was kind of cute on someone else. 'I'll, erm, show you how to do that.'

I had thought Moll and I had been fast but he had the gold in running away.

'What did you do to him?' I asked Moll and Sadie.

They looked at me with large, innocent eyes.

'Hah!' I said.

Then I hurried after the librarian so I could get the letter scanned.

I let the librarian show me how to use the commercial copier-printer set apart from the actual computers to scan the letter and send it to the computer I was using. It turned out that I could have followed the instructions on the control panel myself but I didn't have the heart to tell him I could have done that for myself once he'd started. The only thing I wouldn't have done was approach the copier—if I'd known it did the job, I wouldn't have bothered asking about a scanner.

'Those files should turn up on your computer as jpegs,' he said, staring at the control panel and fiddling with the copier. 'If they don't, just come and get me and I'll do them again.'

'*Diolch*,' I said, picking up the original.

He didn't seem to be in a hurry to return to the girls. They'd obviously scared him, one way or another.

'*Croeso*,' he replied but he didn't sound like he was focussed on me.

I shrugged and sat down to write my email to Marie. Although, once the images of the Institute letter was attached, there wasn't much to say except for pointing out that the date on the letter was a day after I had left Norway. It was unlikely there had been any consideration of the conditions Ben would be returned to given that no-one had come to the farm to verify them—the letter had a reference to his misuse of the Internet, yet my distinct lack of home connection made pandering to any such addiction impossible.

The letter implied there never would be any investigation and, by extension, there would never be a hearing with the Board. I could understand not having a hearing about Ben's future straight away and I expected a negative—I even expected to fight, although I wasn't sure how—but this... This was dismissal. A rude, brief and unequivocal dismissal.

It took about a fortnight for Marie to reply. Well, that's not true. It was just over a fortnight before I could read it as the library—like all council buildings—was shut over Christmas and New Year.

It went by quicker than I expected, in contrast to the slow trickle of time I'd experienced in Norway, although getting things done felt like swimming upstream against the flow of entertaining Conn's daughters. I managed to get them enrolled at the Llados primary school without having to produce any proof of their identity, and survive Christmas without actually having to buy into it.

My shoulder healed, leaving some interesting scars to match those left by the previous six years of werewolf attacks. If it had been likely I could have found someone who wanted to see me naked, I would have worried what it looked like.

I also managed to lose a game of chess to Ben via text message, although I was still waiting for another text that had more in it than the coordinates of a move. I would have thought that Conn or Ben would have texted about the situation, with having Moll and Sadie staying with me, but they didn't. I at least remembered to let them know that Dave's parents intended to come to their son's rescue any time now. I hadn't seen the Williamses since I'd come home.

Anyway, as soon as there was the possibility of the Llareggub library being open, I was there. With Moll and Sadie, both clutching their recently arrived library cards as if they were the greatest prize ever. After a fortnight in the wet Welsh hills, and some help getting them through the books they'd borrowed, they agreed that books were pretty good entertainment after all.

It was the librarian from our last visit on duty. I was pretty noisy taking the books we'd borrowed on my card out of my back-pack and putting them on the counter in front of him. He didn't look up from the book he was reading.

'*Helo*,' I said.

He murmured something that might have been '*helo*' back.

'May I use a computer?' I asked.

He looked at me. As soon as he recognised me he checked who I was with and saw the girls. He paled but Moll and Sadie smiled up at him as angelically as they knew how. They chorused one of the few Welsh words I'd bothered to teach them with enthusiasm, '*Helo*!'

'Okay,' he said and put his head back in the book.

All he needed was a 'Please do not disturb' sign on the counter.

'Do you two think you can behave yourselves in the children's book section?' I asked Moll and Sadie.

They turned their angelic smiles on me.

'By which I mean put all the books back where you found them, in the condition you found them?'

'Yes,' said Moll.

She grabbed Sadie's hand and dragged her off at a run. The librarian looked up and after them.

'Congratulations,' I said, 'You have two new converts.'

It wasn't like he or I had taught them to read. Someone else had been teaching them to read—in English—and we had just managed to show the girls it could be a kind of fun. Conn wasn't quite as negligent as expected.

'Yeah,' muttered the librarian, but he didn't look up.

'Good book?' I asked, just because.

He grunted from behind the book, determined to avoid me. I shrugged and left for a computer.

And that's how I found out that Marie, Ida Marie Bakken who had interviewed me along with two police officers, wasn't employed by the Norwegian police after all. Well, not directly.

Her business card and the email address should perhaps have been a giveaway but, because of the Norwegian spellings and my own stupidity, I didn't grasp it properly until I email and saw the domain name, valemonogeftf.no, broken down into words, 'Valemon & Eftf.', in the email signature.

The email itself was brief—little more than 'please read the attached letters through'. There was something about one having been sent to Olsen and the second being specifically for me in order to progress Ben's case. I wondered how I was supposed to understand the letter for Olsen and ignored it, opening the attachment with my name on it.

For a change, I didn't scream or roar at the contents, presented to me in both English and Norwegian. I decided to pretend it didn't exist and opened the letter to Olsen instead.

It was also in both English and Norwegian. It was written on 'behalf of our client', though the translation may have been off because it never made it clear just exactly who was the client because it used Elkie Bernstein and Benjamin Lloyd where the letter talked about us, and suggested that Ben's mental health and potential return to society needed a full and careful consideration. There was plenty of language that worked around the theme but it eventually came to the same point as the letter officially intended for me.

Valemon and Eftf., whatever name that was short for, were interested in Ben's return to his own life. Circumstances and legal niceties would suggest that was living on the farm he grew up in, although that now belonged to his good friend—they meant me. In order to appease any doubts that Olsen's Institute might have about my ability to provide for Ben, Valemon and Eftf. proposed to send their consultant psychologist, Marie, to do a home inspection.

Two inspections, technically, as they mentioned repeating the home visit about a month after Ben had regained his freedom to monitor his condition. Although, again, the English went a bit woolly in translation, referring to Valemon and Eftf.'s agent.

'Great,' I said, 'I'm being vetted to see whether I'm suitable to adopt a grown man.'

I reopened the letter addressed to me and the details important to me were much as they'd been presented to Olsen—that Marie had, for reasons I couldn't guess, decided to fight my corner and part of that was examining my house, and possibly my life. This visit would result in a report that would be presented as part of Ben's hearing with the Institute board meeting required to get his release. Olsen would probably get to read it a lot sooner than the other board members, though, as it would actually be presented to show there were no legitimate reasons to keep Ben locked up.

'May I print off some documents?' I asked the librarian, pulling his attention away from his book again.

I was a little surprised that nobody else seemed to have arrived to disturb him but it was only three days after New Year and I guess most people didn't need to borrow books.

'OK,' he said, putting the book aside. 'I'll come and show

you how to connect to the printer.'

I kept my attention on the book so I didn't start growling at him. I didn't need him to show me how to do it, I just needed to pay and get the code to put in the computer. And he, of course, had that grumpy look that meant he was stewing in resentment at my disturbing him and making him do any work. I wasn't sure which response would be just deserts for his assumption. It took a moment but I decided to be truthful.

'I just need the code,' I said. 'I've done it before. So may I just pay you for...'—I added up the number of pages in English—'...four pages?'

He looked at his book, gave another heavy sigh and basically ignored everything I just said. Aside from letting me pay for four sheets of paper, of course. Another person might have assumed he thought they were incompetent. I just thought he was curious to see what letters I'd got in return for the one I'd scanned in. I was pretty certain he'd been scanning it as much as the copier had on the last visit.

'So what's your book about?' I asked.

He looked at me over the copier. 'It's okay. Bit more girly than I expected. I prefer less soap opera and more action. Thrillers and that. But it's new in.'

I looked at him, the kind of person who hid indoors all the time and probably had allergies. He liked 'action' because he hadn't tried anything like that in real life. 'Action' isn't the fun it's cracked up to be. It leaves you waking up at odd times, startling at small noises and hoping that the constantly churning guts don't turn in to anything medically serious. Not that I was a huge fan of soap operas and making dramas out of everything.

'Oh,' was the only response I could muster. Then, '*diolch*,' when he handed me my letters.

This time, I didn't get a '*croeso*' in response. He just walked off and left me. He walked away faster than he'd come over, so maybe the book was more interesting to him than he was letting on.

I sent an email back to Marie, starting with 'thank you for your help', which I decided not to question, and finishing with a 'please let me know when you intend to visit'. I didn't expect it to be in the next couple of weeks, given how much organising a trip would take. At least I didn't have any piles of dead bodies to clear out the way. Not any more, anyway. That silver eventually turned werewolves into dust turned out to be one of the most useful tricks Ben's games had ever taught me. Well, for a given value of 'useful'.

I browsed for some reading of my own and picked up some non-fiction—the only book in the library on chess in the hopes it would improve my game and a couple of books about vegetable gardening in the hopes that it would save me some money in the coming year. The librarian barely looked at them as he checked them out.

When the books were stowed in my back-pack, I hovered by the children's section and watched Moll and Sadie still struggling to narrow it down to just three books each.

'We're coming back next week, you know,' I said.

'But I want all of them now,' said Sadie.

She clutched a whole set of picture books to her chest.

'You get three. We can come back for more next week.'

We wouldn't read them all through in a week. It wasn't just the help they both needed with reading, it was the need for repetition. We'd read the same two books at bedtime for the last week and I'm pretty sure the girls had read the same two books during the day, even though I'd seen them reading the other four we'd borrowed last week.

'Well, if you work out what you both want to read,' I said, 'You can share six books that you both want.'

'I don't want to read about a silly rabbit,' said Moll.

'I'm learning how to hunt them better!' Sadie protested.

I hid my smile. This was the puppy version of 'be the rabbit' as she learnt about her prey. She hadn't realised, or didn't care, that real rabbits didn't wear clothes or speak like the white rabbit in the books.

'That's silly,' said Moll.

'No, it's not!'

The smile vanished, chased away by a groan and a sudden pounding in my temples that had me holding the bridge of my nose.

'Yes, it is!'

'You take that back!'

I cleared my throat. They stopped and looked at me. They didn't quite manage the wide eyes and angelic smiles of before. Behaving myself in front of Marie was going to be difficult with these two around. The Deity or whatever powers that be help me if she started questions about why I'd been left in charge of them. She was bound to, though wasn't she? I started a mental swear list.

'You can each have three books. Start working out if you want to share them or not.'

The girls looked at each other and Moll already had that half-snarl that said she wasn't going to be persuaded around to books about little white bunnies.

'Quietly,' I said. 'This is a library.'

Lie 13: I'm A Responsible Adult

I was wrong about Marie taking a while to come over. A mistake compounded by promising Moll and Sadie that I'd not go to the library without them, just go into town for boring things like food shopping. As I was strapped for funds, this was mostly done in the combined Llados Post Office and village shop until Mum could take me to the big supermarket in Sweet for a big, monthly run. Other than the couple of times people fell silent when I walked into the Post Office, there was nothing remarkable or difficult about going for an extra loaf of bread or bottle of milk. More fresh vegetables would have been nice but was beyond their range.

So, I found out the date of Marie's home check by opening the door. I stood there with the door open trying to think of something to say while wondering if closing the door and running was an appropriate response.

'Hurry up,' said Moll, 'We're going to miss the bus.'

'We've only got today. It's closed tomorrow and we're at school on Monday,' added Sadie.

I cleared my throat. 'Hello.'

'Hello,' said Marie.

A neat suit, sensibly flat office shoes, hair in a bun, that neat little leather document case of hers. I guess she knew my address from the scan of the Institute's letter to me.

'I didn't realise you'd be here today,' I said.

She looked me up and down. A brief, amused glance. 'Clearly.'

Moll and Sadie went from pushing against me to hiding behind me. Conn had kept their world small but a fortnight in North Wales hadn't exactly made it any larger.

'Moll. Sadie,' I said. 'This is Ida Marie Bakken. She's here to have a look at how we live.'

Moll and Sadie just held on to my legs more tightly. On the plus side, they thought well enough of me to hide behind me when strangers come and trust me over the mysterious 'them'.

'This is Margaret and Sarah Jones,' I said to Marie, indicating which was which. 'Moll and Sadie.'

'Hello, Moll. Hello, Sadie.'

Marie had the soft, easy tones of someone who has worked with children—as opposed to the soft, easy tones of someone who thinks children are just mentally defective human beings. Depending on how long she stayed, she might even manage to win them around.

'I haven't had a chance to read my emails since last week,' I said, inching my way out of the doorway and back into the house. 'Will you be staying here?'

Marie laughed. 'It's okay. My company found me a hotel room in Sweet. I thought you'd be too busy with the farm to want me underfoot.'

I nodded. 'Come in and have a cup of tea.'

'Thank you,' said Marie.

'I want to go to the library,' said Moll, although it was muffled against my leg.

'It's open until five,' I said. 'We can go this afternoon.'

'But—'

I cleared my throat. Moll stopped and looked up at me.

'We're going to have a cup of tea with our guest,' I said.

'Library later?' asked Sadie.

I nodded.

'Promise?' asked Moll.

I crossed my heart. I needed some new-to-me books, too.

'Can we have a cup of tea?' asked Sadie.

'Sure,' I said.

She happily let go of me to get mugs out of the cupboard. She counted them out loudly in welsh. *Un. Dau. Tri. Pedwar.*

Moll, less cheerfully, sat down at the table. I gestured towards another chair, indicating that Marie should sit down while I made the brews.

'Can I get the milk out?' Sadie asked.

I shrugged. 'Carefully.'

She ran to the fridge, pulled out the plastic bottle and brought it to me. She sat down next to Moll looking pleased with herself.

I leant against the counter remembering used-to-bes. When the Lloyds had lived here, this had been a dairy farm. They used to keep little urns in the fridge, ones that held a couple of pints of just pasteurised, non-homogenised, full fat milk with the cream floating on top. Maybe one of the local farmers was still in a position to supply that. I certainly couldn't and I'd never done the dairy farming side of things, even if I could afford it. I'd need to ask around now we were starting to find our feet and get into routines.

'I didn't think you'd be making house calls this soon,' I said to Marie.

Or maybe I should sell some land off, if anyone was buying, and small hold. Get a couple of cows or goats or something.

'It seemed like a good idea to keep going rather than slow down and let Olsen dictate what happens. If we delay, your Benjamin Lloyd could be in the Institute indefinitely.'

Which all sounded very smooth. Aside from the slight stumble over the Welsh double-l. At least she tried.

'Who's Benjamin Lloyd? You mentioned him before,' said Moll, who had a full week of going to a Welsh-speaking primary school to both traumatise her for the rest of her life and teach her how to say a proper double-l.

If it weren't the only option, I wouldn't have sent the girls to it. That said, I wasn't a first language Welsh speaker, didn't even know any Welsh when Mum and I arrived in Llados, and I'd managed to keep up okay.

I smiled. 'Someone who used to live here.'

'With you?' Moll asked.

I shook my head. 'When I used to live in that cottage I showed you.'

'Down the lane that leads to that other farm?' she asked.

I nodded.

'Moll and Sadie live here with you?' Marie asked.

Maybe it was getting into the rhythm of answering Moll and Sadie's regular questions that had my 'yes' out before I thought about the implications. Maybe it was just that I very rarely thought about the outcome of anything I did. I was going to have to work on that some more.

'We're her sisters,' said Sadie.

She wore the same look of being pleased with herself that she'd had when she got the milk out. I knew it was because it was another chore she enjoyed getting right—and we'd been asked about our purported relationship a lot of late—as much as because she was proud of our false pack.

Marie nodded. 'There's certainly a resemblance.'

I felt a little satisfied, like Sadie. Few people ever questioned further than that and it was unlikely there would ever be actual social workers on my door provided we did all the normal things. So far, we were succeeding at acting normal—or close enough not to attract undue attention.

'We're here until our father gets a new job,' said Moll.

I hid my frown. I hadn't heard her say anything like that before, although she always seemed to be the sister on the verge of telling everyone our little pack was a lie she didn't approve of. Maybe it was the being a year older that brought that stubborn streak. I couldn't really blame her—we weren't family and a month or so ago I'd been a total stranger.

Marie looked at me and then leant in to Moll. 'Who's your father?'

It was Sadie that answered, 'Connor MacLochlann.'

Her week at school had made the ch sound closer to the Welsh and Scottish sound than the ck sound she'd used before.

Marie frowned as if she couldn't place the name. Part of me wanted her to stay ignorant, part of me wanted to supply the missing information just because I could.

'Conn,' said Moll. 'Everyone calls him Conn.'

And Marie understood. Sort of. She looked at me and I could see cogs turning about what this meant for the Institute. From what I read in that one glance, there was no way she was on Olsen's side in any argument. She'd rather swear the sky was green than agree with him or help him.

I swallowed. 'Why don't you two show Marie around the house? Your teas won't have cooled much by the time you've walked around.'

The teas were half made on the side and steaming hot. I hadn't put the milk in yet and both Moll and Sadie didn't seem to mind drinking the milk-scared-by-a-tea-bag that Mum had restricted them to cold.

'Can we show her the horses?' asked Sadie.

'They're not ours,' I said to Marie, 'I have let out the stables as livery.'

But she was gone, dragged away and out the door by two

eager young girls. I sat down and rested my head on the kitchen table, tea to one side. I sat up straight and looked presentable when the girls dragged Marie back through to show her each of the downstairs rooms. I was back to collapsing over the table when they made it upstairs to the bedrooms. Some of the things I could just hear had me turning the resting into a small, rhythmic thump.

'This is our room.'

'You share a room?'

'We like being together.'

'This is Elkie's room.'

I clearly heard Moll and Sadie throw the door open and march in, just as they did in a morning if I wasn't already up. I have no idea whether Marie followed them, she was too light of foot.

'And this will be Daddy's room when he comes.'

More throwing open of doors.

Then movement and whispering so I could only guess what they said. Probably 'And this is May's room.' The threat of being attacked by an adult wolf not ready to be dragged out of bed had sunk in where my bleary-eyed swearing had not.

Marie asked, 'Who's May?'

I didn't hear Moll and Sadie's response. I could only hope it didn't include the factually correct 'bitch'.

May was out. She'd apparently found some money from somewhere and she was out most days. I had a suspicion it was only a matter of time before she moved out to somewhere she considered more fitting. Whether that was the Greywolves' place or around here was less certain.

There were a number of her fashion magazines piled on the end of the kitchen table and I pulled one over to idly flick through it. Every time May came back, she looked a little more like one of the women in these, a little more townie and a little less... whatever the checked shirts and jeans of the Greywolves was. I'd even noticed her carrying a new leather briefcase the other day. I suspect she would have killed for Marie's sleeker version. She had an income, a job, and would rather be doing her own thing than babysitting me and the girls as instructed by the Greywolves. It was unlikely they'd given her other errands to run.

I pushed Marie's tea towards her as she came back into the kitchen. The girls were further behind, talking between themselves on the stairs so that I could hear the edge of their whispers but not what they were saying. They, on the other hand—or paw—would be able to hear everything we said.

'Moll? Sadie? Your tea.'

Might as well have them where I could see them. Hopefully Marie hadn't noticed their dog hairs being all over their bedding and mine.

'May's a guest of ours. Her family are friends of Conn,' I said. I pointed upwards. 'The floors aren't much more than a layer of floor boards in places. I heard you ask.'

Marie nodded and sipped at her tea.

'I'm not sure how long she's here for but it's just while she sets up on her own.'

'And you have no phone line and no tv,' Marie said.

I grinned. 'Moll and Sadie have been complaining? I just can't afford the connection for one and the licence for the other at the moment.'

'Must make it difficult looking after two children without a distraction or a way to contact the emergency services.'

'I have my mobile,' I said, 'And I'll maybe sort it out in the long run, finances allowing. Seeing as my business partnership has collapsed, I don't have to worry about organising alternative care for them, either. It seems to be working out.'

Arguably, no phone line was a good thing if Ben were coming home. He couldn't abuse an Internet connection if we didn't have one. After second and third thoughts, I said as much.

Marie nodded. 'There certainly isn't as much risk to Mr Lloyd or others as there would be in a major city.'

She watched me carefully as she said it. I wasn't sure what she was watching for, what she thought she knew or thought I knew.

'Still, it's pleasant out here. Do you get much snow?'

'Not usually,' I said. 'Mostly it's just rain but we get some harsh weather for a week or two every now and again. Some neighbours lost a lot of sheep the year before last.'

And that was it, all probing questions finished as we

dissolved into gentle small talk about the weather and the outdoors in general.

Marie's visit lasted a couple hours, much to the girls' disgust, but she was kind enough to give us a lift to Llareggub in her hire car. It was, coincidentally, the very same car Conn had hired for us. I recognised the license plate, and so did Moll.

'Isn't that our car?'

I smiled. 'No, Moll. But it is the car Conn hired for us. Well spotted.'

She puffed up a little.

'You don't have a car?' Marie asked.

I opened up my arms to indicate the whole farm yard. 'My business partners decided they don't want to be my partners any more. Seeing as I left their son in Olsen's Institute, I suppose that's only fair. They took the farm Landie with them when they took everything that was theirs.'

I even managed not to sound bitter.

'Ah,' said Marie, 'Mr Williams' parents.'

I nodded, although 'Mr Williams' was always going to be Dave's dad as far as I was concerned.

''They seem a nice enough couple,' she said.

I stopped, in the middle of the pouring rain, while Marie and the girls were opening car doors.

'You've met them?' I asked, too quietly to be heard over the rain. I repeated myself more loudly.

'Yes. They were at Mr Williams' initial hearing in court.'

They'd sold the farm and no-one had told me. Maybe those silences when I walked into the village shop hadn't been about Conn's daughters, after all. Maybe it had been about scaring my ex-lover and his parents—my former business partners—off. Nor had anyone mentioned who had bought the Williams' place, or the animals, or the machinery. Not that I could have afforded it.

'Are they staying at the Institute?' I asked.

I slid into the front passenger seat wetter than the other three put together and steaming up the window with my mere presence.

'I would assume so,' Marie said.

I gave directions to the library.

'Will Mr MacLochlann be helping out with the farm when he moves in?' Marie asked.

I shrugged. 'I suppose so. I don't know if it's his kind of thing.'

'But work needs doing...' Marie's words tailed off and threw a questioning look at me before her attention returned to the wet road.

'Yes,' I agreed.

And if he was staying, his help would be appreciated. I still had no idea if he would be, though.

'How long are you staying for?' I asked as she parked up near enough for Moll, Sadie and I to make a dash for the library doors.

'My flight is on Monday. I'm driving to Manchester tomorrow evening.'

It was more information than I wanted, really, but there's no polite way to tell someone that you don't care.

'Come for dinner tomorrow afternoon, then, before you set off,' I said.

Marie looked at me.

I shrugged. 'Sunday dinner is a tradition, even if Sundays aren't the family's holy day.'

There wasn't an answer except for fidgeting from Moll and Sadie. A glance over my shoulder showed me the sort of expressions that indicated they neither knew nor cared to know Marie. I ignored them.

'If nothing else, you can say you gave me a thorough inspection before you call the social services,' I added.

'My visit has nothing to do with the British social services,' Marie said without even a hint of humour.

It was a relief but I didn't let it show.

'What time?' Marie asked. 'What time do you want me there?'

'Noon?' I guessed.

It was my first time doing a proper roast dinner in the stove in my own house. I used to share the cooking with Mum when we lived in the cottage, then I'd been in the

Williams' home and then, well, there just wasn't any point cooking big meals for one. I was out of practice and I had no idea if it was going to work. Inviting a stranger just made it even more... panic-attack inducing.

I hid the panic-attacks by having Mum, May, Moll and Sadie sit in one of the living rooms. 'I'm fine', 'I'm better off doing it on my own so I know what's going on', and 'Please don't get underfoot' kept them out of the kitchen. In between cooking steps, I held on to the kitchen counter with a white-knuckle grip as if letting go would have me spinning off the planet.

I didn't hear Marie knock on the door—which was a change for me because ordinarily the sound of an unknown vehicle turning off the road would have been enough to make me check what ad hoc weapon was close to hand. When Moll brought Marie to me, I didn't know whether to be grateful for the way my thumping heart had drowned out everything outside of the kitchen or not.

'How long until dinner?' Marie asked.

I stood and blinked at her. It wasn't exactly a typical conversation opener.

'You look like you could do with a break,' she said, 'And if everything is in the oven...'

'Yes,' I said, although it made no sense. And then, 'I'm fine.'

Marie raised her eyebrows.

'Moll, why don't you go and play with Sadie in the other room.'

Moll gave me a black look before leaving us, which I guess meant there wasn't much playing going on with May and Mum watching over them. Although Mum didn't mind playing, she'd banned shape shifting in her presence. May, on the other hand, didn't mind the puppy thing but had no interest in playing. For that matter, it was still a bit of a surprise that she hadn't sloped off today. I hadn't expected her to be in for dinner. I was still expecting her to declare she was moving to somewhere more cosmopolitan at any minute.

'Cup of tea?' I asked Marie, gesturing to a chair at the kitchen table.

‘This is an English thing, isn’t it?’

‘British. Yes.’

She sat, folding gracefully. She was still in a suit, wearing the air of concerned professionalism. She was a psychologist and apparently it was her job to care about me.

‘I’m fine,’ I said, ‘I’m just...’

‘Panicking,’ Marie said.

‘I’ll get over it.’

There were two choices, survival or not, and I wasn’t going to choose the second one. One way or another, I would come to terms with fighting things that went bump in the night and having strange things happen around me.

‘And the dinner preparations are going okay,’ I added.

It was more the idea of having Mum, May, Marie, Moll and Sadie sitting down to dinner together that was panicking me. What could each one let slip that I didn’t want the others to know? How much of what they knew was potentially life threatening? Also, far too many names beginning with M.

I put a cup of tea in front of Marie and sat down behind another. ‘So how’s the report coming?’

‘Well, it would certainly be difficult for Mr Lloyd to anything untoward out here. I have concerns about the nature of your relationship, though. From the sounds of the incident that resulted in his disconnection from Internet privileges, Mr Lloyd has been... abusive?’

‘Boredom and lack of company,’ I dismissed. ‘If I’d been there, he wouldn’t have sent the emails he did.’

‘I’m relieved to know that you have supportive family,’ Marie continued.

I nodded. I did. I just avoided leaning on Mum and had since werewolves had turned out to be real. If I could have found a way to explain something she hadn’t seen, maybe I would have done.

‘It’s certainly an interesting coincidence,’ Marie said, ‘That Mr MacLochlann turns out to be your father.’

I nodded again. ‘Yeah.’

‘I would never have considered the resemblance until you mentioned the relationship.’

‘No,’ I said. ‘There’s more the similarity between me and the girls.’

It's what put the excuse in my head and the only reason to keep pretending was to make sure Moll and Sadie were looked after.

'Have you had much contact with your father?'

I paused. This was one of those tests or trick questions. 'No.'

'And he gave you care of his two youngest. That shows a lot of faith. He must think highly of you.'

I smiled. He'd intended to send them to a strange part-wolf family in the company of a sodding werewolf. Sometimes Conn seemed to have even less common sense than I did.

'It's probably not a good idea to talk about Conn in front of or with my mum,' I said.

Marie's face was all gentle concern and I couldn't help wondering if it hid a totally opposite reaction, the urge to dig away for more information.

'She never really talks about my dad,' I added.

'Ah. A bad end to the relationship and it makes her uncomfortable.'

I shrugged. 'I wouldn't know. She never told me anything.'

Marie nodded.

'So, the report,' I said. 'When it's done, it gets sent to Olsen?'

'Yes. And the Board of Directors, along with a request to have a hearing about Mr Lloyd's fitness for release and the care he will be released into.'

So everyone would likely know, or think they knew, Conn was my father and I'd end up in charge of a bored werewolf—who didn't want to be a werewolf or on a farm in the middle of nowhere. I didn't know how to stop him being a werewolf short of killing him and I wasn't sure *I* considered him safe to be anywhere but the middle of nowhere, never mind what a panel of specialists thought.

I looked down at my empty cup. No more excuses for sitting here out of everyone else's way. 'I guess it's time to introduce you to the other adults in the house.'

'So they can keep me out the way while you hang on to the counter like it's the only thing in the world?' Marie asked.

'Something like that.'

'You know you can talk to me, right?' she prodded. 'If you

need to talk about what happened in Norway—'

I cut her off. 'I'm fine.'

It wasn't Giovanni I needed to talk about. Well, not only Giovanni. It was all those others who died in front of me, mostly because of me, and didn't have any names. Well, not all of them.

I stood and put my empty cup in the sink, next to the things I'd dirtied cooking. I could use the washing up as an excuse to get out of the way.

I waited for Marie to stand and showed her through to the others in the living room.

'Mum, this is Ida Marie Bakken. Marie, this is my mother, Rebecca Bernstein, and our friend, May Greywolf.'

Four pairs of eyes turned to look. Moll and Sadie disregarded Marie almost straight away. May turned predatory, eyeing the suit and shoes as I'd expected. Mum was a little more welcoming.

'Hello, Marie.'

'Hello, Ms Bernstein.'

'Um... I need to go do the washing up,' I said and started backing out of the door.

'Elkie, it can wait,' said Mum.

Moll and Sadie's response was 'We can do it!'

'You can wash the plates after,' I said. 'But there'll be too much for you if I leave all of it, so I'll wash the stuff I've dirtied with cooking now.'

I kept my exit to a sedate walk but I had to lean against the door and take deep breaths as soon as I was out of there. It had felt almost as hard as every meeting I'd had with Olsen rolled into one. Normal things shouldn't be that hard.

'I worry about her,' I heard Mum say through the wooden door. 'Things started to go wrong for her about the time that Lloyd boy left and it doesn't matter what she does, it never seems to come right again.'

An Honest Bit, or: Intermission

I didn't expect to hear or see Marie again for some time. Despite how quickly she had moved with the inspections, the idea that professional organisations were big and bureaucratic—and that bureaucracies move slowly—was there. I was wrong.

The report was emailed through as an attachment for our next visit to the library the following weekend. I couldn't bring myself to open it, not daring to know what Marie had thought of me and my home. The email was bland, mentioning the attached report and another attached document, a cover letter sent to Olsen and his board of directors, and the possibility of organising a hearing 'as soon as possible'. There were references to Valemon and Eftf.'s 'client', to me and to Ben.

It was all heading in the direction I needed and I wondered whether it was worth texting Ben, and Conn, to let them know that things were moving. It would make a change from the chess moves that came through eight or nine times a day—and the getting beaten. Although, on the plus side, the fact that I wasn't outright bombarded meant Ben was showing some self-control.

'You should have a hearing about getting out of the Institute soon,' I texted to Ben.

I tapped out, 'Conn might be about to get some big news.'

My thumb hovered over 'send', then over 'clear'. I saved it as a draft and put my phone away. I picked up the girls from the children's book section, got out some more books on gardening and chicken care, and walked back into what was rapidly becoming my normal life. At least my contact with werewolves was being kept to a bare minimum.

In between the working out if I could take on more livery customers, marking out a vegetable plot and entertaining Conn's daughters—when not at school—I managed to pretend I was busy enough not to think about the report or the likely reactions to it.

Three weeks later, though, some part of that had to change. I told Mum first.

'Marie wants me to go back to Norway.'

'Something to do with Ben or Dave?' she guessed.

I nodded then, realising she wouldn't be able to see me as she was cooking, 'Yeah. It looks like she's been able to arrange a hearing for Ben.'

I felt a shiver hiding at the base of my spine. I didn't want Ben home. There was nowhere else for him to be, unless I wanted him with Olsen, potentially building an army of werewolves like Eric and Simon—and that mysterious third I'd never identified. I couldn't hand Olsen that kind of power.

'What about Dave?' Mum asked.

'I don't know. I haven't heard anything.'

I hadn't asked, either. Just like I hadn't heard or asked about what had happened to the Williams' farm.

Mum cocked her head as if listening. Maybe my thoughts were rattling a bit too much. 'So, are you going?'

'Where are we going?' asked Sadie.

Moll watched from the doorway.

'You want another drink?' I asked, automatically refilling their mugs.

'We're not going anywhere,' I answered Mum. 'But I've been asked to go back to the Institute.'

'To see Daddy?'

'Will he come back with you?' Mum asked.

I shrugged. I didn't think so. I wasn't sure he'd be letting me come back in one piece if he'd read the report or heard about it. Maybe I was lucky and Marie hadn't mentioned I was effectively raising his daughters—my purported sisters—in his current absence. Maybe I could just hide in a corner somewhere and eat chocolate hazelnut spread without anyone questioning me.

'I'm not sure I can afford to go,' I lied.

Marie had asked for my passport details so Valemon and Eftf. could organise my travel. Not her personally but the company. They would cover the cost. It was in everyone's best interests I attend, or so she had written. I couldn't see how this would benefit me.

'And it's not like I can leave Moll and Sadie on their own,'

I said.

Mum just nodded. There would be no volunteering to look after a strange man's children from her. Technically, there was a readily available babysitter in May but she hadn't shown any interest in fulfilling her pack's demands that the girls and I be watched and I wasn't sure I could trust her with the girls, anyway. Would she take them and run for Surrey if I left?

As if knowing exactly the wrong thing to say, Sadie cuddled up to Mum and said, 'We could stay here with Rebecca.'

'There's only one bedroom here, sweetie,' I said. 'And Mum can't stay at our house. She has to get to work.'

'I work shifts,' Mum added.

Sadie looked as if she didn't know whether to cry or ask 'Why?'

'Her work hours don't fit around school,' I explained.

'How long would you be gone for?' Mum asked as if Moll and Sadie weren't a problem.

'I dunno.'

Marie's email had said a week to a fortnight. Not in those exact words, of course. She'd also suggested I get in touch with my father and ask if I could stay with him, rather than at the Institute, assuming his quarters were not within the Institute building itself. Of course, she meant Conn, not my actual father, but it had taken me a couple of heartbeats to work that out.

'Talk to your house-mate,' Mum said. 'You said she isn't doing anything work-wise, didn't you?'

My brain ticked over, considering possibilities. May was hardly ever around and she didn't seem to do anything but shopping. She only ever came back with more magazines and, occasionally, the kind of clothes that said she aspired to being Marie's clone rather than Will Greywolf's. Either she was certain I was safe to look after Moll and Sadie, so babysitting wasn't required or she had no interest in following orders. Maybe the three of them would still be here when I got back.

'Moll and Sadie don't like her. May, I mean. They don't like May,' I said.

'She's doing something she shouldn't,' said Moll.

'Really?' Mum asked. 'What?'

Moll's mouth thinned and she shrugged as if adults should

magically know the answers without her input. It was a feeling I remembered having a long time ago, before werewolves came to North Wales and my life changed from its expected course to the mess of reaction and self-defence I found myself in.

'I'm not sure she's a good idea,' I said.

If Moll didn't trust her, then there had to be something behind my own dislike. Dogs have instincts for these sorts of things. Part-dogs presumably had the same instincts.

'Moll and Sadie don't like her. I can't leave them in the care of someone they don't like.'

'Did they like you before they got used to you?' Mum asked.

I crossed my arms. 'You make it sound like some kind of Stockholm Syndrome.'

'Well, I doubt you mistreated them...' There was a pause with an implied 'knowingly' before Mum continued, 'But they didn't exactly know you before you came home with them. You only met their father recently.'

And their father seemed to be pretty good at handing them over to people without checking whether it was a good idea, too.

'What are you trying to say?' I asked.

'They don't know May. Of course they don't like her.'

'And it isn't as if she's put any effort into being likeable,' I muttered.

Moll snorted. Sadie just hugged up against Mum.

I wanted to say, 'Don't be reasonable. I don't want to go. I don't really want Ben here being possibly dangerous. Tell me that werewolves don't exist and that everything's fine over at the Institute. Tell me I don't have to do this.'

Unsurprisingly, she didn't—and even if she could have read my mind she probably wouldn't have said it. I remembered enough about how threatening I'd found Olsen to know whatever it took to get Ben away from him was the right thing to do. The thing I had to do, even if I didn't want to.

'Fine,' I said. 'I'll ask.'

Not that she'd be in when we got back to the farm. Not that I'd remember to mention it when I see her. Not that she'd agree.

Except that she was there when we got in and 'Would you be able to babysit for a while?' was pretty much the first thing out of my mouth.

Golden hazel wolf eyes stared at me from a human face. One of the reasons I didn't like May was because looks like that made me feel about two feet tall and pathetic. That and I was never sure if she was planning how to rip my throat out.

'Why?' May asked.

I wanted to attempt the same disdain back and say, 'That isn't any of your business.' But I didn't. There was no point in antagonising May when I wanted her to care for Moll and Sadie. It had been over four weeks since she'd come back with us, since I'd basically said her family wasn't good enough. I couldn't afford to upset her more if I was going to leave her with Conn's daughters.

'I've been asked to go back to Norway,' I said. 'To sort out some business.'

She smiled, a wolf smile without humour that told me she didn't think I was capable of anything even vaguely resembling business. It made Moll and Sadie cling to me as if I could protect them from the canine teeth that seemed to grow longer as we looked.

'So this would be for a while?' May asked.

'Yeah,' I said. 'A few days.'

There wasn't really anywhere for her to go except back to her family. I knew where they lived if she took the girls away and she didn't have a car of her own—as yet. She wouldn't do anything to hurt Moll and Sadie—if Conn trusted her family, that meant she wouldn't do anything extreme and things couldn't turn out all bad. She was just enjoying making us uncomfortable.

'Are you admitting that Greywolves are good enough to look after Conn's daughters?' she asked.

I shrugged. 'I think you—that's you May, not you your whole family—can probably manage.'

She glared at me.

'I know where the pack lives,' I said. 'So don't go taking them back to Surrey.'

'Oh, we know they're safest here in the wilds of North

Wales,' said May.

She looked smug. She knew something I didn't. Maybe several things that I didn't.

'Are you admitting that *I'm* good enough to look after Conn's daughters?' I fired back.

May ignored me. 'It'll be good for the girls to learn something about being who they are instead of reliving your lonely childhood in the rain.'

I opened and then shut my mouth a couple of times.

'I don't like her,' Moll whispered into my side.

Sadie may have whimpered.

I should have taken comfort in the small things, that Conn's daughters had bonded with me so well and quickly that they wanted and expected me to protect them from this person they didn't like. Instead, I just found myself wondering what I'd done that was so different from May.

'It'll be fine,' I said to Moll.

I concentrated on feeling calm and I stroked the girls' hair as if that was enough to set the world right.

'Why is she here if she doesn't like it?' asked Moll.

'Because sometimes adults have to do things they don't like,' I said.

I had a weird feeling of being here before, only last time it had been me asking something similar of my mother and getting told that adulthood was basically getting on with your life. I was going to Norway because it was the right thing to do, even if I didn't want to. May would look after Moll and Sadie for much the same reasons.

'Why don't you two go play in the living room?' I suggested.

'Can we have a cup of tea?' Sadie asked, looking up with big brown eyes. 'Aunty Rebecca doesn't have to know if you don't tell her.'

I smiled and hoped it got further than my mouth. 'No. But you can have some warm milk and honey. How about that?'

Sadie nodded.

It took a few minutes to sort the girls out and hustle them out of the way before I could ask, 'So why are you here if you don't like it?'

May raised a single eyebrow—a gesture that must have taken hours of practice. 'Greywolf was entrusted with the care of the pups. You don't think you're the only one who takes orders from their pack leader do you?'

There were two responses that sprang to mind. 'Conn isn't my pack leader' didn't seem like a good idea.

'So why you?'

'So I learn to live among humans,' said May.

And that was obviously going so well...

Lie 14: It Doesn't Matter If People Find Out The Truth

There must have been some kind of time dilation or anomaly in the North Sea because things went weird again before I touched down. By weird, I mean I went from not having enough time in the day—despite having a life that came down to the bare minimum that housekeeping and child-rearing would let me get away with—to having minutes that seemed to take forever to go by. Just like it had been the last time I visited Norway.

I don't suppose that the language barrier helped. Not that anyone set out to creep me out by not talking English but the whole not understanding a word the people ignoring me were saying added to my panicky almost-run through the airport. The ticket printout I'd run off at the Llareggub library looked as if it had been dragged through several hedges backwards by the time I made it on to officially Norwegian soil.

'Elkie?'

Conn was standing there, hands in pockets and nonchalant, like this wasn't a big deal. Maybe he's had more practice. I didn't know whether to run to him or run for the nearest exit.

'*Helo*,' I croaked and swallowed and hoped he didn't ask—

'How are Moll and Sadie?'

'Okay,' I said. 'We have a Greywolf staying with us and she's looking after them while I'm here.'

Conn looked around as if checking who could hear him. I guess there were some words it didn't do to string together in a place where Olsen could either overhear or hear about it.

'Is she a good person to be leavin' my children with?'

'She can't be any less trustworthy than the whole damn family you wanted me to abandon them with,' I said, more sharply than I probably should.

'How about you?' he asked.

I sighed. 'I'm fine. Thank you for asking.'

'No,' he said slowly. 'I meant are you any more trustworthy than a Greywolf?'

I opened my mouth and closed it again, my grip white-knuckling on my back-pack.

'I've known them longer than I've known you,' he said.

I had to look away and down.

'They keep their word,' he said.

I shuffled my feet.

'And runnin' off with my kids isn't exactly a good way of winning my trust,' he added.

'It was a wolf farm,' I said. 'They're breeding—'

'Themselves?' Conn suggested.

'They weren't going to give Moll and Sadie a choice. They were going to groom them—'

'Are you sure? How do you know? What proof do you have?'

'Do we have to do this here?' I asked quietly.

Conn ran his hands through his hair. There was a moment where I could almost see him rein everything back in. 'In the car.'

I obediently trudged after him as he strode off.

'Don't wind up the dogs just standin' there.'

He opened the driver's door and sat down.

'Bag on the back seat.'

He watched me with a slight turn of his head and an almost frown tucked between his eyebrows.

'Sit in the front.'

He was holding the wheel. He had the look of someone who was already driving down the road to somewhere he'd rather be.

'So why the hell have you invited yourself into my house instead of goin' back to the Institute?'

I winced at the use of 'hell'. 'Ben's hearing...'

My uncertainty made it more of a question than a statement, and Conn batted it away. 'That's why you're back in Norway, not why you insist on stayin' under my roof.'

'I don't want to be under Olsen's roof,' I said tightly.

Conn looked at me as if I were an idiot. 'He provides my roof, too, you know.'

'Marie thought it was a good idea.'

'Marie? You mean Bakken, the psychologist that interviewed us?'

I nodded.

'And why the hell would she think that?'

I winced again. Not just because of his choice of words, though.

'Have you seen the report she prepared?' I asked.

'Why?' Conn asked back. 'It has nothing to do with me. It's Olsen and his board's decision. Not mine.'

'She was looking at conditions at home. What Ben would be sent back to,' I said.

Conn's knuckles went white. 'Why would she need to report on your living conditions, Elkie? And why the hell would she have to do it when my children are there?'

'So it was obvious that Ben couldn't cause any problems if he wasn't in the Institute,' I half-said, half-asked.

Conn let out something that could have been a muted scream of frustration or a growl. After a few heartbeats, he started to drive, reversing out of the parking spot and pointing us in the direction of... well, home.

'If Ben has at least as good care and control as he does in the Institute, there's less reason for the board to object to his leaving,' I said, when I thought my being annoying might not be a dangerous distraction from driving.

'And your consultant psychologist thought it would be a good idea to prove you can do that?'

Marie and I hadn't discussed the matter. It wasn't exactly the standard client-consultant relationship.

I shrugged. 'You put her on to me.'

'You do know the company she works for competes with Olsen for business, right?'

Which would be why Conn had thought she could help me. He just hadn't expected it to go this far.

'Is that important?'

Conn sighed. 'Probably not. Well, not to you and Ben. You're just a minor skirmish in an ongoin' rivalry.'

'She's not a werewolf,' I said.

This was a fact I could be certain of, given that women did not and could not change like that.

'No,' said Conn. 'And the company she works for probably has no idea what they're gettin' in to. I thought having their backin' might give you some leverage against Olsen but this could get out of hand.'

'You mean they want to slap Olsen down?'

'I mean Olsen will want to kill them for gettin' in his way.'

I said the first thing that came into my head, 'That isn't my problem.'

Particularly if I managed to get Dave away from Olsen's power, too. Not that a change of management, if it came to that, would affect Dave's obvious status as an inmate. It might even be better for him if Valemon and Eftf. didn't want to kill him.

'I suppose not.'

'You don't have to stay there,' I said. 'Shouldn't you be somewhere else protecting your daughters?'

And not leaving other people to look after them.

Conn's jaw tightened and he stared ahead like ignoring me would make me disappear. I'd seen the same look on Moll's face a couple of times but this time I decided to humour it, waiting until we were parking outside Conn's cottage to try again.

I cleared my throat. 'The thing about the report...'

'What?' he snarled at me.

There was nothing I could do but blink at him and try to remember where the door handle was.

He closed his eyes and took a deep breath and then looked at me. 'Sorry. That was unnecessary.'

I didn't reply. I'd never seen Conn as a werewolf before, despite knowing he was. Now I had and I wasn't sure I'd done anything like the right thing. Or maybe I had and his daughters were better off miles away from both Conn and his Greywolf friends.

'What's in the report that I need to know about?' he asked, his tone carefully level.

'I don't know for sure,' I said. 'I haven't read it.'

Conn raised his eyebrows. Which meant he was calming down because anger would have made them go the other way.

'I— Everyone has been assuming Moll and Sadie are my sisters,' I said.

Conn's eyes narrowed and his eyebrows drew down. I inched my hand towards the door handle, or where I thought the door handle was, anyway. With the other hand, I reached in my pocket for the silver cross.

'I'm not going to do anything to you, Elkie,' he said.

I had the urge to repeat Dave's cliché, the only good werewolf is a dead one, but didn't. Conn knew enough about what I'd been through to know he was scaring me and he was doing his best to control it. I'd known, or thought I had, that he didn't have anything that would set off his obsession. Except he did after all, just as Olsen had said in his off-hand way, Conn was obsessed with his ex-mate. It stood to reason that Conn would be just as protective over their offspring when the mate was no longer there.

'I'm sorry,' I said, meaning sorry for pressing buttons I hadn't intended to.

'What have you done?' he asked.

'Nothing, really, I just...'

'You just what, Elkie?'

I swallowed. 'I let people believe I was your daughter.'

Actually, I'd been actively telling them so for the last three months or more.

Conn got out of the car and shut the door behind with quiet control. He stood next to the car for a moment, looking down at his feet, then he walked off to the cottage door.

'Well, say something,' I shouted after him as I got my back-pack out of the car and let the pack of mongrels out of the back.

He ignored me. I trailed after him and watched him rummage through a kitchen cupboard. He eventually pulled out a bottle of whiskey.

'At this hour?' I asked.

He gave me a look that trapped a squeak in my throat and had me sitting down at the kitchen table before he'd turned his back on me again.

'I guess three in the afternoon isn't that early,' I muttered.

Conn didn't actually say anything until he'd drunk what must have been a double of whiskey, down in one go.

'You told people I was your father?'

'I said I let them believe,' I dissembled.

I got another look for my troubles. He knew there were occasions when I'd been specifically asked about my connection to Moll and Sadie, and I would have answered.

Dishonestly.

'And you told Bakken this?'

'Me? No,' I said.

'You've got Moll and Sadie parroting your soddin' lies?'

'People ask questions. They need to be able to give an explanation of being in my care that doesn't have social services taking them away.'

'So the report says we're... related.'

I pushed my hands out wide into an open gesture. 'Congratulations. It's a girl.'

'And Olsen and his entire board will have read this report.'

'I dunno,' I said. 'How often do they read more than the email or covering letter?'

It's not like I'd read it, although I had a fair idea what was in it and was too scared to find out.

'Olsen's going to know I'm your father,' said Conn. 'If not now, then by the end of Ben's hearing.'

He poured another smaller serving of whiskey and sipped.

'Or think he knows, anyway,' he added.

He ran a hand through his hair and the mix of salt and pepper curled around his fingers. Fathers are human, too. Even borrowed ones.

'And the girls. He'll know about the girls. He'll know who their mother is. He'll guess. So then he'll know that breeding is possible for people like Alex.'

Was it such a small step from knowing that one werewolf-canine had been able to have children to thinking there might be others out there? Or worse, deciding to breed some of his own. Olsen had at least one werewolf who would be happy to try, seeing as Philip was probably this Alex's father. I felt sick.

'I need to rehome the hellhounds. I can't put them through quarantine. I need to hand my notice in. I guess I'll worry about work when I get back to the UK.'

'I'm sorry,' I said. 'I wasn't thinking. Well, beyond making sure I could keep Moll and Sadie safe.'

'You need to start thinkin' longer term,' was all he said in response.

Thinking more than one move ahead was definitely a problem with my chess playing. Who knew it was going to be an issue in real life, too?

'I guess this means you're going home,' I said, assuming he'd be going back to the North of England after he picked up the girls.

'Yam,' said Conn. 'Gan' yam wi'out a yam to ga to.'

'I have no idea what you just said.'

He raised his head and there was so much pain in his face, I might as well have been ripping off his arms.

'"Home",' he said, repeating himself without the accent. '"Goin' home without a home to go to".'

'You can come to Wales,' I said without thinking.

I'm not entirely sure how we made it through an evening and a night in the same cottage. Conn left me to do whatever it was that needed him over at the Institute—security stuff, I guess—for a couple of hours. When he came back, he avoided me. We didn't actually speak again until breakfast.

'When's the hearin'?' Conn asked.

'Ben's?'

Conn nodded.

'Tomorrow.'

He nodded again, as if it wasn't a big deal.

'Can I go see Ben today?' I asked.

Conn looked at the clock as if the answer had something to do with the time. Maybe it did.

'Come over to reception about eleven,' he said. 'I'll arrange for you to be able to visit.'

'And could I see Dave before I leave?'

'Are you sure that's smart?' Conn asked.

I shrugged. Chances were it was very stupid but I'd never wanted to leave Dave in Olsen's power, no more than I wanted to leave Ben here. Well, not since I found out Olsen had plans that seemed suspiciously like making a master race of werewolves.

'I'll see what I can do,' said Conn. 'But it probably won't be today. How long are we here for?'

I shrugged. 'As soon after Ben's hearing as we can arrange for, I guess. Depending on the outcome.'

'Regardless of the outcome. There's no way either of us are

safe here once Olsen thinks I'm your father.'

'And what about Ben?' I asked. 'Or Dave?'

If it wasn't safe for me, it wouldn't be safe for them.

'I'm pretty sure they can manage their own survival,' said Conn.

'Yeah, right. While they're locked up in Olsen's Institute. Sure they can.'

He didn't answer, just left me to finish my breakfast.

'Yeah, right,' I said again.

The dogs snuffled and sighed as they settled in a pile of blankets. It was as interactive as they got and I basically spent my morning watching the clock until it was time to go the Institute as instructed.

'Hi,' I said to the receptionists.

I didn't recognise either of them, but it had been about three months since the last time I was here. Even if they were the same people, I'd forgotten them.

'Hi,' the nearest said back without much of a smile.

'I'm Elkie Bernstein,' I said. 'Conn MacLochlann said I could see one of the, erm, special cases? Benjamin Lloyd?'

Some time about the moment I was obviously speaking English, the smile disappeared. I probably should have said something like 'Sorry, I don't speak Norwegian'. It would only have been polite. I practised smiling to make up for it.

'I'll have to check,' the receptionist said and ducked his head to watch his computer screen as if it was the most interesting thing in the world.

His colleague, on the other hand, cleared her throat and stood up with a pasted on smile. 'Mr and Mrs Williams. How lovely to see you today!'

I didn't manage to stop the 'shit!' that jumped out of my mouth, but I did manage to keep it down a volume that only the receptionists heard. The man's mouth twitched into a slight smile although his attention was apparently fixed to the computer screen. His colleague didn't react but did look at me for a fraction of a second. It was enough to bring my ex-business partner's attention my way.

I turned. '*Helo.*'

They had never been the most cheerful looking people I'd ever met but Dave's arrest and hearing seemed to have taken whatever joy they had left in their lives, as well as twenty years.

'Hello, Elkie,' Mrs Williams said.

Her husband went with, 'What the hell are you doing here?'

I winced. 'Here to see Ben and Dave.'

'No, you're not,' he said.

Mrs Williams was more talkative. 'You'll not be seeing Dave ever again. You got him in this mess. I always knew you were a bad influence, Elkie Bernstein.'

'Yes,' I said drily, 'I'm the one that decided to cheat, lie and murder. I'm the bad influence.'

Well, in that it was my idea to hide the first body and not inform the police we'd killed a werewolf the very first time, I suppose I was. There hadn't been anything to say that Dave had to *keep* doing it, though.

'You ungrateful b—'

'Mrs Williams,' Conn interrupted. I hadn't even realised he was there. I guess he'd just arrived, too. 'If you'd just like to go to your son's ward, security are aware that you're on your way.'

Mrs Williams shut her mouth so quickly, the snap was audible.

'If you'd prefer,' he added, 'I can show you the way?'

'Thank you but I know where I'm going,' Mrs Williams said, with that forced politeness that sounds ruder than a lack of manners.

Dave's parents followed instructions. It should have been a march but the recent changes in their life had brought their shoulders down. Neither of them seemed to have the fire to straighten their spines, even in anger. I could have cried. For a long time, they'd been my family and now they were... this.

'Thank you for paging me,' Conn said to the receptionist who'd been dealing with me.

The other man nodded and gave a quick smile.

'Ready?' Conn asked me.

'Sure.'

As we walked away, I wondered aloud, 'Isn't anyone happy to be working here?'

Something I hadn't thought about my first time here. I'd

simply assumed that everyone was somehow displeased with me for being British, not that they were stressed through working conditions. It couldn't be great both living and working in a building intended for more people. Particularly if Olsen was inclined to risking the business on his obsessive collecting of werewolves—which, it had turned out, he wasn't very good at. There was a possibility that Conn had been keeping him that way.

'It's... strained,' Conn answered.

He led me to the werewolf wing, to the security office manned by three men I might have met before but didn't recognise, and past the inmates I'd seen before. Alejandro still rocked in his cell, dressed up as a deformed dog. Philip was, like the first time I'd seen him, pressing his nose up against the holes in the transparent plastic and whining as if I were a juicy bone.

'Pretty!' he whined at me in Welsh.

Conn's face was carefully blank but his eyes were averted, ignoring Philip. I guess it's the only way to survive knowing your mate's father is a pervert.

'Bugger off,' I muttered at Philip.

He didn't but we were past him and outside Ben's run by then, anyway.

'What you lot all need,' I muttered, hoping there was no audio connection between us and the security office, 'Is de-furring.'

'Destroying the fur-skin didn't do anything,' said Conn. 'Ben and I are both still werewolves.'

It was hearing his name that made Ben raise his head from the bed. 'Conn?'

He blinked like someone had turned a spotlight on him and looked at me. 'Elkie? I sent you texts yesterday and you didn't answer.'

'I turned my phone off when I got to the airport,' I said. 'I thought I'd surprise you today instead of checking.'

It's not like I didn't expect there to be messages. We were on about ten a day with his need to keep the chess games going.

'How about you tell me what the move was and we pick up the game from there?' I suggested as Conn opened the door and let me in.

'You mean you can't tell just by looking at the board?' Ben asked as if I'd just said something stupid.

I walked over to the board and looked down. I hadn't a clue but I didn't want to admit weakness.

'My go, right?' I asked.

'I'll see you later,' Conn said.

'Wait a minute, I forgot to ask you something,' I said as I continued to stare down at the board. How long did I have to do this before it looked like I was stalling? 'I take it Marie hasn't seen this?'

'Who's Marie?' asked Ben.

'Bakken?' Conn asked. 'No. If she'd asked to see Ben, she would have interviewed him in one of the offices.'

I nodded. 'Of course. Couldn't have her seeing Alejandro.'

Or Philip. Not that I'd worked out why he found me a special treat on some days and uninteresting on others. Would he react the same to Marie?

'Who's Marie?' Ben asked again.

I could barely work out which colour I was supposed to be on Ben's copy of our game. I couldn't remember what moves I'd made. Except the black pieces had the king castled and that was something I did a lot that Ben rarely did. That side must me. I fingered one of the black pieces as if considering a move.

'You're white,' Ben said.

'Ummm,' I replied, as if thinking. I let my finger tips linger a little longer, to show it hadn't been a mistake, that I'd been thinking. 'Ida Marie Bakken is a psychologist working for another company.'

'You mean not Olsen's?' Ben asked.

'Yeah. She's been putting together a case for your release.'

'Release?'

'You know, going home,' I said.

'Home?'

I looked up. 'Back to the farm.'

'Do I have to?' Ben asked in Welsh.

'You'd rather stay here?' I replied in the same language.

I picked up a white knight and moved it as if I were totally confident in the move.

Ben watched me rather than the board. He continued in Welsh. 'I guess not.'

He moved the black queen into a square that had become safe with my knight's move. 'Check. What about the dork?'

I swore and stared at the vulnerable white king. I really had to start seeing what the whole board was doing, not just one piece at a time.

'What about him?' I asked.

'Aren't you going to try and take him home with you, too?'

There would have been a time when that thought would have been normal enough for me to assume the answer was 'Yes'. It hadn't been that way in a while. After all, I'd brought Dave with me to Norway the first time to get him out of my hair. He'd just complicated matters by killing a werewolf in front of Conn.

In retrospect, this wasn't necessarily a bad thing. Dave actually employed here, like he'd wanted to be, would have been far worse. Not only werewolves were obsessive.

'His parents have turned up to look after him,' I said.

I moved the white king behind something more useful and waited for Ben to find a way to win again. Although I should probably be thinking of a way to get Dave out of here, too, I doubted his parents would want me to point out things they already knew, like there were mental institutes nearer to North Wales.

'And this Marie Bakken person,' Ben said. 'How did you meet a Norwegian psychologist that doesn't work for Olsen? I thought you went home from here?'

He moved a black piece and trapped my king. It wasn't check but there was nowhere else to move him to to make him safer. At least it gave me a legitimate reason to make insane moves without thinking too much about the future.

'She was the psychologist the police brought in to question me and Dave and Conn. About Giovanni.'

I made a ridiculous move with the white queen that took a black bishop down. Ben naturally took the white queen out with the nearest piece to hand, a pawn.

'She's a consultant,' I added, 'From another company.'

'Another company?'

I nodded and killed the offending black pawn in a fit of

revenge with a knight that should be safe for at least another move.

'And she does police work,' Ben said.

'Yeah.'

He moved something to somewhere else. I'd stopped paying attention for a moment, distracted by Conn's earlier comments about rivalry.

'Think it'll work?' Ben asked.

'What?'

'My hearing,' he said patiently. 'Do you think Olsen will let me go?'

'That depends on whether he controls the board, doesn't it? I'm not even sure which board it is. I mean, if it's the people who bankroll this place, they're in charge, right? But if it's a board of doctors that work for him...'

Shit. I'd just sacrificed Conn's position for a quick win. It was the real life equivalent of taking a pawn with a knight with multiple pieces waiting to leap on it. All in the hopes of freeing up the king piece that couldn't go anywhere but might turn out to be important.

Without thinking, I moved a white piece.

'Check mate,' said Ben.

Lie 15: I Don't Mind Waiting

'I hate Mondays,' Conn said over breakfast.

I grunted into my cup of tea. I'd never had a job when Monday had been the start of my working week. I'd either worked shifts or been on a farm, where work was every day. From what I could gather, what with there being visitors' hours at the Institute over the weekend, Conn wasn't working that kind of job, either.

'It's a day for office workers who think they know better than everybody to start expressin' their opinion again,' he added, as if I'd actually said some of that aloud. Maybe I had. 'They make bad things happen on Mondays.'

'Is that what the board is? Office workers?' I asked.

'Olsen and most of the higher ups only work Monday to Friday.'

The sinking feeling I'd got yesterday over chess returned with a vengeance. I wanted to say sorry and beg Conn's forgiveness for ruining his job. I reminded myself that his real daughters needed him and he wasn't able to look after them if he was busy working for Olsen while they were hidden.

'So the board will be Olsen and some of his pet shrinks?'

Conn shrugged. 'I have no idea. I guess so. I only deal with huntin' werewolves.'

What he did with them was left hanging. There was at least one instance—his mate—where he'd kept the hunted object away from Olsen. There were another two—the Greywolves and his own children—where Conn had kept them hidden altogether. If there were only three other werewolves in Olsen's possession, how many had Conn found and brought back. Why had he allowed them to be brought back if he considered Olsen dangerous? Because those other werewolves were too dangerous to be allowed out?

And then there were Eric and Simon. Conn hadn't let me meet them, although I had run into them later. He'd said, 'They're both killers, Elkie. They're hunters.' Like all the other werewolves I'd met, and disposed of.

'Sup up,' Conn-in-the-now said, 'We're due at that hearin' in fifteen minutes.'

'"We"?'

He picked up an envelope I hadn't noticed and waved it. 'I have my notice to hand in to Olsen, if nothing else. I'm supposed to give a month but I haven't taken holidays in years. I'm due.'

I swallowed some tea to stop myself from saying sorry. I'd said it enough since yesterday morning and was starting to annoy him even more.

'Okay, I'm ready.' I pushed my chair away from the kitchen table. 'Dad.'

He glared at me. 'Never call me that again.'

I opened my mouth.

'Never,' he said.

I have a question about Philip,' I said.

'Oh?'

'He tells you things, right?' I asked and watched as Conn nodded. 'So how come you don't know everything Olsen does with his "special cases"?'

'What kind of things?'

'Like him sending Eric and Simon after me when I left for home last time.'

Conn cursed.

'It's okay. They're dead,' I said.

Conn swore some more before saying, 'I guess Olsen scares him more than I do.'

I shut my mouth and kept it firmly that way until we got into the Institute reception. We must have looked a little odd, striding in through the doors side-by-side wearing an almost uniform—jeans, t-shirts, shirts, walking boots, and jackets for the short walk from Conn's cottage to the big house. Maybe we looked like we were related.

'Hello, Elkie,' said Marie. 'Hello, Mr MacLochlann.'

She looked like she'd walked straight out of one of May's magazines, neat and well presented in a dark suit.

'Bakken.'

'Hello, Marie.'

'Are you ready?' Marie asked.

I shrugged. 'As I'll ever be.'

'I need to talk to Olsen,' said Conn. 'You might have a delayed start.'

He walked off, each movement defined and with intent. Borrowed fathers can be heroic, too.

'What's going on?' Marie asked.

'He's handing in his notice.'

The receptionists' heads jerked up as if I'd slapped them both across the ears. Maybe I had.

Marie nodded. 'Going home to his daughters.'

I swear the receptionists' ears twitched, like cats zoning in on their next squeaking victim.

'Yeah,' I said. Then to the receptionists, 'Excuse me, but where do we go for Ben Lloyd's hearing?'

The receptionists looked at each other and mouthed 'Floyd?' at each other and shrugged. I guess they'd never heard the Welsh 'll' before. I certainly didn't remember having talked to them before, so I suppose there was no reason why they should have.

'Professor Olsen will come down,' said Marie.

'You're that important?' I asked.

She smiled. 'I suspect it's the director who's coming that's important. He doesn't want us contaminating board members with our opinions.'

Or stories that might suggest there was more to the Institute than clinical lycanthropy. Not that I'd dream of mentioning it to Marie, let alone some director I'd never met.

'It will be fine,' said Marie. 'They have no reason to turn down Ben's release. He has never been characterised as a dangerous patient and all that was needed was a responsible home to go to.'

'I'm responsible?' I asked.

Marie laughed. 'Yes. And so is Mr MacLochlann, as a trusted employee who is only handing in his notice to look after his daughters.'

I wasn't convinced but it depended more on what power Olsen held over his board. He wouldn't want to give up Ben. Not only was Ben a member of Olsen's collected werewolf pack, Ben would be able to find more werewolves to increase the pack size. Ben was valuable.

'Unless there is something else you think I ought to know,' said Marie.

'Did you come and visit Ben when you put the report

together?' I asked.

'I interviewed him. He seemed a nice young man.'

I walked a few paces away from the reception counter. The receptionists were listening so closely, I bet they could hear our hair growing and our hearts beating.

'They brought him to an interview room for you,' I said, more or less repeating Conn from yesterday.

Only Conn hadn't known it had actually happened, which meant either security didn't always have to go through him or Olsen didn't want him to know. Or both. Exactly as and why Olsen had hidden Eric and Simon's movements from Conn. And the unknown werewolf Eric and Simon had killed. And the scared Philip didn't tell all the tales in case some of them got back to Olsen.

'*Ja*,' said Marie.

'You didn't see how Ben's kept. It's almost like solitary confinement. He's on a corridor with a bunch of others that never go out.'

'But you've seen it,' Marie said, and she looked at me carefully as if I had suddenly become a most interesting specimen. 'They've let you go where I wasn't given clearance.'

'Maybe it doesn't matter what I see.'

'Hmm.'

She opened her mouth to add something more to the unconvinced sound but never got the chance to say anything.

'Doctor Bakken. A pleasure to see you again.'

Olsen had arrived and did his best to dominate the space immediately. Behind him, Conn stood with his arms folded and head bowed.

'Professor Olsen,' Marie smiled, tighter than she had with me.

There must have been some level of rivalry there beyond her parent company's interests. It was the sort of thing that made me wish I played games better.

'As you're here, you might as well come up to the meeting room,' said Olsen.

'We're ready to begin?' Marie asked.

'No, but we can discuss your report while we wait for Mr Lange and Mr Lloyd.'

Olsen, it seemed, also hadn't heard the Welsh 'll'. But it

wouldn't bother him if he knew he'd mispronounced it. He wasn't that kind of person.

He cupped Marie's elbow and they turned away. I started to follow.

'No, Miss Bernstein, you can wait here with your father. If we need your evidence for the hearing, we'll call for you.'

If I'd been an animal, I would have put my ears down and back, submissive but angry. I might have even got away with growling or hissing and spitting. As a human, all I could do was stand there looking after them.

'So he read the report, then,' I said eventually.

'Yeah,' said Conn.

'I'm sorry.'

'You need to stop saying that.'

'Sor—' I cleared my throat. 'So what do we do now?'

'We wait,' said Conn. 'How about a cup of tea in the canteen?'

'Can we wait here?' I asked.

There was a small seating area and I wanted to see what this Mr Lange, director, looked like.

'Fine,' said Conn.

We sat opposite each other like distorted mirror images. I stared out of the nearest window, admiring the patchwork of white and green, and wondering how long the snow stayed on the ground round here.

'I'm being paranoid, aren't I?' I asked a few minutes later.

'About what?'

'About Olsen. He can't do anything to her just because he's walked off with her. Marie, I mean.'

Conn raised his eyebrows and said nothing.

'People have seen her arrive, people expect to see her leave. If anything happens, even if he makes it look like an accident or whatever, the Institute will be investigated.'

I tried not to think about the possibility of inmate suicide, the fate I expected for Dave if his parents didn't eventually get him out of there. That would surely be investigated, too, but would be harder to prove was anything but self-inflicted.

'He can't physically do anything to Marie,' I added.

He was a man, living in the human world, with a documented life and location. Unless he started stalking her and made sure nothing pointed to him when she was found dead miles away, there was nothing he could do. There was certainly nothing he could do *now*.

'But he can say that Ben has to stay here,' said Conn. 'And ruin whatever play it is her company's got goin' on.'

I didn't know how to answer. I didn't want to think in terms of long-term strategy because it made me think of pieces being sacrificed.

'And he can give me a bad reference,' Conn added.

It wasn't easy getting a new job. It wouldn't be easy for Conn, seeing as he was moving to another country and was definitely in the middle-aged bracket. I felt sick again.

If I had a working farm, I'd have offered him a job. As it was, I was still trying to work things out for myself. Sell some land and small hold was turning out to be the closest to a plan. But I kind of felt I needed to talk it over with Ben before I started selling off what used to be his family's property.

'Don't say sorry,' Conn growled.

'I wasn't going to,' I lied. Movement caught my eye and I lied some more. 'I was going to ask if that was the missing Director Lange.'

A large car was parking on the hard-standing in front of the equally large entrance. The suited man who got out of the car was built to a similar scale.

'Never met the man,' said Conn but he shifted his position so he could look.

'Anyone would think that Olsen kept you in the dark,' I said with as light a tone as I could manage.

'Anyone would be right. Olsen doesn't like telling anyone anything.'

'Like with Eric and Simon,' I said.

Conn gave me a sharp look but I was focussing on the tall, white haired man as he strode into the place like he owned it. If he was here representing Olsen's financial backers, he effectively did.

'I suppose there's always a chance that he'll think keeping Ben's a waste of money,' I considered. 'I mean, it can't be cheap to keep someone who isn't a threat and has a home to go to.'

'Probably not,' said Conn.

The receptionists both stood up and conversation I felt I should be able to understand but couldn't commenced.

'That'll be Lange, then,' said Conn.

It was another couple of minutes before Olsen came to guide Lange to the meeting room. There was some quiet one-upmanship with hands being gripped and back slapped. There was no need to cup Lange's elbow and drag him off.

'Too important to leave it to someone else?' I asked, although Olsen had also come for Marie.

'How many people do you think Olsen actually employs?' Conn asked back.

After a while, I said, 'One less today than yesterday, I guess.'

'Not quite. I'm here until your flight and then I'm officially on holiday until this time next month.'

A bit later I asked, 'Do you think they'll call for us?'

Conn snorted. 'They'll only invite me in if Olsen feels like humiliatin' me in front of Lange.'

I went back to staring at the patchwork of snow and spring grass. If I walked out the door and kept walking, would anyone else notice?

Neither Conn nor I got called into the hearing so we sat in the reception, slumped and staring out of the windows. I can't answer for Conn, but I was watching to see if anyone else came up to the Institute—and whether they would be another enemy.

'There are times when the resemblance between you two is obvious,' said Marie.

I blinked away the watch for the unseen enemies and turned to look at her. She wasn't smiling. Ben, however, had a smirk on his pallid face. I straightened in my seat.

'Does this mean we won?' I asked, nodding at Ben.

'The board are discussing their decision,' Marie said. 'They simply agreed that Mr Lloyd wasn't a danger to others here in the Institute while they talk.'

'So you're babysitting?' I asked.

Ben's smirk became a scowl.

Conn pinched the bridge of his nose. 'How about that cup of tea, Elkie.'

He wasn't asking, he was telling me to behave and not wind up Ben.

'Coffee,' said Marie. 'Make it a coffee and we'll join you.'

Conn led the way, Marie and I followed, Ben trailed behind stopping to look at every picture and out of every window.

'He doesn't get out much,' I said apologetically.

Marie smiled. 'You said.'

'How's it lookin'?' asked Conn. 'Will Ben be goin' home?'

Marie didn't answer.

'Who's on the board? Aside from Olsen and Lange, that is,' I asked.

'There were a couple of other shrinks,' said Ben. 'One brought all my pictures.'

I wondered just how many times he'd painted me, him and Dave holding back the flood of werewolves. Maybe there'd been some variety. Enough to make Ben seem slightly less obsessive.

'Bad luck,' I said, only half joking.

'There was significant interest from Lange as to why an external psychologist was involved in Ben's case,' Marie said. 'I explained about our meeting with Olsen when you were here last. About how not having an acknowledged home to go to was the main issue.'

I nodded. 'Must be expensive, keeping an otherwise healthy young man in a secure cell.'

It's not like Olsen could reveal the existence of werewolves, that Ben was one, or how Olsen was intent on collecting them all.

Marie laughed.

'I think that's what Lange said,' Ben muttered.

After that, we talked of inconsequential things over our drinks—like how Moll and Sadie were doing in the Welsh language primary school, and the unexpected coincidence of visiting another country and finding your biological father. Conn and Ben said very little.

'Well, I had met him already,' I said.

Marie raised her eyebrows. 'Oh?'

'Conn brought the paperwork for the farm,' I said. 'When Ben signed it over.'

She leant forward, engrossed. 'And you found out then?'

Conn shook his head slightly and stared into his cup as if it were infinitely more interesting that the story. Ben was fiddling with his teaspoon.

'There aren't that many Bernsteins in North Wales,' I said.

Except neither Mum nor Conn were from North Wales, and I was only raised there. I'm not entirely sure where we came from, only that I had an aunt and a father/uncle in Oxford. Even before I knew about the father/uncle thing, I started to sound like the worst kind of white trash if I mentioned my family background.

'Ah, so Conn recognised the family name and —'

'Dr Bakken,' Mrs Williams cut through whatever Marie had been going to say.

Marie looked up and around, smiling automatically. 'Mrs Williams. Hello.'

The smile seemed natural, not at all business like or strained. I felt like an idiot. Marie was a consultant psychologist from a company in some kind of competition with Olsen, and she was not my friend. The fact that she could summon a warm smile at will was making me forget the game playing side of things.

'Are you here to see Dave?' asked Mrs Williams, her husband looming behind her. 'He was ill last time you came but he's better now.'

Ben and Conn both raised their heads, looking at Mr and Mrs Williams. I didn't understand the sudden interest.

'Not today,' Marie said.

'Why not?' Mrs Williams demanded.

'Today I'm here for Mr Lloyd's hearing.'

She nodded towards Ben.

'Hello, Mr and Mrs Williams,' said Ben.

They looked at him and there was a moment of trying to work out who he was. For whatever reason, they dismissed him and stared at Marie again. Marie could get Dave out of here so she was more important.

'But you'll check on him later, won't you?' Mr Williams said.

Marie's smile remained apparently natural and warm. 'If I have time and Professor Olsen will allow it, I don't see why not. I don't have anything to discuss with your son but I'm sure some company would do him some good.'

Mr Williams put his arm around his wife, a barrier against the worst Olsen could offer. This was a good sign, no matter how annoying it was to be ignored. If the Williamses were involving Marie, they were trying to get Dave away from Olsen. Dave might just live without me doing anything, even though Conn had promised to help me get Dave out of here.

'How they can keep him in that little suite,' Mrs Williams said. 'It's barbaric.'

'Barbaric,' Ben echoed.

Unfortunately, it made Mrs Williams look around the table and so she finally noticed I was there. 'Elkie Bernstein! How dare you come back here! After you put Dave in this—this horrible situation. How dare y—'

'Wait a minute,' I said. 'Dave killed someone and I'm the one to blame?'

'Elkie!' Conn warned me.

'It wouldn't have happened if you hadn't brought him here,' Mrs Williams screamed at me.

I felt a moment of guilt. I'd set Dave up to stay here, even before he'd killed someone, even before I'd known Olsen had some odd ideas. I'd known he was a specialist in clinical lycanthropy and that Dave's firm belief in werewolves might have been enough to attract Olsen's attention. Mind you, at that time, I'd thought it was the best place for Ben, too.

'Dave chose to come here,' I said. 'He wanted to meet his professional sodding hero. I couldn't get him to stay away once he knew where I was going.'

The idiot had invited himself along, against his girlfriend's better judgement. Remembering that made my brain freeze for a moment and then I was talking over whatever it was Mrs Williams was justifying her son's behaviour with.

'What happened to his girlfriend?' I asked. 'Why isn't she here supporting him in his hour of need?'

Conn gave a look that could easily be translated to 'Now? You have to ask that *now*?'

Things went quiet. Whatever she'd done, it wasn't something the Williamses approved of. It probably involved pointing out she was too good for a murderer.

'Well?' I asked.

Mr and Mrs Williams turned and walked away, backs bent and shoulders down. It wasn't me that had done that to them, it was the result of Dave's determination to get rid of werewolves.

'Elkie,' said Conn. 'You really need to start thinking before you speak.'

'What? What did I do that was wrong?'

'You really need me to tell you that?' he asked.

I stared down at my empty cup, a sullen copy of him just a few minutes before.

'It wasn't the most appropriate response but the whole situation is very difficult to deal with,' said Marie.

I risked looking up at her and that well faked smile was turned on me. Somewhat late in the proceedings, I wondered what was in this for her. *Let it just be an advantage over Olsen*, I thought.

Conn hmphed.

'Witnessing a murder and the people you think of as family dropping you as soon as things got difficult,' said Marie.

Ben was looking up at the ceiling, stretched out as much as the wooden canteen chairs would allow. 'Hardly your first kill, was it?' he said in Welsh. 'And the only reason the dork's parents stuck with you when he got another girlfriend was because you did their work for them.'

'Not important,' I lied to Marie and Conn when they looked at Ben and then me. 'He's talking to himself about the Williamses. Memories, you know?'

Conn raised his eyebrows at me again.

'Ben and Dave never got on,' I added.

Conn's eyebrows came down to normal levels. I almost sighed with relief.

'When did Dave dump you, anyway?' Ben asked in English.

I flushed so much I felt like I'd sat on a fire. Conn smiled at my discomfort and didn't bother to hide it. Marie looked like she was studying us for another report.

'It was part of his graduation ceremony,' I said tightly, 'About the same time he let me know he'd been seeing someone at university.'

'Ouch. Cheap shot.'

'Yeah,' I said.

'Typical Dave, though.'

'Like you would know. You haven't seen him in, what, six years?'

'How long did the board say they needed to come to a decision?' asked Conn.

Which, I guess, meant 'How long do I have to cope with these two?'

Marie checked an elegant little watch I hadn't noticed, hidden under her suit sleeve. May would have been asking where to buy something similar. 'They didn't but I hope they make up their minds soon.'

I was sure Olsen had already made up his mind. We were just hoping someone else would have the power to override his decision.

'Elkie tells me you're leaving the Institute,' Marie said to Conn.

'Aye,' he said. 'I decided I was better spendin' time with my girls instead of missin' their childhood.'

I opened my mouth and then shut it again.

'What?' Conn asked.

I forced a bright smile. 'Cup of tea?'

I didn't wait for an answer but loaded up the tray with the empties and took it back to the counter to get refills. I tried to take as long as possible but the lack of other customers in the canteen meant I was back in the time it took to pour out a couple of coffees and some hot water for tea. I came back to find the others had fallen into silence, and it seemed smarter to fall right into it with them.

I was just starting to consider asking if I should get another round of drinks when Conn buzzed. He shifted in his seat, pulling out an old pager. He didn't bother to look at it, just tapped a button that made the buzzing stopped.

'Reception,' he said. 'They don't bother sending messages, it's just a good way of attracting my attention when I'm needed.'

'Don't forget to hand it back in when we leave,' I found myself saying.

He gave me a tight smile. 'I think they'll want all of us. Well, I think we're supposed to be there for the decision. They may not actually want us.'

He strode away like a man on a mission. Getting away from the uncomfortable silence seemed like a decent enough mission and I joined him on it. I slowed when I saw Olsen waiting in the reception, Marie and Ben walking past me as if nothing important was going on.

I looked out of a window to look at the hard standing. Lange's car was gone. A decision had been made. I was about to get into one of those lose-lose situations that I hated. Ben was either coming home with me or he was staying here to be used and abused by the self-appointed werewolf king.

I hung back as Olsen said something to Conn, and then something more when Marie and Ben reached him. He looked at me and I just knew that, if the people of the Institute hadn't been present, he would have leapt for me and ripped my throat out with his teeth. And that was without putting on his fur-skin-thing. He stalked off, back to his office.

'We did it,' said Ben and he lifted me in a bear hug.

We hadn't had that much contact since he'd thrown me across a room, saving me from another werewolf back when we were sixteen.

'Did what?' I asked, numbly.

He grinned. 'Got me out of prison.'

'Oh. Good.' I turned to Marie. 'Thank you for your help.'

She smiled, that warm smile but with a hint of victory. 'You're welcome. I'll have my office organise your flights home and I'll meet you at the airport on Thursday morning.'

Lie 16: Everyone Is Important

'We need to keep you away from Olsen until we leave,' was pretty much Conn's only response to the situation. I had a feeling that would have been the plan regardless of how the hearing had turned out.

'Okay,' I said, and resigned myself to hiding in Conn's cottage for two days, packing up his belongings.

At least in Conn's house I didn't have to worry about anyone sneaking up on me. I had a pack of dogs as an early warning system.

'What are you going to do with all of these boxes?' I asked in the evening, having already turned his book collection into a wall of cardboard boxes.

'I'll organise somethin',' he said but didn't say what.

The morning after the hearing, I was working on the girls' bedroom. There were signs two young children had been here—and red dog hairs everywhere. They hadn't made a squeak about missing the stuffed toys that still covered every available surface.

'Maybe we should drive home,' I said, loudly enough to be heard by Conn in his own room. 'It's a long way but it would save you getting it delivered.'

Conn laughed. 'It's a very long way. The nearest passenger ferry to the UK is in Denmark. It's not happenin'.'

'Oh.'

I'd thought there would have been something nearer.

'The important thing is getting my stuff out of here before Olsen moves in my replacement.'

'He's replaced you already?' I asked.

'No. But he doesn't like leaving the Institute unless he considers it necessary. He'll want someone to do the house calls.'

'A dog warden,' I said, suddenly realising what Conn had meant back in December.

'Save the green rabbits,' said Conn. 'I'll put those in my bag for the flight.'

I'd already packed them. I fished them out again.

'I'm taking you over to see Williams after lunch,' Conn said.

I jumped. He was in the doorway, not on the other side of the bedroom wall. So much for nobody sneaking up on me in Conn's house.

'Hopefully, his parents have gotten out of the way by then and Olsen will be nowhere near.'

'They said he'd been ill,' I said. 'Yesterday when we were in the canteen with Marie. Do you know anything about that?'

Conn shrugged. 'The human patients have never been any of my business.'

I sat back from the boxes. 'Whoever he replaces you with is going to need to know about werewolves. I don't know of any well-trained enough to make house calls on his behalf. I'm not even sure Olsen should be allowed out.'

'Well, the cottage won't necessarily go to my direct replacement,' Conn said. 'Just another employee who needs some privacy. But my replacement doesn't need to be a werewolf, just aware of them.'

I was aware of werewolves. There was no way I'd work for Olsen. But I guess that didn't mean everyone else felt the same way.

'Lunch,' said Conn.

By the time I stood up, he was down the stairs and on his way to the kitchen.

'How did you manage to keep so many teddies?' I asked when I caught up.

He didn't look up from getting food out of cupboards. 'What?'

'Moll and Sadie. They kill teddy bears. How come you have so many that haven't been ritually disembowelled?'

This time he did turn to look at me. 'What?'

'They do this really neat incision from the throat to the groin,' I said, gesturing. 'Then they pile all the stuffing to one side. Then they pull the stitching apart.'

It was the sort of thing I hoped anyone else never found out, otherwise they'd be in front of child psychologists so fast their feet wouldn't even touch the ground. Or paws, seeing as they did it in dog form.

'They've been told not to destroy their toys,' Conn said. 'You shouldn't let them get away with it.'

'What am I supposed to do? Hit them on the nose with a rolled up newspaper?'

He gave me a black look and returned to putting our lunch together. 'How do you keep them in stuffed toys, then?'

'Charity shops. Fifty pee a teddy. Although I'll have to teach them how to sew them back together and re-stuff them when North Wales has run out of sacrificial victims.'

Conn snorted but my attempt to talk about something other than the institute fell flat because he didn't say anything back and I couldn't think of anything more to add.

He left me at the security room. Not the one for Ben's corridor, the land of the 'special cases', but the one for Dave's.

'I don't have clearance for this place,' said Conn.

'Oh,' I said.

I wanted to ask him to come with me anyway. I didn't really want to see Dave, I just needed to see what condition Olsen was keeping him in. How difficult it might be for there to be an alleged suicide.

'Well, I guess I better throw myself on the mercy of the security team, then,' I said.

Conn smiled, a tight movement that didn't reach his eyes. 'I'll be in reception. You can find your way back?'

'I think so.'

The place wasn't quite as confusing as it used to be. I could keep myself orientated enough to know, for example, that I was in a completely different wing than Ben. There was no possibility of mixing up the people who thought they were werewolves and the people who knew they were.

'Look after her,' he said to the three security guards on duty.

They barely acknowledged us, three tall and blandly attractive people in uniform doing work that they found not very interesting or entertaining. I might have seen them before on duty on the other corridor. I might not. I couldn't be sure and I don't suppose it mattered.

One of them, a man, stood. 'Come. I'll take you to Williams.'

He opened the door to the corridor and I was hit with déjà vu. Blank wall on one side, rooms with clear plastic walls to the other. The only things that stood out from the plastic background was air-holes, handles and keypads. Except there was a pattern, a rhythm to their placement that meant the individual detail was lost.

We marched the length of the corridor and I counted off thirteen cells, not something that standing in the doorway had made possible. Or, for that matter, visiting Ben—assuming his corridor was as like this one as it seemed. All of the cells were occupied and all of the men inside cat-called and whistled or otherwise drew attention to the fact that I was a woman. Most of them got insulting when I didn't respond.

'Are they always like this?' I asked the guard.

He didn't answer.

The only cell not emitting calls and whistles was the last. I would have assumed it was empty if I hadn't known better, if I hadn't been here to see someone specific. The guard turned and touched the keypad.

'Behind the bars,' he said.

He sounded bored but, then, he must do this every day with Dave's parents and any other visitors the men on this corridor had. Which only made it obvious how little contact Ben and his fellow werewolves had, if the security guards posted there were so happy to see a new face.

I looked in through the clear plastic wall. It was virtually identical to Ben's cell, a room partitioned by metal bars into living area and hobby room. Except where Ben had games consoles and computers all over the place, Dave so far had nothing more than a shelf of thick books. The other notable difference was a grey fur thrown over the single metal bed. The partition rumbled shut.

'I don't want to do this,' I said to the guard. 'I've changed my mind.'

Dave smiled from behind his metal bars. 'Oh, don't be like that, Elkie. Why come all this way to see me and bottle it now?'

'You're down for a half hour visit,' the guard said.

'Half an hour? That's not long. It's barely any time at all for two friends to catch up,' Dave said.

He was using a soothing tone that was as close to purring as a human throat would allow. Why didn't the guard see how creepy this was and get me out of there?

'I'll leave the bars closed,' the guard said. 'He can't get to you. Just take a seat in the observation room.'

The otherwise invisible door opened and I stepped through on autopilot. The hairs on the back of my neck were up and my instincts were sending my brain into a spin.

'Good girl,' said Dave.

I looked back, hoping the guard would do something heroic and get me out of there. He pulled a face at Dave's tone but didn't say or do anything, just closed me in with only some bars to keep me away from this... werewolf.

'You were ill,' I said, inanely.

'A couple of weeks under the weather.'

'But, they can't have kept you here for everyone to see,' I said. 'And if you'd been with... the special cases, Ben would have known...'

Dave's smile widened into a grin.

'Do your parents know?' I asked.

He shrugged and the grin stayed exactly where it was. He always had enjoyed knowing more than me. He just made it more obvious than he ever had before.

'But you hate werewolves,' I said. '"The only good werewolf is a dead werewolf".'

He laughed. 'There's no such thing as werewolves, Elkie. Better be careful what you say or you'll find yourself in one of these.'

He tapped the bars between us.

'Fine,' I said, 'You don't like fake fur. Or you didn't. What happened?'

'I didn't like being taken advantage of. Now I'm strong and no-one will ever take advantage of me again.'

Great. Like this had all been about him.

'Really? When did *you* get taken advantage of?'

'They ruined my life, Elkie. Them and you.'

'What? We were fifteen! And you carried on just fine,

going off to university, getting a degree, cheating on me with another woman! How is that ruining your life?'

Dave was growling through the bars, teeth bared and spit flying. 'Knowing there were potential killers around every corner? That there were people out there who were bigger and stronger and could impose their will on me regardless of my consent?'

I stepped back until I was pressed against the plastic wall. His emotional frustration, his rage, was all about how he couldn't impose his own will and someone else could. This was about doing stuff because he could. 'So campaign for equality. "No means no". Don't sink to their sodding level.'

Not that Dave had been especially good at taking 'no' for an answer himself. We'd just been... heading in the same direction so I'd been okay with agreeing. Until he turned out to be a cheating bastard.

'You think this is funny?' he snarled and a droplet of spit landed on my cheek.

I wiped it away.

'You don't get taken advantage of because you're weak,' I said. 'You get taken advantage of because you're too blind to see the situation and because someone else is happy to use it as an opportunity. This doesn't solve anything.'

'I'm strong!' Dave roared.

It seemed like the metal bars he held bent a little. I could have imagined it.

'You're a fucking idiot,' I said, 'Blinded by the need to prove yourself as good as any other man. Olsen's going to take advantage of you while you're busy proving how high you can piss up a wall.'

Not that Dave could go anywhere, right? He'd murdered someone, and was here because blaming it on the existence of werewolves got him out of a proper prison. He was on a secure corridor. Dave wouldn't be let out of the Institute any time soon if Olsen didn't want the place put under enough scrutiny to potentially lose everything he worked for.

I banged on the plastic wall.

'I want to leave!' I shouted.

'This is your fault, Elkie,' Dave growled. 'You put me in this situation. You did this to me.'

'Get me out of here now!' I screamed.

'You're being paranoid,' Conn said.

'Really?' I asked, staring at the red paw painting.

Actually, that's not true. I was looking in its direction but I wasn't looking at it. The only reason I knew what it was was because I'd seen it before.

'About Olsen. He can't do anything to you just because you walk in to his office,' said Conn.

I raised my eyebrows and said nothing. I didn't think Olsen would have calmed down that much with a couple of nights sleep and I really didn't want this meeting he'd summoned me for, via my father in all but DNA and time spent raising me.

'People have seen you arrive, people expect to see you leave.'

'You mean, if anything happens to me, even if he makes it look like an accident or whatever, the Institute will be investigated,' I added.

I'd only just worked out that he was repeating everything I'd said about Marie during the hearing, word for word. He was probably enjoying winding me up.

'He can't physically do anythin' to you,' Conn said, 'That much *is* true. Too many questions would be raised.'

'Assuming he's thinking straight. A person can do almost anything in anger. A werewolf...'

A werewolf is obsessed, focussed to the point of forgetting that not all obstacles are legal to overcome.

'Just go in, Elkie. I'll be here on the other side of the door. And I'll be on his side of the door soon, anyway, with my handover meeting.'

I sighed and did as I was told. I still didn't appreciate that I'd been summoned via Conn's ageing pager, never mind facing down another angry werewolf.

'You called for me,' I said in a small voice.

Olsen was stood in front of a window, his back to the door, hands clasped behind his back. It was the kind of stance designed to show that he was in charge and to impose control on the situation. He was certainly more in control than Dave.

I cast a quick look at Conn, who was studiously ignoring me and staring at the blood spatter painting, and closed the door behind me. I could either go with Olsen's little power kicks or I could relax as much as my thumping heart would let me. I considered the two chairs on either side of his desk. The thumping heart almost silenced the voice of mischief but in the end I went with the urge to cause as much trouble as I could before I was taken down.

I sat in the chair on the business side of the desk. I thumbed some buttons on the borrowed mobile phone and put it down on some paperwork.

'In your own time,' I said in a slightly louder and firmer voice as I put my feet up away from the phone.

He turned. I guess his super hearing worked out I wasn't cowering in the doorway.

'You arrogant, English bitch. You —'

'The "English" kind of makes the "arrogant" redundant,' I said.

Olsen's mouth shut so loudly and so quickly that I heard the snap of teeth meeting.

'And the "English" is kind of insulting enough, anyway, seeing as I'm Welsh,' I added. 'More or less.'

Olsen strode forward and leant on his desk, a threatening gesture somewhat ruined by me being in his seat with my feet up. 'What makes you think you can just come here and rearrange all of my plans?'

I put my hands behind my head. Mainly because it hid how much they were shaking. It was a shame I couldn't do anything about the stench of fear that was probably coming off me in a tsunami.

'Which were going so well,' I said. 'How did that conversation go again? You know, the one about how you couldn't find other werewolves?'

'Benjamin Lloyd can find them,' Olsen spat.

'Yes. And there's no way I'm leaving him here with you.'

'Why not? Too concerned that I might prove werewolves are more than just a sick form of entertainment?'

'I beg your pardon?' I asked, shocked into my mother's manners.

'It's what you do, isn't it? Kill werewolves? Are you sure

you aren't just taking Lloyd home so he can find you more people to kill?'

'I'm not a killer,' I said. 'Everyone I've killed attacked me first.'

'You've killed. You're a killer.'

I forced myself to stay in the fake relaxed and oh so exposed position. He wouldn't attack me if he thought himself better than me, right?

'You have dangerous werewolves under your care and you're worried about me?' I asked. 'I think you need to sort out your priorities.'

'And you plan on letting one of them—the one who organised those eighteen so called attacks you're so upset about—free. Why would you do that, Miss Bernstein?'

Eighteen? He didn't realise that Eric and Simon were dead, then. Maybe he hadn't given them any way of contacting him. Maybe he was giving them more time. I gave up resisting the urge to protect my belly and sat forward in the chair, my feet on the floor and my elbows on the desk.

'Because I don't think you're a good person to leave him with,' I answered honestly.

Olsen stopped as if I'd slapped him. There was a fleck of spittle in the corner of his mouth and the whites of his eyes seemed overly large. He was still angry and I had no choice but to keep fighting, even if his attacks weren't physical.

'I don't trust you,' I said.

He'd given me no reason to, once we'd gotten past the trappings of authority the Institute gave him. He valued the lives of my attackers over mine. He'd turned Dave into a werewolf.

'You brought both Lloyd and Williams to me,' he said.

'Dave,' I said. 'I brought you Dave. That Ben came to your attention thanks to my actions was just a happy accident.'

I'd taken copies of Ben's stalker-like emails, the ones that mentioned my next attackers would be coming soon, to the Police. Ben had been moved from one mental health facility to another. That was all I'd known at the time. It wasn't my fault.

'Hah! You're Conn's daughter.'

And how long ago had Olsen found that out? Had he read

the report before the hearing? He had to have done. He must have been waiting for Conn to slip up or do something about it.

'It's not like we knew each other at the time,' I said. 'And it's not like Conn told me about you.'

'I should have known he was hiding things from me. I should have known there was more than his bitch. And now you're looking after their... whatever they are. Do they look like puppies or humans or both?'

I couldn't afford to let Olsen question what else Conn was hiding or had hidden in the past. Not that it didn't need questioning as Conn apparently had a talent for keeping things quiet—things like offspring and Greywolves. Maybe he'd kept the lives and deaths of a few werewolves quiet, too. It was just that Olsen was not the person to be finding answers.

'I don't know what you're talking about,' I lied.

'You lied to me,' Olsen shouted.

He thumped the desk between us. I half-rose, half-flinched before returning to my previous position.

'You betrayed me,' he said more quietly. 'Both of you.'

I said nothing. It wasn't betrayal if I hadn't been on his side in the first place—or him on mine.

'You're trying to take my people from me.'

I felt the need to correct him. 'Technically, we've succeeded. Not the Ben was ever "your people".'

'He's a werewolf,' Olsen snarled. 'You know nothing about looking after our kind, about showing him what he can become.'

'And you do?' I asked.

Although part of me wanted to point out that Conn was likely to be as capable as Olsen. It wasn't like they'd had a massive amount of success. One of the werewolves Dave had killed, Diarmuid, was the only one Conn had spoken of as if he might have fitted in with humanity. If Dave hadn't got to him first.

'You're not a werewolf. You know nothing about it. You don't know what it's like...'

Olsen turned and he was staring out the window again. This time he was trying for more of a 'the whole world is against me' look.

'Probably not. I wouldn't want to. It's hard enough being a human being.'

'Weak, useless, ineffectual,' Olsen sneered.

'Weak,' I agreed. 'But not useless. Otherwise you wouldn't think I was dangerous.'

Olsen turned and his teeth were bared. 'You're nothing but a big game hunter. You stack the odds in your favour and you kill my people just because you can.'

'I don't hunt werewolves,' I said. 'Those I killed came looking for me, not the other way around.'

It wasn't like I was that difficult to find, I lived in the same village I'd been in for most of my life. I had nowhere to run to.

'You don't give them a chance.'

'To what? Eat me?'

'Werewolves are rare,' said Olsen. 'And you've killed eighteen of them.'

I rested my head on my hands. Twenty, although Olsen didn't know about Eric and Simon. Yet.

'I will never be able to replace them,' said Olsen. He turned and smiled. It was scarier than his overt anger. 'Well, I will, thanks to you giving me the idea but I will never replace those eighteen individuals that you stole from me.'

There would always be men hungry for the perceived power of becoming an almost-wolf. Up until yesterday, I would never have expected Dave to be one of them but it just went to show how true it was. There were more out there if Olsen looked.

'Twenty,' I said.

'Conn and Lloyd haven't left yet.'

My stomach squeezed. That wasn't what I'd meant. 'Doctor Bakken is meeting us at the airport tomorrow.'

Someone was expecting us, someone with enough clout to fight back, and someone with the knowledge of how to do so.

'Yes. You're using that Valemon consultant,' Olsen said. 'Don't expect it to do you any good in the long run.'

'Oh?' I asked.

'It's all about business. *Valemon og efterfølgere* are an old company. For some reason, they think the Institute is taking away their business.'

'Is it?' I asked.

Olsen gave a bark of laughter. 'They know nothing about werewolves and letting them have those cases would be gross negligence. Not that they care, any more than they care what happens to you.'

'I'm of use to them until at least tomorrow,' I said firmly. 'We're meeting Marie at the airport. We're expected.'

'They won't protect you forever—and they don't even know what they're protecting you from.'

'And then what?' I asked. 'You send more werewolves to kill me?'

Olsen looked at me. Werewolf life is too precious to risk versus this one is too much of a threat to werewolves to leave alive.

'Let's make a deal,' I said.

Olsen sneered and looked back out of the window.

'If you promise that none of "your people"—werewolves from the Institute—attack me or my pack, I promise not to kill them,' I said.

And, really, what reason would a werewolf have for wandering around middle of nowhere North Wales without having been pointed in that direction by Ben or Olsen? Ben had, hopefully, given up that particular game, which only left Olsen and revenge.

'I don't want to stop the work you do with men like Alejandro and Philip,' I said. 'Just keep them and Dave and the rest of their kind away from me.'

Not that I had a professional opinion on their mental health but Alejandro and Philip would never be in a fit state to help take over the world. Someone like Ben or Dave... These must have been the decisions Conn had made every time he'd met a werewolf or people like the Greywolves, questioning whether they would be dangerous to humanity under Olsen's protection.

'Okay,' said Olsen. 'I agree.'

Well, it might not be a world-wide peace but it was an amnesty for me. That was enough for the moment. Maybe for the rest of my life. I picked up the mobile and pressed buttons to stop it recording. I left before Olsen could work out what was going on.

Lie 17: Everything's Going To Be All Right

Conn and I stowed all of his boxes in a van that turned up way too early on the Thursday morning. The driver and I asked where various things would go and Conn grunted or bollocked us as necessary.

We had a cup of tea—well, the driver had coffee—before sending the driver on his way. He wouldn't personally be delivering the boxes all the way to North Wales but he had all the papers clutched in his gloved hands as he got back in the vehicle.

All that remained of us in the cottage was the dirty mugs and two back-packs. I could just see an oversized, green bunny ear sticking out of Conn's. After several minutes of me checking that all the furniture and utensils were definitely the Institute's, even the back-packs were gone as Conn flung them into the back seat of his estate car.

'Your dogs?' I asked.

Five mixed breeds of varying sizes and degrees of fluffiness watched us, heads cocked. Where tails remained, they thumped on the wooden hallway floor.

'In the boot. They have a temporary home and we pass it on the way to the airport,' said Conn.

I stepped out of the doorway and there was a minor charge for the car boot. Conn opened it without a word and the dogs jumped in as if instructions were given telepathically. Conn smiled sadly as he shut the boot behind them. 'They think we're going for a walk somewhere else.'

'Well, we are,' I said.

He put his hands in his pockets and stared at the ground.

'You could get them sent over,' I suggested. 'There's plenty of room on the farm.'

'They'd have to go through quarantine.'

'What about a pet passport?'

He shook his head. 'Didn't have enough time to get the paperwork and injections sorted.'

'You could leave some money and instructions with the

temporary home, though, right?'

He sighed.

I guess it was one of those things that would be difficult either way. Maybe he couldn't afford it or maybe he thought they'd be better off here. Well, nearer to here.

'I've done as much as I can to help them,' he said, finally. 'They're going to a good foster home and might end up there permanently.'

I closed the cottage door and handed him the key.

'I don't keep dogs permanently. I just teach them some manners and find them a better home,' he added.

'Do you keep any of your waifs and strays permanently?'I asked.

He looked at me. 'The only one I ever wanted to keep forever wouldn't and then couldn't let me.'

My stomach flipped. Obsession. Romantic love. It's a fine line. Not that I ever got to experience it.

'Time catches everyone out,' I said. 'And you have two daughters to look after, so I think you've got them for the rest of your life.'

'Get in the car.'

We drove the embarrassingly short distance to the Institute's front door. There was a small, pale figure sat on the steps, clutching a plastic carrier bag. Pulling up took away the illusion of small but did nothing for the paleness. It also made it more obvious that the old, worn clothes didn't really fit. Maybe they were the clothes he'd been taken away in, was it seven years ago? Maybe they were just second hand clothes replacing the ones he'd had when he'd arrived. They weren't what he'd been wearing in his cell.

'*Bore da*, Ben,' I called from the car. 'Ready to go?'

He stood and turned to look up at the building that had held him for however long. I wasn't sure if it was the year since he'd got connected to the Internet again—only to lose it with my first visit in December—or if he'd been here since before Dave went to university. Either way, it was a long time to be kept in one room with almost no relief.

'Stop staring,' I called, 'Time to go out into the big, wide world.'

Ben walked slowly down the steps and got in the back,

throwing the crappy little plastic carrier bag against the two rugged back-packs.

'Llados isn't the big, wide world,' he said.

Conn started the car and we were officially free. If I hadn't been strapped in with a seat belt, I would have started jumping just to let some of the energy of relief and happiness out.

'Well, I like it,' I said.

And I'd loved being a farmer, when I'd had a working farm. Another one of those points I'd have to sit down and discuss with Ben eventually even though he no longer owned anything.

'So. Plastic bag,' I said. 'Bit harsh.'

'I don't own anything,' Ben said, echoing my thoughts.

I frowned. 'So the consoles and everything?'

'Were the Institute's. Or Olsen's, I guess,' said Ben.

I turned around to look at him over the back rest of the front passenger seat. 'Did you manage to get my mobile phone out of there?'

'I got it yesterday,' said Conn. 'Consider it a straight swap for mine. Now sit forward.'

I did as I was told.

'What did you do to her?' asked Ben. 'She's never been good at taking orders.'

I glared over my shoulder. 'They're not orders. They're suggestions.'

Ben raised his hands. 'Whatever makes you feel better.'

'Are you two going to be like this all the way to the airport?' Conn asked.

Ben smirked.

'Worse,' I said. 'We're going to be like this all the way home.'

'And then what?' Conn asked.

'We'll keep on arguing,' said Ben. 'She's always been sparky.'

I glared again. 'That is so bloody condescending! "Sparky"!'

'Shit,' said Conn.

'Do you realise how patronising that sounded?' I asked Ben.

He grinned at me. 'Yes.'

I sighed. 'Well, I suppose I should be grateful you've grown up since the days of calling me a "Yid bitch".'

Ben shrugged. Conn's hands tightened on the wheel enough for me to see white knuckles.

'Although it was probably as factually inaccurate as calling me an "inbred hill-billy".'

'You and Dave always looked a lot alike,' Ben said. 'Maybe it was just the second-hand clothes and the greasy hair.'

'He really is a charmer,' Conn muttered.

'Stuck in his teenager-hood,' I said.

'I am not.' Then, eventually, 'Is that even a real word?'

'I have no idea,' I said.

'If you two are going to talk, could you at least talk about something useful or interesting?' Conn asked.

I grinned. 'So no asking if we're there yet?'

Ben laughed.

'You better bloody not,' Conn growled.

I thought for a minute. I hadn't told Conn about Eric and Simon, or my two meetings, but then he hadn't asked, either. Did the results count as useful?

'We didn't manage everything,' I said. 'Dave's still locked up.'

Conn raised his eyebrows. 'Oh? What are you trying to tell me?'

'That I don't mind you getting two puppies for the price of one,' I replied.

Conn white-knuckled again. 'I'm not going back for him.'

'He has his parents to fight for him,' Ben said.

'He's not worth fighting for,' I corrected.

The mongrels in the boot wuffed and muttered and barked a bit, as if reminding the noisy humans of their presence. We'd probably ignored them for too long.

Conn, the man who collected waifs and strays, asked, 'What do you mean?'

'Dave's a werewolf,' I said.

Conn's concentration wavered enough for him to swerve the car. It was only for a heartbeat but it was a rather anxious heartbeat.

'Since when?' he asked.

Ben snorted. 'I'm surprised the dork took that long. When's he moving to the special wing?'

'Since that illness his mum mentioned,' I said to Conn, and to Ben, 'What do you mean?'

'You mean you never noticed that he's all about proving himself better than everyone else? What else is he going to do when given the chance to become a big, strong wearer of fake fur?'

I'd opened my mouth to answer but the phrase 'fake fur' caught my attention. I'd only used it a couple of days ago myself.

'Not that it'll make him especially big or strong,' Ben added.

I had to admit that none of the werewolves I'd seen had changed size just because they'd put their fur-skins on.

'But it wasn't you that bit him?' I asked. 'And you didn't see him on your corridor?'

'I couldn't see anything on that corridor. But I didn't hear him or smell him, either,' Ben said.

Along with that mysterious third werewolf that Eric and Simon actually defended me from, Olsen had a few others up his sleeve. Unless he'd let Alejandro or Philip do the honours.

'It's probably not a big deal,' said Conn.

'Really? Why not?' Ben challenged.

'As far as the human world is concerned, your friend has just been locked up in a mental institute for committing murder while not of sound mind. It's not like Olsen can release him or let him do anything.'

I said nothing.

'I managed quite a bit from the same situation,' Ben said.

He seemed a bit too smug about it.

'I stopped you,' I said firmly.

He smiled, not quite as smug but still proud—as if he'd made me.

'Yeah,' he said, 'You did.'

'And Olsen allowed Eric and Simon out despite apparently needing to be locked up,' I said.

Conn cursed.

'They're not a problem now,' I added.

Conn looked at me and Ben cheered.

'How did you get them?' my former crush asked.

'Silver.'

He nodded.

'Olsen promised me that he wouldn't let any of his people bother me,' I said quietly. 'Including Dave.'

Conn nodded. Maybe in acknowledgement of maybe he'd heard through Olsen's door.

'In return for what?' asked Ben.

'For me not killing any of them.'

'You really think you could take more werewolves?' Ben asked, sitting forward in his seat.

'Sit back!' Conn barked.

Ben ignored him and watched me, waiting for an answer.

'No,' I said honestly, 'So don't get any ideas. Also, don't set any werewolves on me because Olsen considers you all "his people". It might be enough to break the truce.'

'I'm not a werewolf,' said Ben.

Conn looked at Ben in the rear-view mirror. 'Oh? Really?'

'I don't want to be,' Ben clarified.

Conn cleared his throat. 'So, if you kill another werewolf, you're on Olsen's shit list again but if you can stay clean, he'll leave you alone and not let others—'

'You mean Dave?' asked Ben.

'Aye, Dave,' said Conn. 'He'll not let insane idiots who think they have a point to prove, like Dave, come after you.'

'Did you shake on it?' asked Ben. 'I'm not sure it counts if you didn't shake on it.'

Conn let out a dry bark of laughter, the kind that only serves to show how mad things are getting. 'Shake? I'm not even sure that agreement would be worth anything if it were on paper.'

'How about if I have the conversation recorded?' I asked.

'Make sure there are copies made and left somewhere safe with instructions for them to be released if anything happens to you,' said Conn. 'And remind Olsen they exist on a regular basis. It may even work.'

Ben sat back in his seat. 'What about the rest of us? Did you make Olsen promise to leave us alone? Or say we wouldn't play with his toys?'

'Don't,' Conn warned.

'I'm just asking.'

'Don't even think it,' I said.

'So you didn't.'

'No.'

Ben smiled and closed his eyes.

'Don't play that game, Ben,' I said. 'Please?'

The smile faded and he shrugged. I'd have to take that as agreement.

'I asked him to leave "my pack" alone,' I said to Conn.

Conn looked at me briefly before returning his attention to the road. 'So the agreement includes me and the girls.'

'And Ben, I guess. Anyone else that's in my household or family. Although whether he's going to bother staying up-to-date on who's who is unlikely.'

'So I'm free,' said Ben.

'So we're all free,' I said.

I needed this. I deserved this. I didn't care what happened to the rest of the world as long as werewolves left me alone. It was my turn to have things turn out right for a change.

Printed in Great Britain
by Amazon

51197719R00136